MADAM CHARLIE

Written by

SAHARA KELLY

Ellora's Cave Publishing, Inc.
PO Box 787
Hudson, OH 44236-0787

ISBN # 1-84360-572-4

Madam Charlie edited by Briana St. James.
Cover art by Darrell King.

Warning: The following material contains strong sexual
content meant for mature readers. *MADAM CHARLIE* has
been rated NC-17, erotic, by a minimum of three
independent reviewers. We strongly suggest storing this
book in a place where young readers not meant to view it
are unlikely to happen upon it. That said, enjoy...

What the critics are saying

Prologue

The Evening Gazette, Fleet Street, London, 1814:

Authorities reported to the Home Office today that the Investigation into the Fire that claimed the Life of Philip, Earl of Calverton, and his young Bride, was of Accidental Origin. The Dreadful Damage inflicted by the Horrendous Conflagration occasioned the long delay between the Sad Demise of His Lordship and the Final Finding in this Matter.

The Lord Lieutenant of the County, The Right Honorable Matthew Ffortescue, informed the Secretary that in his Opinion, the Earl and his Bride had been overcome by Terrible Fumes when a Log fell onto a Rug in His Lordship's Chamber. The Consuming Blaze devoured much of the East Wing of Calverton Chase and left Little for Investigators of this Tragedy.

The Heir to the Calverton Estate, formerly Colonel Jordan Lyndhurst, now the Seventh Earl, has been recalled from the Continent where he was serving under the Duke of Wellington's Command, earning Distinctions for his Conduct. He is quoted as saying:

"I am surprised and saddened by His Lordship's passing. Although I had no knowledge of his marriage, my sympathies are, of course, also extended to his wife's family. I deeply appreciate the honour of receiving His Royal Highness's sentiments on this matter."

The Seventh Earl is scheduled to return to His Native Shores next Month, just in time for the Season. As the Son of a very Distant Relative of the Calverton line, this must surely be a Pleasant Change in Circumstances for the Distinguished Soldier. His Arrival will be Eagerly Awaited by the Ton. Colonel Lyndhurst is Unwed, and Reputed to be of Handsome Countenance. We wonder if the Military Strategies he has Created for our Brave and Noble Wellington can compare to the Romantic Strategies which Doubtless will be Created by The Fairer Sex?"

A pair of slim hands folded the paper and set it back on the table. The buzz and rumble of another London day continued unabated beneath the window, but the person in the room did not move.

The ornate mirror on the opposite wall reflected a slender lad, in nondescript clothing. An unkempt shirt straggled out of a pair of well-worn breeches and a dark jacket was flung over a nearby chair. Long gold hair was tied back into a serviceable bundle and the lad's cheeks were smooth and showed no hint of a beard.

Raucous laughter echoed outside the room. It was early yet, but here, in the elegantly erotic rooms of 14 Beaulieu Crescent, the women were stirring. Soon their customers would be thronging the streets of London, and within hours of sunset, the entire mansion would be alive with seekers of pleasure.

The figure rose and crossed the room to gaze from the mullioned window onto the thoroughfare below. An occasional carriage clattered by, and some vendors passed, having made their daily deliveries.

For the moment, all was as it should be.

The figure shrugged. For a slip of a lad named Charlie, who had spent the last few years quietly working around the "Crescent" as it was known, this was an ordinary morning.

For Charlotte, Countess of Calverton and widow of the Sixth Earl, this might well be the day her troubles began.

It was very doubtful that Colonel Jordan Lyndhurst would be pleased to find out that Lady Charlotte and Charlie of the Crescent were one and the same. He'd be even more upset to learn that, as of yesterday, the Dowager Countess was now the owner of a house of ill-repute.

But what would really get his blood pounding would be the knowledge that this same Dowager had most likely murdered the Sixth Earl.

Chapter 1

London, 1815

"Don't you worry, none, Susie. Madam Charlie ain't gonna let no one 'urt you."

The Seventh Earl of Calverton, Jordan Lyndhurst, curled his lip as he caught the snatch of conversation outside the door. Clearly "Susie" was new at her job.

"We gets to give the customers what they want, but no rough stuff. It's a 'ouse rule, and Antonio will be there in a sec if you shouts for 'im."

The voices faded away, leaving Jordan slightly puzzled.

This was a brothel. Nothing more, nothing less. Certainly it masqueraded under the trappings of a "discreet house of pleasure", and offered its clients a nice selection of foods, excellent wines, and several well-organized gaming tables.

But beneath the facade of discretion and elegance, there were women willing to trade their bodies for money. Cash. Cold hard cash.

Jordan snorted. There would always be women ready to trade their bodies for cash. Some forced by circumstance, others by greed. His lip curled even more as he lay back on the comfortable divan and watched the fire flicker in the grate.

He devoutly hoped that Susie wouldn't have to shout for Antonio, whoever the hell he was. Probably that mountainous doorman who'd tried to bow politely as he'd been ushered onto the premises earlier. Watching him bow was like watching a whale breach in the ocean. Surprising, enormous and a bit messy on the way down.

He felt that he could fairly assess this place, seeing as he wasn't really here as a customer. Well, not in the strictest sense of the word. He'd be getting serviced this evening, but not sexually.

This was the one place where he could find someone to help him ease the ache in his back. For the last several months, he'd been using the services of Major Ryan Penderly's Japanese manservant. Kasuki's trick of walking up and down Jordan's spine had cracked bones loudly, squashed his intestines into pancakes, and given him enormous relief from the pain he'd suffered intermittently since he'd been thrown from his horse in Belgium.

Now Kasuki was gone, heading home on a packet boat, and he'd learned of a Japanese girl, here at the Crescent, who did the same kind of treatment.

He fidgeted a little, aware of the growing soreness in his spine. Damn. He'd arrived here not a moment too soon.

Of course, he supposed, he could get a quick fuck while he was at it.

It had been nearly a year since the last one, incredible though it seemed.

A year since he'd buried himself between the softly rounded thighs of his soon-to-be fiancée, Daisy Wrothings. A year since he'd suckled the sweet juices from between her legs and felt her come in his face, only to have her tell him afterwards that she was marrying someone else. A Duke. One who had an intact estate, and more money than God. Damn. And damn again. That had been the end of his wenching. Fortunately, it had coincided with the beginning of the hardest work he could remember doing.

The ache in his spine was transferring itself to an aching erection. Maybe he should persuade Miss Japanese Nimble Feet to suck him off while she was here, take care of all the aches at once, as it were.

She probably wouldn't mind, and he could afford the extra cost. Now that Calverton Chase was practically whole, and the estate regaining some of its income, it was getting time to start living some kind of a life again. One that didn't include long hours in the fields with his tenants, days poring over financial papers with his agent and his lawyer, and nights alone with only brandy and exhaustion for company.

Yes, perhaps a quick fuck was just the diversion he needed. Someone young, lithe, who could suck his cock into next week.

Someone eager, someone tall, someone perhaps blonde, someone nice to look at...

Someone like *her*.

He had been so lost in his thoughts that she'd entered the room without him hearing her. His soldier's instincts were horrified by such a lapse of concentration. He frowned at himself.

"Good evening, my Lord."

Her voice was low and refined, her body slender and tall, and she was one mouthwateringly beautiful woman. He wanted her immediately and his cock seconded the notion.

"I must apologize for keeping you waiting. I was not informed until just now that you were asking for Kiko-San."

Jordan rose without even thinking about it. Whatever else she was, this was a woman and deserving of his courtesy at least.

"No matter. I have been quite comfortable, and the staff here is certainly attentive." He waved negligently at the brandy glass, which was nearly empty. "A fine brandy, too, if I may be allowed."

She dipped her head in acknowledgment. "I am gratified. My staff does its best."

"Your staff?"

"That is correct."

The gray eyes looking at him were expressionless, allowing him to see nothing of her feelings, her character, or her personality. Perversely, he wanted to bring a glitter into those eyes. To provoke a reaction from her. To see what she'd look like if he thrust deep into her and pressed her clit just right to topple her off the highest mountain.

"Then you must be…"

"Madam Charlie. Yes." Another polite nod followed these words.

"You own the Crescent?"

"I do."

"You seem very young to have such a responsibility. Have you been a prostitute long?"

He could have sworn a faint sparkle of anger flashed behind her eyes, but it was gone before he could be sure.

She turned away with a pretense of attending to the fire. "Unfortunately, my Lord, Kiko has left our establishment."

The truth? Or a lie to get rid of him after that unpardonable insult? He couldn't tell. Damn. She was very, very good.

"However, we all realized the extraordinary benefits that Kiko's techniques were able to bring her clients. She undertook the task of teaching us a few of her methods. If you would consider another person administering her massage?"

Jordan pretended to consider her offer, while noting every single stitch of clothing she wore so beautifully, every strand of hair, every dip and hollow in her skin that he could see. He catalogued her, thoroughly, effectively, and rapidly.

His soldiering skills might be lapsing in some areas, but others were still invaluable to him, on occasion. This was certainly one of the occasions.

"Well, seeing as my back will only get worse if nothing is done, there seems to be little choice for me in this matter. I would be willing to accept the ministrations of an alternate, if you assure me she is skilled enough to at least do no damage."

"I can assure you of that."

"So tell me, Madam Charlie. Who is this skilful practitioner of the Oriental healing techniques?"

"Me."

* * * * *

Charlie knew that she had finally, utterly, magnificently, lost her mind. None of her inner turmoil showed on her face, however. She had schooled herself far too well for that.

But she had just agreed to offer a service to a customer, something she had sworn never to do. And all because of his eyes.

Those brown pools, glittering with gold flecks, stared past her outer façade and seemed to dig deep into places she'd long thought dead.

He'd looked at her like he wanted to know what she looked like naked, but also that he needed to know what she was thinking *while* she was naked.

It was that particular look that had broken through her resolve.

"If you would care to remove your clothing, my Lord," she gestured to the ornate screen standing in one corner of the large room. "Then please resume your seat. I shall return in a moment."

She didn't give him a chance to respond before whisking herself out of the room and running up the short stairwell to her private quarters.

Her hands were shaking by the time she got there and she shocked the woman in her rooms by bursting in with a gasp.

"Good heavens, Miss Charlie. Whatever's the matter?"

"I have to change. Quick. My silk robe and chemise. The blue ones."

"*Miss Charlie*. Whatever for?"

"Hurry, Matty. I'm going to give a customer Kiko's treatment."

"Oh, Miss. No. You *ain't* gonna…"

"No, Matty. I'm just going to walk his spine for him and give him a quick back massage. Just like Kiko showed me. That is absolutely and completely *all*."

Matty looked at her mistress. "You sure? You're awfully pink."

Charlie deliberately tried to slow her breathing. "I know. He's caught me by surprise. It's the Earl of Calverton."

Matty's jaw dropped and she plopped down on the big bed, heedless of the gown she was crushing beneath her ample hips. "Oooh! Never say."

"Oh yes, Matty. He's here." Charlie struggled with her lacings and slid out of her gown. "He has a back problem and came looking for Kiko. That's all. And before you ask, he doesn't have a clue who I am."

"Well, let's keep it that way, shall we?" said the woman, with the easy familiarity of a long time friend.

Charlie slid her undergarments off and allowed Matty to ease the silk over her head. She knew she'd need her balance to maintain this treatment and Kiko had emphasized over and over again the need for lightness. Lightness in the heart, the mind and the body. No heavy clothes, no intense thoughts, just focus and awareness.

Charlie sighed.

Awareness. *That* wouldn't be a problem.

She was very aware of Jordan Lyndhurst. She just wasn't quite sure why. His frowning expression had caught her attention within seconds of entering that room, and he was firmly fixed within her consciousness.

"So, do you want another girl in with you?" Matty's words jerked her back from her thoughts.

"No, I don't think so. But just in case, who's free?"

Matty paused in her folding and tidying, her brow wrinkling. "Well, let me see, Susie and Grace are entertaining Mr. Johns this evening."

"I remember. He did tell us he'd be here tonight for his usual entertainment. And I think it will be perfect for Susie to start with Grace. A good introduction. "

"Most everyone has a client who has either arrived already or who will be here soon."

Charlie was always amazed at Matty's uncanny ability to stay on top of the doings at the Crescent every single night. She seemed to know instinctively who would be best for whom, and was the single best resource Charlie could have ever imagined. Every item Charlie owned would be happily parted with before she'd let anything happen to Matty.

"The three newer girls are in the billiard room and Antonio is keeping an eye on the crowd in there. It's full again, of course, with a few lined up to get in."

Charlie's newest feature, her "Billiard Room", featured a large green baize table, several cues and three female players, all quite naked.

Customers were permitted a seat around the table, where they might smoke, drink and enjoy the view to their hearts' content. Touching, however, was prohibited.

So far, the room was a screaming success. The sight of three nude lovelies playing billiards was provocative and entrancing. There were few customers who left the establishment after their allotted time in the billiard room. Most of them hurried off to find themselves a partner for the rest of the night. It had proved a handsome moneymaker, the girls liked the respite from other, more athletic duties, and Charlie was generally pleased with the results.

"Oh, you know who's not on tonight is Jane. She's around someplace, but can't service any customers this evening, it's her courses time."

Charlie nodded, aware that one or other of her girls was bound to miss a few days a month. It was calculated into her system, and she'd been amazed at how grateful the girls were.

"And Dr. Ponsonby was by again." Matty's lips curled into a half-sneer. "He was pushing Dora to take him upstairs. Just like he did last time. Antonio saw him off, but I think he's going to be trouble, that one."

Charlie nodded. "It's time to deal with him, I think." She turned towards the door. "Remind me to make an appointment with Ponsonby soon. We'll straighten out this business once and for all. I must go. The Earl will be waiting."

Matty slanted a look at Charlie. "You be careful with that one, sweeting. Jordan Lyndhurst could be very dangerous."

"Not to a London Madam, Matty," she smiled slightly. "That's all he thinks I am. A procurer. Lowest of the low. He asked how long I'd been a prostitute."

Matty gaped. "Why that dirty, rotten-minded piece of..."

"What else should he think? I'm happy he feels that way. Keeps his nose out of our business. He'll pay no more attention to me than he would if I were what he assumes I am."

"You be careful. You hear me?" The other woman's eyes betrayed her worry.

Charlie crossed the room and put her arms around Matty, hugging her hard. "You worry too much."

"And if *I* don't, who's going to, I'd like to know?"

Charlie pulled back and gazed at the woman she loved more than any other on the face of the planet. She raised her hand and gently caressed the savagely wrinkled skin that marred one side of Matty's neck and rose to a sharp point behind one ear. No hair grew there any more.

"Matty, you've done enough for me. Let me do the worrying, and the planning, from now on. Please?"

Matty's eyes filled with tears. "You're more precious to me than any daughter could be, Charlie. I can't help worrying that this life is not right for you. You should be in a fine house with a fine husband and several fine..."

Charlie's finger stopped Matty's speech. "...Children. Yes I know. You've told me. But it's not going to happen. We're here now, making a new life for ourselves, and hopefully making lives better for a few poor unfortunate girls while we're at it. Let's look at it that way, Matty. All right?"

"Oh, go on with you. Go walk up and down that man's back. Tempt the devil if you must, but don't blame me if your feet get singed."

Charlie grinned at Matty and swirled out of the room, a barefoot beauty in swirling blue silk.

Her smile faded as she reached the closed door, behind which lay a very naked Jordan Lyndhurst. Her hand slid to her back and she felt the scars of her own injuries through the softness of her robe. She'd been burned once by this family.

She'd not let it happen again.

Chapter 2

Her light tap on the door stirred his loins and he grunted for her to enter. He'd followed her instructions to the letter.

Naked as the day he was born, he was sprawled on his face along the low divan, which he'd pulled nearer to the fire.

He turned his head and snuggled more comfortably into the pillow as she closed the door quietly behind her. His eyes glittered as he watched her approach from beneath half closed lids.

"I didn't ask you to fuck me, you know."

"I don't intend to."

"Then why the change of clothing?"

Charlie moved out of his line of vision for a few moments then reappeared, clad in her simple blue chemise. She had not realized that standing between him and the fire rendered it all but invisible.

He felt his cock harden, and he shifted uncomfortably against the fabric of the cushions beneath him.

"I understand you have had this treatment before, my Lord. May I ask what your previous practitioner was wearing at the time?"

"Well, blue silk wasn't considered appropriate for a gardener."

She ignored his attempt at humor, busying herself with small jars that she placed over a warming candle.

He shrugged. "Mostly just some kind of cotton robe, now I come to think of it."

"I see. This technique requires focus, concentration and an ability to sense the essence, what is known as the *chi,* if you will, of the patient. Additional layers of clothing inhibit the ability to become one with the patient, to feel the areas of the body that are troubling."

"I can tell you exactly where I'm troubled. Right here." His muscles flexed as he raised his hand behind him and pointed to a spot just above his buttocks. He watched her eyes as she followed his pointing finger to the site of his injury and then wandered a little further, taking a good look at his backside. "See anything? Anything that might need your attention?"

She met his gaze with an expressionless one of her own, then reached for her first pot of massage oil.

"What's that?"

"This? This is fragranced oil, which I shall use to relax your skin and your mind. Releasing the tensions around the injury is one of the first steps to healing it."

His hand lashed out and grabbed her wrist before she could pour the oil onto his body. He raised himself onto his arm as he dragged her toward him.

"Forgive me. I am a naturally cautious man." He pulled her hand closer and sniffed at the bottle. It was light, soothing, and vaguely oriental and he wrinkled his nose as he tried to identify it.

"It is a blend of sandalwood and lotus oils, my Lord. It will not harm you."

He released her wrist, knowing he'd probably held it too tightly, but unable to stop himself. For some reason, his nerves were on a high state of alert around this woman.

"Very well." He lay back with his face down and waited.

As softly as raindrops, he felt the splash of the first dribbles of oil. Soothingly, she rubbed her hands lightly over and around his skin, not quite touching his buttocks, but running her hands all the way up his spine and back down in a gentle circle. It was an amazingly erotic feeling, and yet he knew his body was relaxing beneath her touch.

After several minutes, she added a little more oil, then fetched a damp towel that she had placed near the fire.

"Ouch! That's hot."

"It's meant to be. This will aid the oil in its task and also add another level of relaxation to any muscles that may be tight."

He was tempted to ask for one for his cock too, if she was going to discuss things that were tight.

She moved away from his side, stretching.

He watched, fascinated, as she proceeded to work her way through what looked like a series of cat-like attitudes. She pulled her own muscles, curled them up and then flexed them, bending, resting and standing tall in an odd sequence of movements.

He could almost see her focus intensifying and her eyes reflected her concentration as she returned to his side and removed the towel.

He was so hot for her he could have knocked her off her feet, ripped her chemise from hem to neck and thrust into her right that second. It was a huge surprise to him that he didn't. She was a whore, a Madam. She must be used to that kind of treatment. So what was holding him back?

Why wasn't he, even now, beating his balls against her pussy and sucking on those tender breasts? Why weren't they both screaming out their orgasms together?

Why?

Well, the answer might have been that she did not seem in the slightest bit aware of him as a man. And that fact alone was really aggravating him. He had yet to get any kind of sexual expression out of her. She was almost wooden in her treatment of him, impartial to the point of absurdity.

He made himself a pledge as he felt her hands begin to exert pressure on his sore spine.

He was going to have this woman. He was going to get those eyes to light with the fire of lust, the need for an orgasm that he'd only let her have after she'd screamed out his name and begged him for release.

He was going to make her come like she'd never come before.

And he'd probably do the same thing—just to keep her company, of course.

* * * * *

Charlie needed all the focus and concentration she could muster as she felt his smooth skin beneath her palms.

If he'd had any idea of her internal turmoil, he'd probably have been astounded. She was almost weak at the thought of his body so near hers. The room had seemed to become smaller as she'd run through her warm up exercises, and the heat had flared both in the fireplace and inside her womb.

Something primeval within her sex was pulsing and throbbing in recognition of the urge to mate. To join with this prime specimen that was starting to groan a little under her pressure.

She increased the weight behind her hands, pushing firmly into the muscles on either side of his spine and digging her fingers deep into the solid mass she found there.

The oil slid between them, a silken veil that allowed her to smooth and knead his flesh without impairment.

His body was perfect. In spite of the odd scar here and there, and a much more evident dip at the base of his spine where his back problem must have begun, she could find no fault with the man lying quiescent under her hands.

"May I ask how you received this injury?"

"Salamanca."

"You were shot?"

"Horse threw me. Shell exploded next to us. Blew him off his feet and he fell on me. Killed instantly, poor creature."

"Along with a terrible number of other soldiers too, I understand." Charlie commented quietly.

Jordan shrugged, clearly not anxious to relive past battles, especially that one where Charlie knew so many had died in such carnage.

"And you have had pain since then?"

"Some. It got worse when I returned home and began working at Calverton Chase."

Not by a fraction of a blink did Charlie reveal how familiar this name was to her. "Working? You mean taking care of estate business?"

"No, I mean working." He fidgeted a little as his muscles began to loosen under Charlie's continual pressure. "The damned place had burned while I was gone, almost to the ground. When I inherited it, there was little left standing but one central building and the stables."

Charlie managed not to react. She remembered the terrible fire, the east wing collapsing, but hadn't realized the full extent of the damage.

She needed to stop him. Memories were not what she wanted to indulge in, not with Jordan Lyndhurst lying naked next to her.

"Forgive my forwardness, my Lord. I must straddle your limbs for a short time."

"Help yourself," he muttered settling himself a little more comfortably. His voice sounded relaxed, his breathing even. Her lessons with Kiko had not failed her.

Of course, Kiko had never told her what it would be like to spread one's thighs and straddle a naked man.

Kiko never told her how hot his body would be or how pleasingly rough the hairy skin of his thighs would feel against her soft, silk covered ones. She carefully arranged her garment to prevent their flesh from touching. Charlie was so afraid that if their naked skin came into contact, she'd burst into flames on the spot.

As if he could sense her discomfort, Jordan chuckled and she felt him shake as his laugh rolled through him.

"Are you sure you're not going to fuck me when we're done? I'm certainly developing the urge. Must be that scent or something."

Charlie's mind froze for an instant, as visions passed through her consciousness. Images of sweaty tangled bodies, naked limbs, hot breaths and hotter lips, and the sweetness of flesh meeting flesh.

"You are uncomfortable, my Lord?" she said, beginning her rhythmic pressure up and down his back once again, this time with the full weight of her body behind her hands. Anything to distract her errant thoughts.

"Sweetheart, I have a very hard cock here that would love to make your acquaintance. I told myself that this was strictly a medicinal visit, but your house and your delightful person have reminded me that I'm a man with a man's needs. Perhaps after the treatment is finished, you could..." he waved his hand vaguely in the air.

Charlie worked on him in silence, considering her options. She chewed her lip, knowing that her deepest desire was out of the question. The one that was nagging her to rip off her thin silk chemise and rub her aching breasts over his slippery back. The one that was telling her his cock would feel even better if she rubbed her soft mound against it, or took it into her mouth.

The one that was telling her she had an emptiness deep inside her pussy that would feel a great deal better if Jordan Lyndhurst were to administer large helpings of that cock he was talking about. Large pounding helpings. Deep, long, thrusting helpings.

God, she was getting wet. This would never do. She came to her decision.

"Very well, my Lord. I believe you are ready for the spinal walking treatment, and after that I shall ensure that your needs are met."

* * * * *

The Seventh Earl of Calverton tried very hard not to jump. Jordan could scarcely believe what he'd just heard. Neither could his cock, which had leapt to even greater lengths at her words, and was even now trying to thrust its way through the pillow beneath his belly.

She moved off his thighs, which immediately felt cool and bereft of her warm weight. He listened and tracked her movements as she pulled a small bell and went to the door in response to the almost immediate tap.

A quiet conversation ensued, and strain though he might, he could hear nothing that was said.

"My Lord, I shall now mount your back."

"Darling, I doubt it." His wry humor was wasted. In her cool and efficient way, Madam Charlie had stepped carefully up onto the divan and was placing one small foot firmly on the lowest portion of his back. She steadied her balance and drew in her breath.

The other foot joined the first and he felt her full weight. His muscles were soft and pliable thanks to her massage, and he could almost feel the bones slithering back into alignment as she delicately walked up to a point just below his shoulders, then retraced her steps.

She was completely silent, to the point where he could hear the swish of her silk garment as she moved.

He guessed she was focused on her steps along his spine and he was forced to admit her balance and movements were faultless.

Within moments it was over, and she was carefully stepping off him, back onto the floor.

"You are well, my Lord?"

He moved experimentally. "Yes. Yes indeed. Much of the pain has been relieved. Actually, more than usual. That is quite amazing, Madam Charlie."

He started to roll onto his side, but a firm hand on his shoulder stopped him.

"Not quite yet, my Lord. Your muscles are now very soft and relaxed. We must let them wake up a little, if you will, before putting them to the test."

"And how do 'we' do that?" His lips curved into the pillow.

"With this."

The lightest of touches on his spine told him she was back to massaging him. But this time, rather than the working weight of her hands, she was using something very soft, like a piece of sheepskin.

Slowly, she rubbed his back, up and down and back up again. He very much wanted to purr.

"Why do you run a brothel?" The question slipped out before he had time to think about it.

There was silence for a moment as her rubbing motion continued, unabated. He wondered if she'd answer him at all.

"It is an occupation like any other."

"You are well educated by the sound of your speech. You are attractive, intelligent, and clever enough to run this place and make it profitable, to judge by what I've seen. Surely you'd have plenty to offer a husband?"

For the first time since he'd laid eyes on her, he felt his words cause a reaction. Her hands slipped ever so slightly from their rhythmic stroking.

"And you believe marriage would be preferable to this?"

Jordan snorted. "Better than being a prostitute, albeit a highly paid one, who owns her own whorehouse? Of course."

"In that assumption, my Lord, you are sadly mistaken."

"What do you mean?"

The silence that followed his question was broken by a quiet knock from the hallway.

Madam Charlie removed the fur from his skin with a final pat, and he sighed as she crossed the room to the door.

Now, he thought. Now we're done with the massaging, rubbing and treating. Now I get to return the favor and massage her, rub her and treat her pussy to a good dose of Jordan Lyndhurst.

His mouth watered as he imagined her naked and slippery beneath him, and his mind started wondering if she might enjoy the touch of that furry thing. Perhaps a tickle across her nipples right after he'd grazed them gently with his teeth. Or maybe he'd brush it delicately across her clit, just to warm her up for his tongue. Of course, he'd also like to try the oil. Perhaps pouring it over her belly and rubbing the head of his cock in it might be fun.

Or even better, rubbing it on her back, the way she had done to him. He'd be a little more adventurous of course, and make sure her buttocks were nice and soft and shiny after he was done.

Perhaps he'd even slip some between her cheeks. See how tight her little arse was. He'd never taken a woman that way before, but he'd heard many a campfire discussion amongst his men, most of whom swore there was nothing like it.

For the first time, he wondered if they might be right.

"My Lord?" Her cool, collected voice pierced the miasma of lust that was settling over his brain.

"This is Jane. She is going to tend to your other needs this evening."

"*What?*"

Chapter 3

Charlie had no idea how she kept from laughing. The look on Jordan Lyndhurst's face as he jumped to his feet was a priceless study in shock.

"But I thought…"

"Oh, Sir, I'm ever so good. You won't be disappointed." Jane's eager face gazed at Jordan and fell to his cock, which was standing straight up in military fashion.

He slumped back down onto the divan.

Jane crossed the room and fell to her knees gracefully in front of him, reaching for him with a gentle hand. "Oooh, this is a fine beauty you've got here, Sir. Mind if I give him a kiss?"

The Earl seemed stunned and Charlie could see his skin shiver as Jane bent her head and pressed her lips to his erection.

Charlie turned to leave them alone.

"Madam Charlie."

His voice stopped her in her tracks. She turned and raised an eyebrow, noting that Jane hadn't ceased her actions. On the contrary, she was now getting herself quite comfortable between Jordan's spread thighs.

She refused to admit that the picture of Jane's dark head moving slowly and sensuously over Jordan's cock was arousing, but she felt her womb contract and her own juices moisten her thighs, making a liar out of her.

"My Lord?" Her voice was expressionless.

"I'll double the fee if you stay."

That brought Jane's head up and she shot a quick glance at her mistress. Charlie made a couple of lightning decisions, and nodded at Jane to continue what she was doing.

"Very well, My Lord. If that is your wish. You understand that I shall not participate, of course."

"Of course." The candlelight glinted from his brown eyes. "You will watch, however."

Charlie crossed the room and seated herself on a straight-backed chair, arranging her silk robe carefully.

"You will not remove your eyes from us. Is that understood?"

Charlie met his gaze with a blank one of her own. "Of course, my Lord. Our customers' desires are always honored."

"Not always." Jordan's muttered rejoinder was almost lost as Jane enthusiastically began to suck on his cock, slurping her way down to the thick base and then back up to flutter her tongue beneath the head.

Charlie watched, as directed.

Her nails were clenched so tight she knew she'd be leaving small scars in the palms of her hands, but not by one muscle would she show this man that he affected her.

Not by one twitch would she reveal that the sight of his body sheening with sweat was arousing to her. Nor would she let on that a bead of her own perspiration was trickling down her spine, which she held so rigid in the chair.

His nipples had tightened to small brown nubs as Jane began to caress his balls as well as his cock.

His chest was as well-formed as the rest of him, strong and slightly brown, as if he had indeed been working outside in the sunshine without benefit of a shirt. Knowing how his flesh felt beneath her fingers made Charlie's heart beat faster, and a dull yearning began inside her body.

He slid his hand down to Jane's head, pushing her hair to one side.

"Jane?"

She stopped her movement and glanced up at him over his glistening arousal. "Sir?"

"Jane, loose your breasts for me, I'd like to see them."

"Very good, Sir."

But it was at Charlie that Jordan gazed as Jane shrugged her dress off her shoulders. It was at Charlie's breasts that Jordan stared as he reached out and smoothed Jane's soft flesh, and it was at Charlie that Jordan winked as he pulled Jane to his mouth and suckled her nipple, making her moan.

Charlie was helpless to prevent her body from reacting. She moved very, very slightly, hoping to conceal the fact that her own breasts were about to ignite from the heat his gaze was generating.

She prayed that her own rapidly hardening nipples were not betraying her state. She was hot, wet, and aching, but she'd be damned if she'd let him know.

Jane was rubbing her chest over Jordan's hairy thighs now, having returned to her former occupation of devouring his cock. He gently ran his hand through her hair as he studied Charlie's golden locks.

She refrained from reaching up to see if her elegant coiffeur was intact. His glance flickered down to her breasts again, heating them with the passion she saw within his eyes.

He desired her, that was a given. Why she returned that desire, she had no idea.

Jane was very obviously enjoying herself this evening. Instead of her usual five minute session, she was prolonging this one, bringing him to the brink, then easing off and letting them both catch their breath.

"I would like to help you release yourself shortly, Sir," she breathed finally, rubbing a nipple against his balls.

"I should like that too, Jane. But not in your mouth, if you please. In your hand. That way we can pretend that Madam Charlie over there is actually part of our fun. What do you think?"

"Oh, Sir." Jane giggled, blushing with her own heat. "Madam Charlie doesn't play with the customers, Sir."

Jordan's eyes flashed to Charlie.

"Jane, I think you may finish the Earl now." Charlie's clipped tones reminded Jane of her duties.

"Yes, Madam Charlie. It'll be my pleasure."

"Jane? Try the little pressure point touch we discussed at yesterday's meeting." Charlie could have been ordering wine for the evening meal for all the expression she allowed into her voice.

"Oooh. All right, ma'am." Jane giggled again and bent back to Jordan's cock with enthusiasm.

It took mere seconds this time for her to bring him close to his climax, and Charlie noted the rapid rise and fall of his chest. His eyes were almost closed, but she didn't fool herself that his attention was distracted. This man was dangerous, as Matty had warned, and she knew better than to let down her guard.

Jane removed her mouth with one last loving lick, and let her hand take over. She eased the other beneath his balls and slid it to his tightly puckered arse muscles. His eyes widened.

Charlie never moved a muscle, knowing that now Jane was delicately inserting one finger into his backside and probing to find a certain spot. She could certainly tell when Jane found it.

He grunted and heaved his buttocks off the divan.

Jane held onto his pulsating cock, refusing to give up her rhythm. He threw his head back, neck cords stretched tight.

"Yes, now. *Now* Charlie."

Charlie's mind froze as she heard him cry out *her* name. Not Jane's, not the woman whose hand was fucking him into heaven. But *her* name. Charlie. She realized he was fantasizing about *her*.

Breathless, she watched as the veins in his cock throbbed violently. He grunted again and jets of his seed pulsed high from his cock, probably spurting in time with his heartbeat. Charlie wanted to find out.

She wanted to put her hand on his chest and feel that heart pounding beneath her palm. To rest her head there and listen as it slowed down again.

What had Jane felt, she wondered. How did it feel to hold a man like that while he shouted out his pleasure?

For the first time in her life, Charlie wanted to know.

And her interest couldn't have been aroused by a riskier man. This was truly a case of where curiosity might indeed kill the cat.

"Thank you, Jane. That was an excellent experience."

Jane, who was already straightening her dress and retying her laces, gave him a big smile.

"Well, thank *you*, Sir. It's a pleasure to help out someone as well made as yourself, Sir." She gently mopped him clean of his juices with a damp cloth. The same one, he noted, that Charlie had draped on his back earlier.

"I hope you'll come back and visit again, Sir. I'd be happy to take care of any of your needs. And not just with me mouth, either." Jane gave Jordan a cheeky little grin and nodded respectfully at Charlie as she whisked herself out of the room.

Charlie rose stiffly to her feet, cloaking herself in her protective dignity. It was her customary armor, and she was able to meet Jordan's eyes without a flicker of expression. She felt rather proud of herself. It was not an easy performance, since her own juices were sticky on the inside of her thighs.

Jordan eased his body from the divan. She'd forgotten how tall he was.

He moved towards her with purpose, naked, glistening, his cock nestling flaccid between his legs.

He smiled as he caught her quick glance. "He'll be more than ready for a round with you, Charlie. Just say the word."

Charlie made a production out of glancing down at his manhood. Sure enough, *he* was stirring again.

"No thank you, Lord Calverton. However, if you should wish additional services, I can summon one of our other ladies."

Jordan sighed and stepped even closer to her.

Charlie obstinately held her ground, something telling her that to move back from this man would be to admit weakness. Never allow your weaknesses to show. She'd learned that the hard way. From another Calverton.

With a grin, Jordan brushed past her to the screen where he retrieved his clothes. With unashamed exhibitionism, he dressed slowly in front of her.

"My compliments, Madam Charlie."

"Your back is feeling better?"

"My back, my front, my cock *and* my balls." He grinned at her. If he hoped to shock her with his language, he was fair and far out. "Everything is feeling better. Everything except for one thing."

Charlie tilted her head slightly and allowed her raised eyebrow to ask the question.

"My mind, Charlie. My mind isn't satisfied."

Charlie blinked once as he neared her again. Naked, he was a woman's dream. Dressed, he was overpoweringly handsome and his presence filled her senses.

"My mind is full of you, Charlie. You're a puzzle, an enigma. A mystery. I'm a man who likes to solve mysteries. Who likes to lay them bare. To delve into their darkest secrets and bring them into the light. I like to touch puzzles, Charlie."

He was nearer than he should be for her peace of mind. His eyes were shining as he met her cool gaze. She could almost swear he was enjoying himself more teasing her with his double entendres than he had when Jane sucked him off.

"I like to take them apart, see what makes them tick, how to touch them and smooth them out and make them tick faster. Like your pulse. Just here..." He reached out and laid the very tip of his forefinger on her neck, where her heartbeat was pounding like a racehorse at the finish line.

"Did you realize that a man can tell a lot about a woman just by watching this little spot here?" His finger grazed her skin delicately. It felt like a burning brand to Charlie, who fought an enormous battle with her reflexes not to flinch from his touch.

"It's fluttering like the heart of a captured bird. My God, that's poetic. I don't usually spout things like that. It must be your influence, Charlie."

Back and forth his finger brushed her flesh.

"That, and the fact that I want to fuck you senseless."

Her breath caught in her throat, but she continued to meet his gaze. She knew she was coloring up now under his touch and his words, but she refused to succumb to his seductive manner. This man could well be her sworn enemy. She had to cling to that fact before she melted in a puddle of useless desire at his feet.

"I want you screaming underneath me, Charlie. Have you ever screamed, I wonder? Ever been desperate for a man's cock to thrust into you so that you can take that final step into another world? A world of light and dark, of day and night, a world where nothing exists but pleasure and the pain of finishing, coming, releasing your soul?"

His lips were closer now, and still Charlie refused to move a muscle. She wondered if she'd ever be able to move again. Her body was locked in a furious battle with itself, and she was sure that she'd probably end up as a casualty.

"We'll do it too, Charlie, you and me. We are going to fuck, and it will be soon. Sometimes I just know these things. Then I'll watch your eyes as I suck on your breasts, and I'll watch your eyes as I make you come with my tongue inside your warm cunt. I'll watch your eyes as I pound my cock deep into your wet body, and they'll tell me what I want to know, Charlie. Your eyes will tell me how much you want my cock. They'll betray your secrets, Charlie. All of them. I know. Trust me on this."

He pulled back slightly, as if waiting for a reaction.

She gave him nothing.

"Until then, my sweet." His lips brushed the pulse in her neck. "You'll just have to dream of me. I can assure you I'll be thinking of you." He put the finger that he had rested against her neck into his mouth and sucked it, staring at her all the while. Then he withdrew it slowly, lips curving as he did so. "Soon, Charlie. Soon."

He moved away, shrugging into his jacket and tossed her a grin as he left the room.

She stood motionless, for a full minute, then sank down into the chair, resting her head back against the ornate carving.

She raised a hand tremblingly to her cheeks.

To her surprise, tears were running freely over her skin and splashing onto her blue silk gown.

* * * * *

Jordan had no idea if his legs would carry him down the stairs to the ground floor of the Crescent. He was weak as the proverbial kitten, and not from the effective ministrations of Jane, either.

He was weak from the climax he'd had because *she* was watching him. He'd thought he was pretty well up on most things sexual. Damn, he was a soldier, for God's sake. He'd seen it all and done it all. Or most of it, anyway.

But this night had been the most erotic experience he could ever remember having. Not because of a woman's mouth, or cunt, or even because of her touch. Just because of her eyes.

Because for a little while, those gray eyes had burned. And he'd felt their heat halfway across the room.

What would he feel when they were burning beneath him?

His cock stirred yet again, reminding him that such thoughts were probably best kept for somewhere less public.

He wandered through several of the rooms, sampling some of the excellent brandy and chatting with acquaintances. He told himself he was not waiting for the owner of the establishment to make her appearance.

He also knew he was lying to himself.

"Jordan? Is that you?"

A light voice cut through the babble of conversation as Jordan moved into the large foyer.

"Good God, it is. What on earth are *you* doing here, darling?"

Jordan Lyndhurst would have turned tail and run, if he could. Unfortunately, strategic retreat was not an option.

"Elizabeth. This is a surprise." Jordan watched as Lady Elizabeth Wentworth gracefully swanned her way through the throng to await him at the foot of the stairs.

Beautiful, slightly scandalous and toasted by the Ton, Elizabeth had made no secret of her interest in Jordan. However, he was among several whom she favored, and Jordan could only hope that there were others higher on her list than himself.

He enjoyed her company, and felt there might actually be a nice person underneath all her society fol-de-rol, but wasn't sure if he was ready to play her games this evening. He was off kilter enough as it was.

He watched her black hair and blue eyes garner the attention of the men she passed. She was really quite lovely. He couldn't fathom why she didn't make his pulse race.

Her gown was a masterpiece of understatement, hanging precariously off her beautiful breasts, and giving the impression that if she caught her breath it would completely collapse. "If I'd known you were going to visit, I'd have begged for a place in your carriage, Jordan," she pouted, slipping her arm through his.

"I hardly expected to find you at a place like this, Elizabeth." Jordan managed a slightly reproving tone to his voice.

"Oh, darling, you're too funny. Everyone comes to the Crescent now. Well, not everyone, I suppose. But certainly a lot of people. And they set a very nice table and the gaming room is well run. Besides, I had Tony bring me, because Mother is trying to decide whether she should try to save these 'Poor Unfortunates', and I thought I ought to take a look before she gets *too* involved..." She dropped her voice and glanced around, as did Jordan.

He was vainly looking for a Poor Unfortunate, but couldn't see one.

"You know how Mother is," continued Elizabeth, tugging Jordan along beside her.

"Mother", Jordan knew, was Lady Amanda Wentworth, nicknamed "Armada" Wentworth by some wag, who'd likened her approach to that of the Spanish Armada. A dozen galleons under full sail.

Lady Wentworth liked to busy herself redeeming Poor Unfortunates, as the fallen women of London were called. Seeing as her husband was a prime contributor to the downfall of many a Poor Unfortunate, Jordan supposed it was the right thing to do. There was a certain kind of symmetry about it.

A stir behind him caught his attention.

Madam Charlie was descending the staircase.

"Oh, I'll bet she's one," prattled Elizabeth nosily.

Jordan watched as Charlie, now gowned exquisitely in gray lace and pearls, moved amongst her guests.

"I rather doubt she's poor, Elizabeth. And as for being unfortunate, well, look at her." Jordan's eyes couldn't pull away from the graceful picture Charlie made as she nodded and smiled at friends and offered her hand to new acquaintances. "That's Madam Charlie. Your hostess this evening." He could feel his cock twitching at the mere mention of her name.

"Oh, *that's* her."

Something in Elizabeth's voice caught Jordan's attention and he wrenched his gaze from the tall woman in gray.

"You know of her?"

"Well of course, although not *personally*. Where *have* you been, Jordan? Oh, I forgot..." Her light laugh tinkled across the candles. "You've been in the country. *Working*." She restrained a theatrical shudder.

"Madam Charlie. You said you know her?"

"Well, yes...no, I don't know *her* exactly..."

"Hello, old chap. Getting a bit of cunt...oh, sorry Elizabeth. Didn't see you." A large form appeared next to Jordan and resolved itself into Sir Anthony Douglas.

Under ordinary circumstances, the two men would have exchanged pleasantries, slapped each other on the back, swapped comparisons of the women available for their pleasure and gone their separate ways.

This evening, however, Jordan Lyndhurst gritted his teeth and wished for his dress sword with which to dispose of Sir Anthony Douglas. Elizabeth was about to reveal Charlie's secrets and this...this dunderhead had to butt in.

"Tony, I'm going to let Jordan take me home, now. Do you mind?" She flashed him a dazzling smile. Jordan's heart sank to his highly polished boots.

"Not at all, Elizabeth. Good idea. Think I'll go play some billiards, myself." He nudged Jordan, nearly knocking him off his feet. "If you know what I mean, old man." Receiving a subtle wink and a nudge from a man who easily topped six foot five, must have weighed close to twenty stone and had hair as red as the sunset, was an experience. Something like being run over by an elephant, Jordan imagined.

Elizabeth giggled. "Oh Tony, you naughty boy. Run along then." Tony waved at them both and disappeared through a nearby door. "He's so funny. He thinks I don't know."

"Know what?"

"The Billiards Room?"

Jordan shook his head, not understanding a word of the conversation.

Elizabeth looked at him in surprise. "You really don't know, do you?"

"Know *what*?" he repeated, teeth clenched.

Elizabeth snuggled up against him even closer and stood on tiptoe, breathing into his ear. "The billiard room is where the Poor Unfortunates play billiards." She paused for dramatic effect.

Jordan ruined it. "So?"

Elizabeth sighed. "They do so without the benefit of clothes." Her whisper just reached his hearing as Charlie's gaze passed over his face and stopped.

He froze, an image of Charlie, naked, golden hair spilling over a green baize table as he plowed into her from behind flashing across his mind. He sucked in a breath.

"Yes, isn't it too, *too* dreadful? That's what made Mother wonder if these Poor Unfortunates should be next on her list for assistance."

"Elizabeth. Have someone fetch your cloak. I'll get my carriage and meet you outside." Suddenly he wanted to get away from this place. The air was stifling, he couldn't breathe, and he needed to go somewhere where he could think about Charlie without seeing her laugh and smile and talk to other men.

He moved to the door, where Antonio, the massive butler, was waiting.

"Your account for the evening, My Lord. Would you care to settle now, or shall we send a messenger to your man of business tomorrow?" he asked, passing Jordan a small folded card.

"I'll take care of it now." Jordan pulled out some coins and counted out fifty guineas without a blink. "Your mistress must be quite expensive. That's a sizeable sum for a massage."

"Oh no, my Lord, you are mistaken. The fee is for Jane's services, and was doubled, at your request. Madam Charlie does not accept money for medical treatments that she performs out of the goodness of her heart."

Antonio looked at Jordan as if he was the lowest form of life.

Suddenly, he felt that he was. But then again, he was leaving a whorehouse, no matter how nicely it was gussied up to look like an elegant Salon. How was he supposed to know that its owner looked upon her massages as beneficial medical treatments?

A little voice told him that he might do well to trust the messages his heart was sending to his brain. He ignored the little voice.

"I'm ready, darling. Shall we?" Elizabeth bustled up to Jordan, and grabbing his hand led him through the door and away from 14 Beaulieu Crescent.

Chapter 4

"So, tell me about Madam Charlie."

Elizabeth gazed at Jordan as he shot his order at her, barely waiting for her to settle her gown on the seat opposite him. The carriage rocked into motion and she narrowed her eyes at the man staring at her.

"Why do you want to know?"

"Elizabeth. Don't be annoying."

"I'll make a deal with you. I'll tell you what I know if you touch me while I'm doing it."

"*What?*" Jordan couldn't have been more surprised if the carriage had sprouted wings and flown over London.

"Touch me, Jordan. I've been watching people all night as they brushed up against each other, rubbed each other, kissed each other. It's driving me out of my *mind.*"

"You don't know what you're saying," sputtered Jordan. "And if you think you're going to get me to marry you by some sort of compromising behavior, let me tell you how wrong you are."

Elizabeth sighed. "Damn you, Jordan Lyndhurst. It's not about *you.* Although God only knows I don't seem to be able to convince any man of that fact. I *don't* want to marry you. D'you hear me?"

She was leaning forward now, poking him in the chest with a very rigid forefinger.

"I hear you. So does half of London, a portion of Chiswick and probably a good two thirds of the boats on the Thames."

She ignored his sarcasm. "I have needs, Jordan. A woman has needs. I'm of taking care of them myself. I want to know that I can make a man's cock jump, like that Madam Charlie does."

"What the hell are you talking about? And watch your language." Jordan struggled for words. Elizabeth Wentworth, Incomparable of the Ton, was using words he never thought to hear fall from her elegant lips.

"I watched you watch her, Jordan. She came down those stairs and your breeches nearly exploded. Now look at this..." She leaned nearer and wrenched at the front of her gown.

Her breasts spilled out into the shadows of the carriage, and Jordan had to confess that they were quite beautiful examples of womanly attributes.

"See?"

"Ahem. Yes. I see quite well. Now put them away."

Elizabeth leaned even closer, letting him scent her light fragrance. "No, I'm talking about *this*, Jordan." She laid her palm on his crotch, feeling the bulge that had appeared about the same time as her breasts had swung free.

"Nice, but watch this. If I was to tell you that apparently Madam Charlie likes to have her titties suckled..."

Sure enough, underneath Elizabeth's hand, Jordan's cock leapt to attention, and he cursed his own body for betraying him.

Elizabeth grinned. "Darling, I don't care. If you want to fuck a whore, that's fine with me. It's not about emotions, or love, or marriage or happily-ever-after. It's about me wanting to learn more about pleasure. Wanting to be touched with some warmth and affection. I'm a grown woman, Jordan. I've seen sex all around me tonight and I'd like to have some of my own. From someone I trust. Don't make me find someone else."

She reached for his hand and brought it to the softness of her breast, sighing with pleasure as she rubbed it across her hard nipple. "Please?"

Jordan fought a valiant battle with himself, but he too was on the edge. His mind was full of a gray-eyed beauty, his cock was hardening by the second and a lovely woman was asking him to touch her body.

Hell, he was only human.

"This never leaves this carriage, Elizabeth. Do I make myself clear?"

"Absolutely, Jordan. I certainly don't want the rest of the world knowing I had to beg for sexual favors, do I?" Her wry tone was not lost on Jordan.

"You won't be getting sexual favors. I'll see you get your pleasure, but that's all, Elizabeth."

"That's all I want, darling." She slid over next to him and pressed her breasts against his chest. "I'll even let you pretend I'm her…"

Jordan frowned. "I pay attention to my partners, Elizabeth. I don't play games like that."

Elizabeth giggled. "Very well. But you can't stop me telling you what I know about her, can you? Go ahead, Jordan. Touch me. I won't break."

Jordan sighed. Friendship sometimes put a great strain on a man. He bent his head to Elizabeth's breasts. They were full and firm, and she shivered as he gently kissed the warm swell of her flesh and pulled on a nipple with his lips.

"Oh yes. That's lovely. More please."

He obliged. "So," he breathed on the wetness his tongue had wiped around her nipples, making her shiver. "You were going to tell me about her."

Elizabeth arched her back pushing her breast into his face. "Yes. She's young, you know. Not more than about twenty-two, or so I'm told. Oh God, more of that, yes…right there…"

His lips and teeth were busy nibbling, licking, soothing. He felt her bones melt as he eased his arms around her body and pulled her onto his lap. His hand unfastened the laces at her back and she heaved a sigh of relief as he loosened the bodice of her gown and tugged it free. Elizabeth was a lovely woman.

He warmed to his task.

"She's only been running the Crescent for a little less than a year. Some say she inherited it, some say she bought it outright after working there all her life. Others say it was purchased for her by some man who wanted to buy her off."

Jordan's teeth clamped down hard on a nipple, making Elizabeth squeak.

"Sorry. Go on."

"I will if you will."

Jordan, excellent soldier that he was, followed orders. He slid one hand beneath the loosened silks of her gown and up her thigh, teasing, tickling and stroking the soft flesh he found above her neatly tied garter.

"She...she...oh darling that feels *sooooo* good," Elizabeth wriggled as Jordan's hand cupped her soft mound.

He could feel her moisture dampening his palm and he smoothed his fingers carefully around her woman's folds, learning her likes and dislikes and spreading her juices freely across the swollen flesh.

"Go on," he urged, pressing down on her clit and making her moan.

"She...um...they say she's still a virgin. Others say she's had more men than Messalina. Her girls are highly prized, that's for sure..." Elizabeth sighed as Jordan slid a finger inside her.

"Oh, that's *lovely*. Mmm. Yes...did you know that Pinky Waterston paid two hundred guineas for a night with one of them?" She opened her eyes and glanced at Jordan. "Two hundred guineas. Can you imagine that?"

Jordan sensed that she was getting distracted and slid another finger inside her, reminding her of where she was and what he was doing.

She gasped and swallowed before continuing. "She takes good care of her girls. No one is allowed to harm them in any way. There are very strict rules. Oh, God. Oh Jordan..." Her voice tapered off into a whisper as Jordan deepened his penetration.

Her legs spread even further apart as Jordan's fingers worked their skilled magic on her distended clitoris.

"No more talking, Elizabeth. Not now…"

Guilt drove Jordan to hand-fuck Elizabeth with every iota of talent he possessed. He had no business fantasizing about one woman when another was lying half naked across his lap.

Angry with himself, he suckled her nipples fiercely, pulling her tight against his mouth as his hand moved roughly now against her soaked flesh. He had two fingers deep inside her and his thumb pressed against her aroused clit, and he bit gently on her nipple as he moved his fingers in a rhythmic stroke against her inner channel.

She writhed beneath him, forcing herself against his hand and his mouth. She moaned as his hand found a spot that tightened every muscle in her body. He felt her tension increase as her choppy gasps grew louder.

He increased everything he was doing by a factor of two.

Elizabeth clenched her teeth, straightened her legs and exploded beneath him on a savage sob.

Her cunt trapped his hand, clamping down with such savagery that he reckoned his fingers would be bruised for days.

She shivered and shook, helpless against the onslaught of her orgasm.

He gentled her body, soothing her breasts with soft kisses, riding out the after effects of her orgasm, and easily slipping his hand from her cunt as her juices flowed around his fingers.

"Oh *Jordan*," she breathed. "Thank you."

Jordan felt like slime beneath her feet. "Elizabeth, I…"

She reached up a hand and pressed a finger to his lips. "You did as I asked, Jordan. For that, I thank you. You have given me a gift, tonight. You've made me feel wonderful. You have released my body from the tensions that I've been feeling, and you've given me something to use as a touchstone. Something I can hold on to when I'm alone, and something I can remember if I need a good memory someday." She smiled wickedly. "And you've taught me that Ryan Penderly is an absolutely awful lover."

"*What?*"

Elizabeth straightened her gown and turned her back to him. Jordan was still so stunned that he automatically began doing up her laces without a word.

"Ryan Penderly. Yes. The quiet, landscape-mad, ex-Major, Ryan Penderly. I think I intend to marry him, you know. But I have to teach him a little something about what goes on between a man and a woman. That's why I really needed something to compare him to, you understand?"

Jordan realized that his mouth was still hanging open and shut it with a snap.

"So all this, what we just...you and me, it was all to..."

"To find out if Ryan was any good or not. Yes. Can't make a comparison if you don't have anything to compare, now, can you?"

Jordan felt a grin curving his lips. "Elizabeth, you are the *most* outrageous woman."

Elizabeth grinned back at him. "Yes, I know. And I also know that I really like Ryan Penderly. He's nice. Not that you're not, of course, you're much better at bringing pleasure to a woman, Jordan, and you touched my body divinely. But, and please don't get offended when I say this, you didn't touch my heart."

"I'm not offended." Jordan frowned. "I don't think." He shook his head. "Actually, I don't know what to think about anything any more. This whole evening has been a very confusing one."

"Poor darling. Getting a serious case of lust for a Madam, then getting propositioned on the way home. It has been a rather hard night, hasn't it?"

The enormous lack of sympathy in her voice made him smile.

"Yes. Well fine. Laugh your pretty head off. You've got what you set out for. What do I have to show for tonight?"

"That's a good question, Jordan. What do you have? An interest in an unsuitable woman? A damaged heart? A bruised ego? A major case of lust? What is it about Madam Charlie that has set you off?"

Jordan gazed out at the dark London streets as the carriage slowed its pace.

"I don't know, Elizabeth. And that's the truth. I just don't know."

* * * * *

In the noisy rooms at 14 Beaulieu Crescent, Madam Charlie had no chance for pensive introspection.

People demanded her attention, and her business demanded she respond in kind, with smiles, quick and witty repartee and an aloof air that gave her the special *cachet* that she knew made her an "acceptable" figure.

The Ton was fickle, paying attentions to one person one day and cutting them dead the next. So far, she had been very lucky in attracting the right kind of people to her house, and also in creating an environment where sexual desires could walk hand in hand with sexual curiosity.

Visitors could get a glimpse of hidden treasures without compromising their position in society, and she was thrilled that a few brave women had begun to venture past her doors and not suffered as a consequence of doing so.

It was one of those women who occupied the majority of her private thoughts as she went about the evening's duties. The attractive dark-haired one who had seized Jordan Lyndhurst's arm and not let go.

God knew she had no business even thinking about Jordan Lyndhurst, let alone wondering who the woman had been and what her relationship was to Jordan. But somewhere, somehow, the man had crept under her skin and he was making her itch. In places she'd thought would never itch for any man. Ever.

Her route through her house took her down a quieter corridor where she stopped frequently to check the unobtrusive peepholes into the rooms beyond. She refused to believe that offering sex meant that a girl could be mistreated as well. Anyone wishing to hurt a woman could go elsewhere. 14 Beaulieu Crescent was a house of pleasure, and Charlie's stated intention was that everybody should find it so. Not just the customers.

Sally Trotter was obviously earning her pay that night. Enthusiastic and pretty, Sally had a regular list of clients, two of whom were with her this evening. The Thompson-Ffyfe brothers were tangled up with Sally in a laughing writhing mess of limbs, sprawled across the largest bed in the house. This room was one of those reserved for clients who enjoyed several partners at once, and tonight it belonged to Sally, Ned and Tommy. As Charlie observed the scene, Ned Thompson-Ffyfe freed his legs and plunged hip deep into Sally's cunt, pushing her mouth even further onto brother Tommy's cock.

Tommy clearly appreciated the move, and Sally slurped him out and back in again, all the while moving her hips wantonly against poor Ned who was about to surrender everything he had.

Charlie closed the observation slot on his yell of completion.

The other rooms offered much the same in the way of inhabitants, a variety of men enjoying sex with a variety of women in a variety of ways. Mostly, the men were of the nobility; Charlie's girls were not outrageously expensive, but certainly not for those watching their pennies.

She suppressed a chuckle at Belle's customer, a well-known physician and politician, who was being tickled by an enormous feather. Apparently, only Belle could maintain just the right pressure with the feather combined with some talented manipulation to ensure a rigid erection and a successful conclusion. This particular customer had just increased his visits to three times a week, and Belle was—well—Belle was tickled pink.

Charlie moved on to the last door in the hallway and quietly peeked inside. Here, her newest girl, Susie, had made her "debut" this evening under the skilful guiding hands of Gracie, one of the more experienced residents of the Crescent.

Their customer had been Neville Johns, a successful investor, and a man of quiet manners. Not particularly handsome, Mr. Johns usually allowed his wealth to do his talking, but Charlie had found him pleasant and considerate, and blunt in his self-assessment.

"I enjoy women, Madam Charlie," he'd said when he'd sought her out several months before. "But my appearance does little to attract them. My money, unfortunately, does." He'd grimaced ruefully. "I have no interest in being seduced for my fortune. If I'm going to buy a woman, it will be an honest transaction with all parties quite clear on the nature of the deal. And I understand that your girls are clean, willing and pleasant to be with."

Charlie had nodded her head at his words, knowing that he spoke no less than the truth and proud of the reputation her girls had garnered.

"Therefore, I'd like to request two women at one time. It's been something I've always wondered about, but have been unlikely to experience without professional help." His charming smile had crinkled his eyes, and Charlie had found herself smiling back.

So Mr. Johns had become a regular customer, usually stopping by at least once a fortnight, and most often taking two of her girls upstairs with him for the night. It was expensive, but everyone involved seemed to find it successful.

And to judge by the sight that met her eyes, once again Mr. Johns had had a pleasant night.

Amidst the wrinkled sheets of the large bed, Susie slumbered in a tangle of young limbs. She seemed contented and her breath barely stirred the linens next to her nose.

Neville Johns and Gracie, however, were not done.

Seated on the upholstered blanket chest at the foot of the bed, Johns had Gracie on his lap.

Charlie had to admit that even though Mr. Johns was no longer in the first flush of his youth, his body was still firm and pleasant to look upon. What she could see of it behind Gracie, anyway.

Something held her still, eye pressed to the peephole. Usually she'd simply check that all was well with her girls and finish her rounds. But tonight, something was different. Her needs were different. Her body felt different.

So tonight she watched Gracie as she leaned back against Neville Johns and let him pleasure her.

She had sunk his cock deeply into her arse, Charlie could tell. This alone gave Charlie pause. Gracie had made no secret of the fact that she enjoyed being taken this way, but would permit few customers the opportunity. Mr. Johns must have been very well-behaved this evening for Gracie to go this far. Their bodies were aligned, tipped forward at the groin, allowing Charlie an unobstructed view of Gracie's glistening cunt and swollen flesh.

Gracie moaned and pulled Neville's hand to her breast, as his other one slid between her legs and found her clit.

He moved his hips slightly and Gracie moaned again.

For one blinding instant of time, Charlie was insanely jealous. She wanted to know what it was like. What was Gracie feeling right now? How was it to have a man buried in one's darkness and to want his hands in one's most secret places? She briefly closed her eyes as the image of Jordan Lyndhurst's smile floated in front of her.

A groan from Neville distracted her, and Charlie resumed her watch as he threw his head back, lips curling away from clenched teeth.

Gracie was shivering now, hips thrusting in small but violent moves. She pressed a hand over Neville's as he sunk his fingers deep into her cunt. Clearly their release was upon them.

As Charlie watched, Neville and Gracie tensed, and then Gracie yelled out her climax. Neville was silent but shuddering as Gracie spasmed above him.

The force of their orgasms blasted its way through the door and into an empty space between Charlie's thighs. She ached for the same completion. She closed the peephole with a shaking hand, and smoothed the front of her dress.

What was wrong with her?

She was awfully afraid that the answer had long, firm legs, a very nice backside and brown eyes that tore at her soul.

She sighed and tried to put Jordan Lyndhurst out of her mind.

Her nightly patrol completed, Charlie moved to her quarters. There were still a few customers downstairs, and her girls would be busy for a couple more hours yet. But Charlie's role for the evening was done. If there was a problem she'd be called, if not, Antonio would bar the doors a little after three o'clock in the morning, and the staff would begin the process of shutting down the house for what was left of the night.

"You all right, Miss Charlie?"

She jumped at the sound of Matty's voice. "Matty. You should have gone to bed. Why are you waiting up for me?" Charlie chastised the woman gently, knowing they were both tired.

"It's been an odd night, Miss Charlie, and no mistake. I couldn't rest until I knew you were safe and tucked up in your own bed. Alone."

"*Matty!*" Charlie was shocked. "After all we've been through, you actually thought…"

"It was that Colonel Lyndhurst. He bothered me no end. Just what did he think he was doing, coming here like that?"

Charlie sighed as Matty began brushing her hair. "He has no idea who I am, Matty. None at all. It was sheer coincidence that brought him here. That and a very nasty old injury. I saw the scar."

She closed her eyes and for a second, firm flesh and a pair of well shaped buttocks flashed in front of her mind.

"Well, I don't like it. Not at all, I don't."

"Neither do I, Matty. But we have no choice in the matter. In all probability, we've seen the last of the Earl of Calverton."

"Yes. You're probably right." The woman finished Charlie's hair with a little tug, and settled her onto her own pillow with a small hug. "Of course, dearie, I'm forced to remind you that we said that once before."

Charlie needed no reminder. It was a long time after Matty left before her eyes closed and she let herself surrender to sleep.

Chapter 5

For the next few days, the Earl of Calverton and his man of business were kept fully occupied. Jordan had matters that needed his attention, and a project he wanted to complete.

That project was Madam Charlie.

The efficient Martin Jeffreys, who handled the Calverton business affairs, had demonstrated some surprise at being asked to bend his considerable talents in the direction of detective work.

"You want me to *what*, my Lord?" he'd said, looking dazed.

"I want to find out everything I can about this woman, Martin. You have the contacts. Find out who she is, where she comes from, that sort of thing, and report back to me. In exchange, I promise to sign all this stuff..." He waved his hand at the substantial pile of paperwork in front of him, "...without complaint."

His dark eyes twinkled at his companion.

Jeffreys shook his head. "I'll see what I can do, my Lord. "

"Excellent, my friend. Excellent."

Jordan had rubbed his hands together in anticipation. He'd known after taking one look into those cool gray eyes that he wanted Madam Charlie. What he hadn't realized was that this wanting would become a need, and might become an obsession if he didn't do something about it soon.

For the past days he'd functioned perfectly normally, fulfilling his business obligations, visiting various friends and contacts in the City, organizing the Calverton financial matters to his satisfaction. Yes, things were looking very good for the estate, and his personal wealth was quite acceptable.

But he was constantly aware of a presence. A gray eyed ghost that haunted him. It was worse at night, when his head hit the pillow, his naked body felt the cool sheets and his cock did nothing but ache.

Two nights ago, he'd dreamed.

He was running his hands over her body as she ran her fingertips down his stomach to his groin. Her hair fell against his belly, bringing a moan to his lips and a smile to his face.

Then her mouth closed around him.

Within seconds he'd come, hard and strong, and woken himself up to the fact that he'd actually spent his seed while he slept, like some raw youth.

He'd angrily stripped the bed and put on fresh sheets himself, not wanting to shock the servants too much. They'd know, they always did. But he didn't have to advertise the fact that he had lost control.

He'd slid back into the bed, dropped his head on the pillow and promptly got hard again as those damnable gray eyes laughed at him.

And that, Jordan Lyndhurst admitted to himself, was what he really wanted. He wanted to see those eyes smiling, laughing, and encouraging him on to bigger and better sexual achievements.

He wanted, above all, to see those eyes widen and dilate as she neared her peak, and to watch as they melted when she came with him deep inside her.

That was his ultimate project.

And like any seasoned campaigner, he knew he needed a strategy. Jeffreys was the first part of that strategy. Information was always vital, and never more so than now. With information he could begin to search for a weakness or a vulnerability he could use to achieve his goal.

And his goal was to bed her.

Further than that he couldn't think, because once, Colonel Jordan Lyndhurst was not thinking long-term. His cock was leading this assault, and completely ruling his usually organized and discreet thought processes.

Of course, in the back of his mind was the vague notion of making her his mistress. He didn't have one currently, hadn't had one since he became the Earl, and he thought that Madam Charlie would be ideal. He'd take her down to Calverton, maybe deed over one of the smaller properties to her and together they could while away the years…

Whoa.

Fortunately a knock on the door roused Jordan from a daydream that was looking suspiciously like the parson's mousetrap. He needed a mistress, not a wife, and even if he did, a whore from a brothel was not eligible. In any way whatsoever.

Jeffreys entered with a nod for his employer and a sigh.

"Well, my Lord, I've failed you."

"I beg your pardon?"

"I have failed you, my Lord," repeated Jeffreys, seating himself in the large chair in front of Jordan's desk and pulling a sheaf of papers from his leather satchel.

"In what way, Martin? This is so unlike you." Jordan couldn't help a little humor creeping into his voice. For Jeffreys to fail at something was akin to the Houses of Parliament falling down or the waters of the Thames fading to a trickle. It could never happen.

"I can't find anything out about your Madam Charlie."

Jordan sat up with a rush. "*Nothing?*"

"Well, very little." He balanced a small pair of spectacles on his nose and referred to his notes.

Jordan held his breath.

"She certainly owns number 14, Beaulieu Crescent, free and clear. It was deeded to her as a purchased inheritance from the previous owner, one Anne Brody."

"A purchased inheritance?"

"Yes. There were outstanding debts, which she paid, and the paperwork was then filed as an inheritance. She's owned it for a little over a year now. Before that time, there are only rumors. It is as if this woman never existed until she inherited a brothel."

Jordan exhaled through his teeth. "Impossible, man, impossible."

Jeffreys flashed him a look of annoyance. "Well, of course it's impossible, my Lord. Everybody who exists now has some kind of history. If you'll permit me to continue?"

"Sorry." Chastened, Jordan leaned back in his chair, steepled his fingers and paid close attention.

"Her current financial situation is interesting and worth noting. The house, as I said is hers, free and clear. However, she has little in the way of personal assets other than the property itself. No major accounts, no private accounts, no personal fortune."

"How can that be? That place is a goldmine, I've seen it myself. Always busy, always full of people who can afford to spend what she charges..." Jordan erupted with questions.

"If you'll allow me the chance, my Lord, I'll explain."

"Sorry again."

"My researches at the bank, however, led to a very interesting phenomena. Each girl in the house has an account for herself."

Jordan's mouth fell open.

"You may well look surprised, my Lord. I daresay I looked much the same when I realized this was happening. It would appear that Madam Charlie, who, I should add, personally opens these accounts for her girls, is putting money away for them on a regular basis and has done so for the past year. She is not keeping any of the cash they earn. She pays her expenses promptly and in full, she has no outstanding accounts with any of the local tradespeople that I could find, and the balance goes into the funds of the girls who've earned it."

Jordan shook his head in disbelief.

"Furthermore," continued Jeffreys.

"There's more?"

"Oh yes. This is a very interesting task you set for me, my Lord. I had no idea what I'd find when I began my search for information. Anyway, where was I? Oh yes, furthermore..." He pulled another paper from his satchel.

"Madam Charlie owns three large houses outside of London."

"Aha. More brothels, I assume. That's probably where she gets her money from."

"No."

"No?"

Jeffreys shook his head. "No. These houses were ramshackle old buildings that she bought very inexpensively. She is in the process of having them restored to livable conditions, and the first, which is now completely habitable, she has turned into a combination of Inn and boarding house for — how shall I put this — women of less than spotless reputations."

"Wait a minute," Jordan closed his eyes, trying to grasp what he'd just heard. "You're telling me that not only is she setting aside trust fund type accounts for her girls, she's taking in other whores and giving them a place to live? She doesn't have another brothel, but a boarding house?"

"That is essentially correct, my Lord. Your Madam Charlie may run a brothel, but she is also doing her very best to improve the lot of other women who may not be as fortunate as to work in a place like the Crescent." Jeffreys referred once more to his notes.

"In fact, I understand that the occupancy of the next two buildings is already full, and there are girls on a waiting list to get into the Crescent. That's another interesting thing..." He paused, looking to Jordan for permission to continue.

Jordan nodded weakly.

"Madam Charlie is not your usual abbess. Her girls are carefully schooled, very carefully selected, and are there strictly by their own wishes. No one is forced to become a whore at 14 Beaulieu Crescent, they simply have no other choice and wish to make the best of it. There are no rooms that involve cruel practices, and the girls have the right to refuse any customer's demands if they so choose. And they have, in fact, done so."

"They have?" Jordan was completely fascinated.

"Oh yes." A small smile crossed Jeffreys' usually collected countenance. "It appears that recently a gentleman visited the Crescent without mentioning that he had a decided predilection for play that got rough. He assumed if he was paying for it that he could beat any *girl* he wanted with any *thing* he wanted – in this case his riding crop that he'd hidden in his jacket."

"What happened?"

"Well, apparently he found out that being on the receiving end of such punishment wasn't quite as much fun as he'd thought. His injuries made riding impossible, he had to use his carriage for the next few weeks, and he is rumored to have some interesting scars as souvenirs."

Jordan couldn't help it. He laughed out loud. "Good for her."

Jeffreys' face crinkled into a small grin. "Indeed, my Lord. All my researches into this young lady indicate a very shrewd mind coupled with a very kind, but retiring, personality. I had to look very hard to gather this information, you understand. She has hidden it very well indeed."

"But nothing about her past, eh?"

"That's where I hit a brick wall, my Lord. There are rumors, of course. One has her living at the Crescent for some time prior to her taking over, and dressing as a young man. Hence her nickname, Charlie. But no one seems to have any idea at all where she came from or when, or even if she has any other name. She has always been accompanied by her maidservant, a Mistress Matty Jones, but whether the Jones part is real or not, I couldn't discover, and even if it was, there are too many Joneses for me to make any use of the name to trace their origin further."

"Damn." Jordan stood and paced restlessly to the window.

"There is just one thing, my Lord."

Brown eyes fixed Jeffreys with intense interest.

"I did find out that both Mistress Jones and Madam Charlie share an unusual characteristic."

"They do?"

"Indeed yes. According to the third parlor maid at Lord Duffington's residence, who is stepping out with the knife boy from the Crescent, rumor says that Mistress Jones and Madam Charlie both carry scars. Burn scars. Mistress Jones's are visible on her neck and shoulder, and Madam Charlie's are supposed to be on her back, according to her maid."

Jordan stood still, absorbing this tiny morsel of information. Burns. Scars. God knew he'd seen enough in battle to know the pain they inflicted. The thought of his Charlie being hurt like that was enough to make his breath catch in his throat. The thought that something or someone had brought that kind of agony to her soft skin was unbearable.

Suddenly the room felt close and the air stuffy.

"Jeffreys, you've done splendidly. Keep up the good work. I need a ride."

And Jordan was gone before Jeffreys could pull out the rest of the papers he'd hoped to present to his Lordship that morning.

* * * * *

While Colonel Jordan Lyndhurst had spent the time since their meeting pursuing the interests of his position as the seventh Earl, his project, Madam Charlie, had been busy about her own affairs and trying not to think of the Earl at all. She'd succeeded in the first and failed dismally in the second.

It was her business affairs that had brought her this morning to a discreet residence on Harley Street, where she was facing the unpleasant task of confronting Dr. Ponsonby.

This physician, who regularly attended some of the highest titles in the Ton, had offered an arrangement that seemed useful at the time. His services as physician in exchange for a small financial retainer and "companionship" once a month.

Charlie, eager to protect the health of her girls, had agreed.

Then she'd discovered a few months ago, that the good doctor was not treating her girls with kindness or medical care, but often brutality. His actual doctoring was limited to lancing the occasional boil, leeching anyone who had anything resembling a fever, and dismissing a good number of complaints with the muttered phrase "women's problems".

Charlie had wasted no time in terminating his agreement, and the doctor was not pleased. In fact, he'd attempted to bully both her and her girls on several occasions and his recent visit to Dora was the straw that had broken Charlie's back.

Today would be the end of it.

She marched to his door and rang the bell, leaving her carriage waiting at the curb and one of her maids inside it. For this visit, she'd prefer no audience.

She missed the elegant phaeton that was just turning onto Harley Street as she stepped inside, and never saw the alert gaze of the Earl of Calverton as he drew his horses to a standstill behind her carriage.

Dr. Ponsonby's maid showed Charlie into his waiting room, a dusty and dim salon that could have used a fire and a thorough cleaning.

She heard voices from the next room, and deduced that he was with a patient. She walked across to the grimy window that looked out onto a small garden. Nothing was growing there except a couple of dandelions and some struggling weeds.

Suddenly, Charlie heard a scream.

Without a thought, she ran to the far door and flung it open, gasping at the sight that met her horrified eyes.

A woman was face down on some kind of table, and her back was lacerated in stripes from her shoulders to her waist. An attempt at bandaging had been applied, and was already staining with blood.

But what was worse was the doctor himself. With his breeches around his ankles, the doctor was thrusting himself in and out of the woman's backside, oblivious to her cries.

"What the devil do you think you're doing?" yelled Charlie, outraged beyond belief.

Lost in his lustful activity, the doctor hadn't heard her come in and he jumped, his cock popping out from the girl's arse and waving in the air. There was a trace of blood on it, and a red haze descended over Charlie's vision.

"You filth!" She grabbed the nearest thing she could find, which was a heavy brass paperweight.

She threw it at him with all her strength.

"You disgusting piece of offal," she screamed, angry that he'd ducked her missile.

She seized a lamp from a table. "How dare you treat a woman that way, let alone a patient…"

"Stop this instant, you stupid woman." The doctor had pulled up his pants and apparently found his voice at the same time. "This isn't a patient, she's a whore. She can't pay with money, so we agreed on a trade. What's the matter with you? It's the same sort of thing you do every day."

His lips sneered at her, as his words clunked their ugly sounds into her anger-ridden brain.

"You vile and inhuman bastard…" Beyond speech, Charlie flung the lamp and leapt at him, fists flying.

"Get off me, you whore," roared the doctor, pushing at her with all his strength. And unfortunately, Dr. Ponsonby was a big man.

Charlie went flying across the room to end up in a heap on the floor, with half her dress hanging off her shoulders and the other half in Dr. Ponsonby's grasp. The woman on the table sobbed as Charlie tried to pull the remnants of her dress together across her bosom and stagger to her feet while Dr. Ponsonby spat vile words at her.

And that was the very moment that Jordan Lyndhurst chose to continue his pursuit of Madam Charlie.

Chapter 6

As soon as he stepped over the threshold, Jordan's military senses had gone on the alert. It was too quiet for too long, and the scream and crash that suddenly echoed through the foyer seemed unsurprising.

Instinctively, Jordan reached for his sword. Of course, he was not carrying it, and ended up with a handful of his own jacket, but his fighting instinct was aroused and he hurried towards the sound of the battle.

A door was flung open.

"I'll see you get what's coming to you for this, you bitch. I'll take care of you, don't be fooled into thinking I won't. You'll be lucky to see nightfall."

The blustering threats emerged from a rather unkempt looking man, whose raiment announced him to be the good Dr. Ponsonby. "Good", realized Jordan within seconds, was probably not an adjective applicable to this particular physician.

"Excuse me, Sir. I must leave. There will be no appointments kept today. Some vermin has found its way into my offices. I must have the place fumigated. Nothing for you to worry about. I'll take care of this little problem myself."

Ponsonby pushed past Jordan and disappeared into another part of the house, followed almost immediately by a manservant who had appeared in the foyer at about the same time as Jordan.

A moan from behind the door sent a chill down Jordan's spine and he gritted his teeth as he stepped inside.

A scene of chaos and shambles greeted him.

Charlie was there, all in one piece apparently, and Jordan felt the air seep back into his starved lungs.

She was crooning to a woman who was lying, bloodied, on a long table, and trying to hold bits of her dress together. A bruise was forming on one cheek.

"Charlie, Madam Charlie," said Jordan, hurrying towards her. "Are you all right? What happened?"

Charlie turned to Jordan, eyes no longer cool but hot and angry.

"That...that p-p-pig of a doctor. He *hit* me. After hurting *this* girl. He was supposed to help her, *heal* her, and instead he...he hurt her...shhh, dear, it'll be all right..."

Jordan noticed Charlie's hand start to tremble, and saw the color fade from her face. He'd seen enough battles to know that shock was setting in.

He caught her as she fell.

The door crashed wide as Charlie's maid and Jordan's coachman rushed into the room.

"Miss Charlie? Oh my God, Miss Charlie..." squawked the maid.

"Sir? My Lord?" Jordan's man looked around with wide eyes, fists still clenched and ready.

Jordan, who was still struggling with the fact that he was holding a half-naked Charlie in his arms, pulled his errant thoughts together.

"You, girl, go and see what you can do for that one over there," he nodded at the young woman who had been so badly beaten. "Joseph, help her. Take that young woman out to Madam Charlie's carriage and have her taken to the Crescent. They'll know how best to help her there. Tom is with the horses?"

Joseph nodded as his gaze took in the bloody back of the young woman. He winced in sympathy for her.

"Good. Tom will drive me back to Calver House. I'll take Madam Charlie with me. I don't like the sound of Ponsonby or his threats."

He glanced down at Charlie, and snuggled her against his chest. She was tall, but in his arms she felt like the veriest child. There was little padding on her firm body and in spite of the surroundings, Jordan felt himself hardening.

Silently stifling a curse, he turned to the maid who was now helping the young victim deal with her injuries.

"You, there, what's your name?"

"I'm Amy, my Lord," she bobbed a little curtsey.

"Amy, tell everyone at the Crescent that I am taking Madam Charlie to my place here in London, Calver House, on Farmington Square for her safety. Once she's recovered from her shock, we'll decide where to go from there."

He strode from the room bearing his burden, leaving two servants gaping at each other.

"Well, I never," breathed Amy. "High handed, ain't he?"

"That's the Colonel, for you. Very used to being in command he is. Ain't never seen him offer to take a woman back to Calver House, though. Usually he's only too ready to give 'em the old heave-ho."

"Just wait til Madam Charlie wakes up. She'll give *him* the old heave-ho." Amy grinned at Joseph as she turned back to see how she could help the poor woman whose predicament had started this unusual chain of events.

* * * * *

Within minutes, Jordan had Charlie settled in his carriage, and was on his way back to Calver House. Why he still had her in his arms was something else again, and a question he was not about to ask himself at this point.

Her color was returning a little, and even though her hands were cold and clammy, he felt that she was over the worst of it.

His gaze dropped to her torn dress and for the life of him he couldn't stop staring at the soft flesh it exposed. He'd pulled it together as much as he could to protect her from unwary eyes, but now they were alone, he allowed himself the pleasure of looking at her pale breasts and the way they swelled together into an appealing cleavage.

He desperately wanted to run his tongue between them and taste her skin. She'd be slightly salty, but sweet, he imagined, a mix of wanton woman and sweetness.

His hands shook as he fought his instincts. Instincts that were urging him to ease back the ripped fabric and reveal her nipples. A jolt in the carriage's motion did it for him, and he drew in his breath as one breast fell free of its torn coverings.

The roundness entranced him, the color dazzled him and his heart started hammering a pulse that roused his cock to an amazing level of rigidity. Her areola was a deep rose pink, and larger than he would have imagined given her slender body. Her nipple was perfectly round and rested softly atop her flesh, just begging for the touch of his mouth to wake it to urgent hardness. He could almost taste her as his eyes feasted on her and his cock stirred restlessly beneath her.

She moaned, and the sound brought him out of his sexual haze. With a sigh of regret he covered her, and gathered her against him, letting her scent waft around his nostrils and permeate his mind.

The carriage slowed and he realized that they'd arrived at Calver House. For the next few hours, at least, she would be where he felt she belonged — by his side.

Now if he could just persuade her that it would be even better if they tried another position — the one where he was on top.

* * * * *

Charlie hurt. From her eyelids to her toes she was one big ache. She didn't want to open her eyes in case her eyeballs hurt too, so she snuggled deeper into the soft pillow and lay there, in unusual peace.

The room she was in was quiet, and the linens smelled wrong, although they were soft against her naked skin. Within moments she'd tensed, realizing that wherever she was, it wasn't her own room at the Crescent and she wasn't wearing anything at all.

Cautiously she raised her eyelids. It was dark, and little glimmers of light led her gaze to a fire flickering nicely across the room. There was a low sofa near the fire, and Matty was resting comfortably with her head back, and a woolly blanket covering her legs.

Her mouth was open and she was snoring slightly.

Well, if Matty was here, then wherever "here" was should be acceptable, supposed Charlie. Matty had always known what was best.

Charlie raised her head with a little groan, and that was enough to wake Matty.

"Sweeting, you're awake," she muttered, tossing back the blanket and hurrying to the side of the bed.

"Oh Matty, I'm sorry. I didn't mean to wake you. You were napping so peacefully over there." Charlie raised a hand to her head and felt a large bump behind one ear. "Ow. No wonder I have a headache."

Her vision swam a little and she sank back onto the pillow. "Where are we, and why am I naked?"

"Just you lie there like a good girl, Charlie..." The bed moved as Matty bustled around the room then dipped as she eased an ample hip up next to Charlie's.

Charlie smelled tea. She smiled. Matty's remedy for everything was a nice cup of tea. Most often it worked too.

"Now let me ease you up a bit and you can have a few sips of this nice cup of tea, love," and Matty slid her arm behind Charlie's shoulders. "The doctor says you're going to be fine.

You've got a few bumps and bruises, but nothing that won't heal within a few days."

Charlie removed her lips from the cup and winced. "Matty, this tea isn't up to your usual standards."

"That's because there's a wee bit of medicine in it for you, sweeting. Something to take the worst of the pain away. The Colonel let me use it."

Charlie stilled. "Matty, where are we?" she asked again. More firmly this time.

"Well, see it's like this, after the Colonel rescued you from that beast Ponsonby, you fainted and he whipped you up into his carriage lickety-split, and brought you back here."

"And *where* is 'here'?"

Matty fussed with the cup, not meeting Charlie's eyes. "Um, well, he brought you to the nearest safe place, dear."

"*WHERE?*" Charlie's voice was almost a growl.

"Calver House."

"Oh God. Jordan's London home?"

Matty frowned. "What oh God? Oh God my foot. The Colonel did the best thing he could for you, young lady. You should be thanking your lucky stars he come by and saved you when he did."

Charlie closed her eyes and prayed for patience. "Matty, I need to set a few things straight for you. Firstly, Jordan Lyndhurst didn't *rescue* me, I rescued myself. Secondly, bringing me to Calver House was *not* the best thing he could have done under the circumstances. He should have taken me to the Crescent. And thirdly, where's my nightrail?"

Charlie's eyes narrowed as a shaft of pain spread up her side and across her ribs.

"There now, see what you've done. Your ribs are bruised and you've probably gone and made them ache, haven't you."

Charlie recognized the signs of outrage, worry and guilt when she heard them. She sighed.

"Matty, it's all right. We'll manage. I've never been here before, remember? It's just annoying that I'm not home where I should be. Who's looking after things at the Crescent? Who's taking care of the girls? What happened to that poor thing from the surgery?"

Matty patted her hand and straightened the coverlet around her patient. "Everything is just fine at the Crescent, and I'm going to bring your clothes over in the morning. Things got a bit rushed today, which is why I haven't had chance to fetch your nightclothes. It doesn't matter though, your bruises needed some arnica on them, and so we'd have had to leave it off anyway. I'm taking good care of the place for you and I've told the guests that you're visiting friends away from town for a few days. There's no gossip, and the girls are fine, just missing you. " Matty stopped to take a breath, giving Charlie time to catch up with all the news.

"That young lass, Mary, the one from Ponsonby's?"

Charlie wanted to nod but her head felt just too heavy.

"Well, she'll most likely have some nasty scars, but she's healing up real well. Made some friends at the Crescent, she has, and although I don't think she's interested in working there, she's got a real touch with hair and the girls are already on at her to do their hair for the evening. She's having quite a nice time for herself, and she'll be just fine in spite of everything..."

Charlie tried her best to keep her eyelids open, but they drooped in spite of her efforts.

"Now just you rest, Charlie-love. Everything is going to be just fine."

Matty's voice was soft, and Charlie felt the touch of a gentle hand across her eyebrows. She smiled, remembering how Matty would do that when Charlie was a little girl.

Perhaps she would do as Matty said. What could it hurt if she was to sleep in Calver House? It wasn't like she was in Jordan Lyndhurst's bed or anything. And even though she was naked, it was just for a few hours, anyway, and she was so damn tired…

Chapter 7

Jordan Lyndhurst watched her as she slept in his bed. He'd carried her here without conscious thought, his steps automatically taking him to his own room and his arms laying his precious burden down where he felt she should be—on his pillow.

He'd watched as she'd started to tremble, and gritted his teeth against the urge to strip off his clothes, climb in next to her and hold her tight against him until the fear passed.

Instead, he'd terrorized his household and had them flying every which way in search of his own physician, the softest pillow available, firewood to build up the fire in his room, and messengers to be sent to the Crescent.

The latter had been pretty much unnecessary, as within a very short time of Jordan and Charlie arriving at Calver House, Matty had pounded on the front door and nearly run down his butler in her haste to reach her charge.

Jordan had found himself fascinated by the blend of devotion, love and respect that Matty showed for Madam Charlie. She treated her first like a little girl and then like a grown woman, and it was clear to Jordan that these two had a long history together.

He could not help but notice Matty's scars, but was not allowed to get a glimpse of Charlie's, as Matty shooed him from the room as soon as she began to tend to her patient, and didn't allow him back until Charlie was safely tucked under the covers and wrapped as tightly as any babe in swaddling clothes.

Matty's attitude had initially been hostile and suspicious.

"We'll have her home in next to no time, my Lord." She'd been quite firm in her pronouncement, and it had taken all of Jordan's charm and logic to convince her otherwise.

"Ponsonby is a very real threat, Mistress Matty," he'd finally argued. It was nothing but the truth, after all. "I can guarantee her protection here at Calver House. Can you say the same for the Crescent? I know you have guards, but there are so many people coming in and out. Would you know if Ponsonby's man slipped in? Or if someone he'd hired to do harm to Miss Charlie arrived there?"

Matty had tilted her head and stared at him for so long that he almost felt a blush starting.

"Ponsonby hit her, you know. He was very violent." Jordan wondered if this argument would reinforce his offer of protection.

"Yes. Well, gentlemen do that, don't they?" Matty's acid answer had surprised him.

"No they don't, Mistress Matty."

He'd gotten a snort in response to that, and damned if he was going to let her get away with it.

"Any man who hits a woman is not a gentleman. He may be titled, or rich or whatever, but he's no gentleman. He's a boor, a pig, an animal and worse, but he's not a gentleman. There is no, and I repeat, *NO* excuse for a man to ever raise his hand to a woman. The one time I caught a member of my brigade doing so I had him flogged. By the woman he abused and several of her friends. In public."

Jordan had watched an odd expression cross Matty's face as he delivered his statement. It had begun as one of relief and then turned into a small smile.

"Weeeelll..." She'd tugged on her lower lip, obviously considering him and his words.

He'd smiled and tried to ooze charm and reliability.

"I suppose it wouldn't do no harm to keep her here for a day or two. No one must know, mind you..."

He'd shaken his head firmly.

"She's put up with enough gossip as it is, poor thing. It wouldn't help either of your reputations if it got out that she was staying here."

"No one will breathe a word, Mistress Matty. And you may come and go as you please. If you wish to stay with her—"

"I should, I know," Matty had answered, sending Jordan's guts into a massive clench.

"But other than Charlie, I'm the only one who's on top of things at the Crescent. And it would cause talk if I disappeared too. No," she reached a decision. "I'm going to trust you, Colonel Lyndhurst. Keep her safe and let her heal. Then send her home."

Jordan had promised.

Keep her safe.

Well, he was doing that. Stretched out on the rather lumpy couch under a blanket, he could certainly keep her safe. He'd assigned extra servants to keep an eye on the house and stables, mentioning a rash of recent burglaries in the area. Most of the household knew he'd brought home an injured guest, but few, besides his butler and his valet, knew her identity or even her gender.

The doors had been locked, bolted and double-checked. This room was locked and the windows high up above the garden at the rear of Calver House were secure. Jordan wondered if he was overreacting, but then remembered Ponsonby's face. There was a man who held a grudge, and especially if he thought he'd been bested by a woman, and a whore at that.

Whore. Hah. The woman sleeping in his bed was no more a whore than he was.

That was one thing that Jordan had rapidly realized as he held her shaking body and settled her into his room.

Her eyes had opened and stared blankly at him, the effects of shock still visible in their misty gray depths. Any whore would have been more than used to such violence, because in spite of the enlightened times in which they lived, whores were victimized on a disturbingly regular basis.

Her slim hands had held tight to his lapels, and he'd marveled at the softness of her skin as he'd eased her torn dress away from her shoulders. She was every inch a lady, and no matter what her past, he knew that she was no whore.

Let her heal.

Well, there wasn't much he could do about that. The bruises stood out, livid against her pale flesh, but they were just bruises and would fade. Her reaction to the attack, however, had him a little puzzled. She might not have been a hardened prostitute, accustomed to personal violence, but the level of shock she'd experienced was extreme. Surely she'd had to deal with behavior like Ponsonby's before?

It was a puzzle, and Jordan loved solving puzzles. He licked his lips.

Send her home.

Ah, there was the kicker. He didn't want to send her home. He wanted to keep her.

He leaned back with a sigh and faced the inevitability of the situation. He wanted Madam Charlie so bad his teeth ached.

It was the first time he could remember ever being so obsessed with a female. Even the one he'd almost married, whose name he couldn't now remember. No one had ever made him feel so hot, or so needy inside, desiring something he couldn't even put a name to.

He wanted her body, certainly. He knew that burying himself inside her and pumping his seed deep into her womb would be some kind of amazing marvel, something he'd not experienced before. He wanted to taste her, sip her juices, suckle her breasts and caress her buttocks. He wanted to explore her body like a treasure seeker mining new worlds for gold.

He wanted to see her naked in the sunshine and naked by the firelight. Hell, he just wanted her naked. With him. Skin to skin, mouth to mouth, breasts pressed against him and her cunt hugging his cock.

He muttered to himself and shifted, trying to relieve some of the pressure that his cock was creating as it responded to his imaginings.

Sighing, he stood and stripped, dropping his clothes negligently by the couch and groaning in relief as his cock sprang free of his breeches.

"You're no help," he mumbled, sinking back down and covering himself with the blanket.

He tried to divert his thoughts but a slight sigh from the bed linens across the room brought his attention back to Charlie.

Jordan pondered what sort of woman would acquire the name "Charlie". And have it suit her so well, too. She wasn't an Emily, that's for sure. And Margaret, or Jane, or Daphne — none of them would have fit either.

No, she was Charlie. Proud, elegant, reserved, yet willing to go all out for her girls and secure them a decent life beyond anything they might have expected. A woman with a core of iron ready to take on the vilest beast in order to protect someone weaker than herself.

Charlie. A woman of surprises, contrasts, puzzles, and mysteries. An unusual name for an unusual person.

At that moment, the "unusual person" whimpered.

"Papa?"

* * * * *

Charlie felt the vestiges of the dream sliding away from her like water droplets, and yet the illusion lingered.

Her mind was fuzzy, images blurred and distant, and her body felt heavy and unreal. Perhaps she was still dreaming.

No—there was someone next to her, holding her. It felt good, safe somehow. It must be Papa. He was there for her at last.

"Thank God. Papa. You must listen. Don't make me do this."

"Do what, sweetheart?"

The voice was soft and deep. It didn't sound like Papa, but it was a man's voice.

"Don't make me marry him. You know Mama would never have made me marry him."

Fingers brushed the hair back from her face. "Tell me about him."

"He's so old, Papa." Perhaps this time he'd listen to her. "And the way he looks at me. He wants to get me alone, Papa, and I'm afraid of him. Just the other day when he came for tea…"

"What happened?"

"He t…touched me, Papa. Somewhere he shouldn't have. Somewhere p…p…private."

The fingers paused in their gentle stroking.

"Don't be cross with me, please, Papa. I didn't do anything. I wanted to scream, but I didn't. Reeves came in with the tea tray and he stopped. But Papa, I didn't like it…"

Charlie let out a sob. Why wasn't her father listening? Why was he making her go through with this awful marriage?

"I don't want to marry him. I really don't. Why can't you understand and listen to me? Let me stay here with you and look after you. Please, please Papa. I'll die if you make me go to him."

Warm arms held her close and she could sense the thump of a heart against her befuddled head.

She could almost see her father's face, sadly smiling. She sighed. "I have to, don't I? There's no other choice. He'll ruin you if I don't marry him. And he'll ruin me if I do." She let out a wry laugh. "We're both going to lose."

"Ssshh, it's all right, Charlie, it's all right..." Soothing sounds helped the tension in her shoulders ease, and Charlie sighed in relief.

"Make it all right again, Papa. Make it like it never happened." She giggled a little. "And I like it when you call me Charlie. Mama used to, do you remember? Much more fun than that stuffy old Charlotte."

She sighed and snuggled against the warmth that was spreading all up and down her body.

"Mama used to sing *Charlie is me darlin'*. Do you remember?" She hummed a little tune, letting the memories of her mother slide over her and comfort her. "I miss Mama, don't you, Papa?"

The arms around her tightened.

"Yes, you do, I can tell. I'm sorry I complained. I know I have to marry him. I don't want to, and I don't know if I'll survive, but I will. I'll marry him for you, Papa. And because Mama asked me to take care of you, and I don't know any other way..."

She felt the tears trickling down her face, only to find them whisked away by a warm hand.

"Don't cry, Charlie. It's all over. You're safe now, with me."

Safe. Was she safe?

Her body ached, like it had ached before. But her heart didn't hurt as much.

"Am I safe with you?" She turned her head to find him, her eyes refusing to focus on anything definite, just the pale blur of a face near hers.

"You are safe with me. I will never let anything happen to you, Charlie. You have my word on that."

His voice calmed and soothed her, and for a few seconds a pair of brown eyes with little bits of gold dancing in them swam into her vision.

"Yes. You will keep me safe, won't you?" She felt her mind slowly drift and her body sink into a blissful state of relaxation. "Thank you."

Her eyes closed. Then opened again briefly and found his face once more.

"Jordan," she whispered. "You have beautiful eyes."

She slept.

Chapter 8

Sunlight streaming across her face woke Charlie.

As she stretched, she realized her mouth felt like she'd been licking a carpet for hours, her stomach was rumbling and she had an overwhelming need for a chamber pot.

Raising her head up slightly, she saw the screen across the room and deduced that at least one of her needs could be met.

Her legs were shaky, and her body was sore, but she was pleased and proud of herself for making the short trip behind the screen and back to her bed without stumbling.

She noted that she was now wearing her own nightgown, and smiled as she realized some of her other possessions were scattered around the room. Matty was obviously in command.

As if the thought had summoned her, the door opened, and Matty herself bustled in holding a large tray.

"Oh dearie, look at you. Up already. And I'm sure you must be starving too."

"Thirsty more than hungry, but yes to both, Matty. What time is it? How long have I been sleeping?"

Charlie yawned hugely, and reached high above her head, stretching her shoulders and wincing slightly.

"Still sore?" asked Matty, pouring tea from the pot on the tray she'd brought with her.

"A little. Not much. My head feels a bit cottony though..."

"That's the laudanum. We thought it was a good idea to give you just a few drops."

"Laudanum? Matty, you know I've never touched the stuff." Charlie frowned at the thought. There'd been a time when Matty had encouraged her to take some, but she'd adamantly refused.

"I know, pet, I know. But you were that badly banged about, and we knew if you were awake you'd be fussing over the Crescent and getting home, so we thought it best. Just for the once, sweeting."

"What time is it, then?"

Matty cleared her throat. "It's gone four o'clock."

"Good lord, you mean I've been sleeping for several hours?"

"Well, actually, it's four o'clock on Thursday."

Charlie's jaw dropped. "Good God. I've been sleeping for *two days*?"

Matty nodded and buttered several pieces of toast. "We thought it best. You needed to heal."

Charlie's eyes narrowed even as she gladly took the teacup and allowed Matty to plump up the pillows and get her comfortable.

"I'm hearing a lot of the word 'we'. Who is 'we', Matty?"

Matty offered the toast.

Hunger won out, and Charlie eagerly bit down on the food. "Don't think you can get out of this, my friend," Charlie mumbled around the toast.

"No talking with your mouth full, young lady," said Matty automatically, pouring a second cup of tea and settling her ample hips on the chair which she had drawn up next to the bed. "Now, how are you feeling?"

Charlie polished off her second piece of toast. "Besides bruised and hungry, and headachy, I'm damned anxious to know what's being going on, and why you thought you had to drug me to keep me out of it."

She kept her voice firm and level, and her gaze on Matty.

Ignoring it, Matty leaned forward and wiped a dab of butter off Charlie's chin with the ease and familiarity of a long time friend. She sipped her tea and then straightened her spine in her chair.

"Very well. The Colonel and I felt it would be best for you to sleep for a while. He was very concerned about Ponsonby's threats and felt you were better protected here than you could possibly have been at the Crescent."

Charlie opened her mouth to protest, but Matty's raised hand stopped her.

"Just think a minute, Charlie. Would you have closed the Crescent? Would you have ordered a servant at each and every door to check out the guests as they arrived? How would you have protected the girls if someone had decided to punish them instead of you?"

Charlie closed her mouth.

"Would you at least have stayed in your rooms until Ponsonby either showed his hand or surfaced at his home again?"

"He's gone?"

"Lock, stock and barrel."

"Well, I'll be."

"The Colonel also made sure that his patients knew exactly what had happened, although he kept your name out of it. Just put it around that he'd surprised the doctor abusing a woman who needed medical attention. That was all it took."

"Didn't that put Jordan...I mean his Lordship in danger too?" Charlie's worried question brought an interested gleam to Matty's eyes.

"He didn't seem to think so. He was more worried about you. And he's been taking extra special care to make sure that you're safe, and protected, and that nobody knows you're here." Matty nodded approvingly. "And he's done it, too."

"He has?" Charlie looked at Matty, amazed that for once a man was finding approval in the woman's *very* critical eyes.

"Yes indeed. Tended to you all by hisself, he has. No one but that nice Mr. Arthur knows who you are. He's the valet to the Colonel, you know," Matty leaned forward conversationally.

"Ever such a pleasant man. Says he's been with the Colonel for years now. Ex-batman, now valet. Takes ever such good care of him, and he's been making sure I get in to visit you with no fuss or bother every time I come over."

Charlie swallowed, completely taken aback at Matty's amazing salute to Jordan Lyndhurst. "Really? Well, my goodness. So what did you tell the girls?"

"I told them that you were visiting friends you'd met unexpectedly, and that you were going to spend a few days with them."

"How did they take it? I've never done anything like that before."

"That's probably why they took it so well. Mostly they said about time you took a few days off. A couple said don't hurry back because the men look at them more with you gone."

Charlie grinned.

"And I'm managing to keep everything up and running as best I can. The customers seem to be just fine, a few have inquired about you, men mostly," Matty's mouth turned down, "but overall, things are doing well. No need for you to worry at all."

"And is she worrying, Mistress Matty?"

The deep voice tingled through Charlie's consciousness and instinctively she pulled the covers higher up around her throat.

Apparently, Jordan had noticed her movements, because his eyes followed her hand and his lips twitched into a little grin.

"Lord love you, Sir, of course she is. But I've just finished telling her how things are at the Crescent, so she'll be able to rest and not worry for a little while at least."

Jordan neared the bed and helped himself to the last piece of toast.

* * * * *

It felt like dry sawdust in his mouth, but chewing and swallowing gave him a focus that he might otherwise have lost while staring at Charlie.

He'd had the last forty-eight hours with her, to learn her scent, her sounds, and briefly, the touch of her skin. But now she was fully awake, alert and already pulling down that veil of concealment over her gray eyes.

He was determined not to let that continue. Somehow, some way, he was going to break through Madam Charlie's fortress of control and breach her emotions along with her body.

He licked his lips and was pleased to see a tiny shiver disturb the tousled hair around Charlie's face.

"I would like to give you my word, Madam Charlie, that I will protect you while you are here in my house. You should have no fears on that score. I understand that the Crescent has taken some sensible precautions too. I will be a lot happier when Ponsonby is located, but for right now, I don't believe there is any more we can do."

He leaned against the tall post at the foot of the bed and surveyed her, enjoying the rumpled blonde hair that fell every which way, and the lace gown tied daintily around her neck that did nothing to discourage him from wanting to pull the ribbons until it fell apart.

Or perhaps not even bother, just rip it from hem to trim and expose her heat, her pussy, her beautiful breasts…

Jordan shifted his position and looked away, feeling unaccustomed warmth in his cheeks as he mentally stripped and fucked his houseguest.

"I appreciate all you've done, my Lord. I cannot but believe that I have inconvenienced you."

Charlie's answer was all formality and her eyes were completely unemotional. Yes, she certainly had herself well in hand.

"Not at all. You've spent most of the time sleeping. Not exactly a difficult guest to entertain," grinned Jordan.

"Well, now that I am awake, perhaps we should be making plans for my departure. I really must get back to the Crescent."

Jordan drew a breath but was forestalled by Matty.

"Now, Charlie, let's not rush into any foolish decisions. Right now, no one knows where you are. Give the Colonel a couple more days to see if his agents can locate Ponsonby." She glanced quickly over at Jordan, who nodded slightly in approval. "You see, lovey, Ponsonby's servant has been recognized as an out-and-out villain."

Charlie frowned.

"Indeed, Charlie." Jordan didn't even realize he was calling Charlie by her first name. It just seemed so natural. "As soon as I had my people begin inquiries into Ponsonby's possible whereabouts, we discovered that his servant has a history of violence. Especially against women. There have been stories of missing maidservants in homes where he has worked, and quite a bit of verifiable brutality. It appears the man is abusive without doubt, and possibly a killer into the bargain."

Charlie paled slightly. "Dear heavens. And we never knew."

"How could you? And under the normal course of affairs, you'd never have contact with him anyway. But now, seeing as Ponsonby is on the run from authorities who'd like to talk about his medical practices, and the whole collapse of his affairs began with a woman, we have no clue what his servant might be thinking or doing or encouraging Ponsonby to do. It's a frightening situation, and one that we simply cannot control at this time. You are safest right where you are."

Charlie's gaze flickered from Matty to Jordan and back again. Jordan held his breath as he watched her considering the problem from a variety of different perspectives.

Her face remained impassive, her eyes calm and collected. But he had become attuned to her body language over the past two days, and he could tell from the tiny flicker of the pulse in her neck that she was disturbed by his revelations. The covers rose and fell over her breasts as she drew a deep breath.

"It seems that at present I have no choice but to accept your hospitality. I thank you, my Lord. I shall, however, reserve the right to leave as soon as this situation is resolved. In the meantime, I think I should dress and perhaps take care of some of the Crescent paperwork. I'm sure Matty wouldn't mind bringing it along with her when she returns? I shall need her constantly by my side, of course…"

Jordan stifled a grin. His Charlie was attempting to neatly circumvent the possibility of his presence disturbing her. And he knew it did. Knew it as sure as he could feel his heart beating. The woman had many strategies for keeping herself aloof, uninvolved. He was going to enjoy defeating every single one of them. It was time to begin.

"I understand." He smiled politely. "However, I should point out that Mistress Matty has been running the Crescent in your absence. Do you have someone in mind to replace her while she stays here watching you?"

Having neatly reminded Charlie of her business obligations and also implied that Matty would be doing nothing more than fussing over Charlie, he waited to see how she would respond.

She didn't disappoint him.

Her chin went up a couple of notches and she met his gaze with tolerance. Not a hint of what must have been a huge internal struggle showed in the clear gray eyes.

"You are correct in your assumptions, my Lord. I should have considered all the possibilities before I spoke."

Charlie turned to Matty.

"Matty, I shall be forced to rely on you for a while longer, it seems. I would still like to have the paperwork brought over. The business end must be attended to and I can certainly do that without jeopardizing anything or anyone. If his Lordship would be kind enough to allow me the use of a desk…?"

One pale eyebrow arched in query.

"Of course. Although you've not had chance to explore, this suite does have a small sitting room through that door..." He gestured slightly. "You are welcome to use it for as long as you need to."

"There you are, dearie. Now my mind can rest. Just look at this as a little holiday. Heaven knows you haven't had one, and you've needed one ever since..."

"Ever since I took over the Crescent. Yes Matty, thank you."

Charlie's interruption had been rapid and deliberate. Jordan mentally noted it down on the little list he'd begun in his mind. It was devoted to solving the puzzle that was Charlie.

It was right next to the one that was already filled with ideas on ways to fuck Charlie.

"Now I must be off, the dinner menu needs to be finished up and the girls always feel better after I get back."

Matty bustled around, collecting her shawl and her bonnet.

"Matty, I..." Charlie hesitated, as if loath to see Matty leave.

"Now you just let the Colonel take care of everything, sweeting," soothed Matty.

"Indeed, Madam Charlie, there is nothing to concern yourself over. I have requested a bath be prepared for you shortly. Perhaps you would care to join me for a small informal meal later. I understand from Matty that you play chess..."

Jordan tilted his head, presenting the veriest picture of innocence. He could have been doing nothing more than being a polite host. In fact, his innocence radiated so strongly from him that the proverbial butter not only wouldn't have melted in his mouth, it would have kept there for a se'nnight.

He devoutly hoped that Charlie was fooled. There was nothing innocent about his goals. They were simple and fundamental. Fuck Charlie. Understand Charlie. Make Charlie smile, then make Charlie scream. Oh, and then fuck her some more.

For Colonel Jordan Lyndhurst, Earl of Calverton, the battle was commencing. The strategies he'd use would be devious and skillful. His campaign would involve every tool at his command. His goals would be worth the fight, and Charlie's surrender would be a prize beyond price.

He never actually considered the possibility that there might be casualties.

Chapter 9

Charlie listened as the bumping and rattling in the next room told her of a bath being prepared.

Her skin itched, she swore she could smell her own sweat, and she was dying to sink into its warmth. A woman of fastidious habits, Charlie was used to a daily bath, be it small, quick, cool or whatever was available for her convenience. She'd missed it.

She waited, until the sounds receded and the room was quiet. Gingerly she crept from her bed through the doorway into the sitting room of the suite.

A warm fire was crackling in the hearth and the curtains had been drawn against the rain that had set in earlier and turned the outside world to an early twilight.

A large hip bath was drawn in front of the fireplace, with a small stool to one side upon which rested neatly-folded towels, a bar of soap and several small cloths.

With a sigh of relief, Charlie ran her hand through the water and found it just the right temperature. She crossed the room, threw the lock on the door and within seconds was immersed to her neck in the tub.

She felt her worries ease as the warmth of the water soothed her body and relaxed her mind. Her eyes wandered around the room, noting the fine carpet, a small desk to one side, a very comfortable looking sofa and a couple of well-used armchairs. Clearly this was one suite where guests had spent considerable time relaxing.

She could understand why. The painting over the mantelpiece was a wonderful seascape, empty of everything except a gull, some blades of seagrass and a deserted beach. It begged one to imagine oneself strolling along the sand.

A small clock ticked away the minutes as Charlie soaked, and the fire crackled its approval in the hearth.

The sound of six chimes recalled Charlie to a sense of where she was. She reached for the soap and began her bath, feeling cleaner by the second and noting that her bruises had faded away to almost nothing.

She pushed her hair up further on her head, wishing she could wash that too, but there was so much of it, and her shoulder was still somewhat sore.

She jumped at least a foot and slopped water over the sides of the tub when a deep voice spoke behind her.

"Why don't you let me help you with that?"

Charlie froze. Instinctively she slithered down in the tub until barely her nose was showing. She turned angry eyes to Jordan Lyndhurst, who was negligently leaning against the doorjamb with two buckets at his feet.

"You forgot to lock the bedroom door."

She narrowed her eyes and raised her mouth from the water. "What are you doing in here? I'm taking a bath, for heaven's sake. This is extremely inappropriate."

"I know." His grin was pure seduction, and Charlie fought the urge to squirm.

"Someone had to bring up more hot water for your hair. I wasn't about to let any of my servants in. This sight is reserved for my eyes alone."

His gaze swept across the soapy water.

Charlie glanced down. She was mostly covered with bubbles and the water was not as clear as it had been earlier. She doubted Jordan could see much of anything. Her thighs locked together, however, just in case.

He neared the tub.

"I have warm water to help you rinse your hair. Are you going to allow me to assist you? Or are you too particular in your habits to let a humble man touch your head?"

Charlie's chin went up. "It's not a matter of being particular. I simply think this is an extremely improper situation. And I wouldn't describe you as humble." She muttered that last comment as she pushed a handful of hair out of her eyes and grimaced as she realized it really was quite filthy.

She cursed inwardly. He'd caught her once again with his logic and his straightforward conversation. "Damn you. I have no choice, do I?"

"There's always a choice, Charlie. Just make sure it's the right one."

She glared at him, for once allowing some of her anger to show.

Jordan nodded. "Very well."

Her eyes widened as Jordan proceeded to remove his coat, his vest, untie his cravat, slip that off, and then unbutton his shirt.

Charlie's voice returned when he got to the fourth button. "What on earth do you think you're doing?" She refused to believe that she'd squeaked, but was secretly afraid that she had. There was something stuck in her throat that was getting larger as more of Jordan's chest was exposed to her gaze.

"I intend to help you wash your hair. To do that I will need to lather it, and rinse it well. You, Miss Charlie..." He tugged on a wayward curl, "...have enough hair for at least three women. It is likely to be a difficult task. I'm not even sure if a humble man such as myself is up to the challenge."

He sighed dramatically and removed his shirt.

Charlie gaped.

"I really would prefer not to soak my clothes. Particularly my jacket, which I've been told is a very fashionable shade of green. The vest, well, I'm not sure about that, but the shirt is one of my favorites. You know how it is when you have a favorite item of clothing. You just seem to want to wear it all the time. I certainly don't want dirty bathwater or soapsuds splashed willy-nilly over it. It is linen, you know."

Charlie was having enormous difficulty following his words, because he'd brought the buckets over to the side of the tub. His chest had come with him.

And what a chest it was.

Solid, nicely muscled, with a delightful mat of hair spreading from just below his neck to the vicinity of his waist. Flat nipples could be seen lurking within this soft jungle and Charlie was astounded to feel her fingers curling beneath the water. She wanted to touch. For the first time in her life, she wanted to run her hands over his chest and feel all the different textures there for herself.

She licked her lips.

* * * * *

The second his hands touched her tumble of golden hair, Jordan was lost. He slipped his hands across her scalp, seeking tangled hair pins and removing them until the last lock was free and the silken mass was hanging loose across the water and down the back of the tub.

He had spoken nothing but the truth when he'd likened her hair to that of three women. It was thick, lustrous, and had a mind of its own.

He took a breath and gathered the unruly curls into his hands, pushing them into the water around her neck.

"Take a breath…" He warned.

"Mmmph…" She gurgled, as he pressed down on her head and dunked her. She came up sputtering.

"Good God, are you trying to kill me?" She spat water angrily from her mouth.

"I did tell you to take a breath," he said reasonably, as he began to soap her hair.

"Well, yes…but…oh my."

Jordan's fingers worked lazy circles over her scalp and encouraged more lather to build between his hands and her hair. He massaged and soothed and rubbed her head and felt the muscles relax beneath his touch.

"Oh God, Jordan, that feels like bliss," she sighed.

Jordan sighed too as the pressure of his swollen cock began to turn into pain.

"And what would a lovely young woman like you know of bliss, might I inquire?"

There was no answer for some moments, just the sound of his hands working the lather and the ticking of the clock on the mantel.

"Nothing."

The answer was nearly a whisper.

"I know nothing of bliss. I can only assume that this sense of relaxation and warmth approximates what others might call bliss."

"Not hardly," he chuckled. "There is much more to it than that."

Charlie moved her head slightly to get his hands working just behind her ear and flicked a bit of soap away from her nose.

"You are talking sexually, I assume." All of a sudden she was Miss Prim Hoity-Toity.

"Among other things. But yes, sexual bliss is the best kind of bliss there is."

Again, the silence fell.

"I wouldn't know."

The confession dropped into the quiet room like tiny explosions, turning Jordan's rigid cock to marble. There was so much he wanted, and it was all within inches of his hands, and mouth, and cock, and it was all wet and slippery and naked.

He was probably going to have heart failure within the next five minutes. The Times would have to work hard to phrase his obituary so that the entire world didn't find out he died of a severe case of unrequited lust.

He wondered if cocks had ever exploded.

He was afraid he was about to find out.

"Let me show you, Charlie." The words slipped out before he could catch them, straight from his heart and his loins.

She froze under his hands. "I do not want to have sex with you, my Lord."

"Are you sure?"

Her neck straightened so fast he could have sworn he heard the bones crack into place.

"I never want to have sex. With you or anyone. It's a pastime I fully believe is best left to others. Yes, it's my business, but not my pleasure. I have no interest in such things."

"None at all?"

"'That's correct. None at all. Now, if you're quite finished with my hair…"

Jordan reached for the spare bucket of water and tested the temperature. His mind was spinning, working out the logistics of his next move.

He pulled her hair back from her face and tipped the water through it, encouraging her to sit forward. Her breasts rose to the surface as her body swayed forward.

She coughed as Jordan, attention distracted, poured water over her face by mistake.

"Sorry." He pulled his mind back to his task, making sure that all the soap was rinsed clear of the sodden yellow mass floating in the tub.

He caught up a towel and squeezed the worst of the moisture from her hair, bundling it up into a turban, as nurses and nannies had been doing since time began.

"Thank you, my L…" She began, only to have her words cut off.

"Charlie, I have a proposal. An experiment for you, if you will."

She raised one eyebrow.

"You say you have never experienced bliss. And you don't intend to become sexually involved with anyone. Ever."

A slight color invaded her cheeks, but her eyes remained cool and alert. "That's essentially correct."

"What if you let me demonstrate what bliss is?"

He could see the denials and outrage about to erupt from her mouth. He stayed her words with a finger.

"I will not touch you, Charlie." He moved his finger until it was a scant inch from her lips.

"I will show you bliss. Right here, right now. And I will not have to touch you to do it."

Charlie snorted, disbelief clearly evident in her expression. "I really doubt that such a thing is possible, my Lord." She looked down her nose at him. "Even if it were, I doubt that you'd find me at all responsive. Why I'd bet…"

Jordan's ears perked up. "What would you bet, Charlie?"

"Nothing. I didn't mean to say bet…"

"Yes you did. You said 'I'd bet'. I heard you quite clearly. So you're a gamester are you?"

Charlie bit her lip and stared down into the water, for once apparently unwilling to let Jordan see her gaze.

"What shall we bet, Charlie? I bet I can bring you to a woman's bliss, in this tub, right now, without touching you. If I lose, what shall my forfeit be?"

He looked at her willing her to raise her head and meet his gaze.

"I…don't think this is such a good idea," she muttered, not moving.

"Scared you'll lose?"

That brought her head up. "Of course not. The whole idea is preposterous. And very inappropriate too."

Jordan chuckled. "We passed inappropriate some time ago, Charlie. I have it—" He snapped his fingers. "That girl you rescued. If I lose this bet, I will provide a home and a job for her in the country. We'll get her trained as a lady's maid. What do you say?"

He knew he'd played a trump card. Charlie's commitment to bettering the lives of her "poor unfortunates" was a major factor in his decision to place this particular wager. He was certain she couldn't refuse.

"And if you win?"

She wasn't going to give in without a fight, thought Jordan ruefully.

"If I win, then I will undertake to get *two* of your girls into maidservant training." He grinned.

She sighed and shrugged her shoulders, sending little ripples across the surface of the water. "Very well."

He grinned some more.

"Do your worst." She lay back in the bathtub, making sure that her entire body was submerged. Her chin hit the water, and her eyes followed him as he sank down onto the carpet next to the tub and hooked one arm over the side, swishing the water around. "You are not to touch me, is that understood?"

Jordan felt the heat sear his crotch and wished he had taken his pants off as well. His cock was tenting the fabric in a very uncomfortable way.

"Close your eyes, Charlie," he answered, slipping his free hand to the fastenings of his breeches.

She obeyed, settling her head on the high back of the tub. He stifled a sigh of relief as his cock surged free.

"I will not touch you. I gave you my word, and believe it or not, my word counts for something. But I will give you bliss like you've never known. All I ask is that you let go."

Chapter 10

He wanted her to let go. Charlie stifled an internal snicker.

He couldn't know that she never let go. Ever.

Her experiences with her late husband had made sure of that. Of course, it was certainly very relaxing lying in the warm water next to the fire, feeling clean and fresh, and with a nice male body next to the tub.

But let go? Absolutely not.

She tensed slightly as Jordan's hand breached the surface of the water and he moved it around, setting up little currents.

"Remember, Jordan. No touching." Smugly she settled herself a little more comfortably. This was one bet she'd have no problem winning. Her mind slipped to which girl deserved the chance to get away from the Crescent and accompany her newly rescued charge to the country.

Then she became conscious of a warm breeze.

"I won't touch you with my hands, Charlie, never fear. I promised. I won't touch you with any part of my body, although I'd certainly like to."

His breath fluttered against her ear.

"I'd like to touch this little piece of skin here with just the tip of my tongue."

He blew a soft stream of air over the sensitive whorls, making her shiver. What was he doing?

"You see, a woman's ear is a place of endless fascination. Full of intricate curves and dips and little secret caves…"

Once again the warmth of his breath caressed her. Charlie froze, afraid that if she moved a scant inch he'd be inside her ear.

"It's a very sexual place, Charlie."

She wriggled ever so slightly, dipping down even more and devoutly hoping that he didn't notice the fact that her nipples were getting harder by the second.

"A woman's ear is not unlike another sexual place. Mysterious, dark, warm, just waiting for the touch of a lover's tongue."

His hand swirled in the water again and the ripples lapped seductively against her body.

"Have you ever had a man caress your ears with his tongue, Charlie? Ever let him take a long slow lick down the outside and then swirl…" His hot breath filled her ear, "…swirl around and around in tighter circles until you feel he's in your brain and your body and your cunt?"

Charlie jumped and frowned at his language.

"Shocked, my sweet? Why? You have heard words like that before, I'm sure. Haven't you, Charlie? Haven't the girls told you how their customers slip into their cunts and how it feels? How their customers' cocks can move quickly or slowly, and some even bring pleasure? How the pounding of their bodies against each other can release powerful drives that turn two people into roaring infernos?"

Jordan's hand continued its swirling motion, and now Charlie could feel every single ripple and current beneath the water.

"Have you ever watched, Charlie? I'm sure you have the security peepholes in place. You must observe the rooms now and again, you're too good a businesswoman and too protective of your girls not to. So tell me, Charlie. Have you watched?"

Charlie's mind flew back to the night she'd done just that. Fortunately, her eyes were still closed, or she knew that her expression would have given her away.

Jordan's hand moved slightly and she sensed him withdraw. Then the water slurped and she opened her eyes to see him ladling out some of the bathwater into a bucket.

"What are you doing?"

"Just lowering the water level slightly. When you reach your bliss you'll probably move around a lot, and I don't want to ruin my Aubusson carpet."

Charlie snorted. "Don't take too much out, I'll get cold."

"I doubt that."

Damn the arrogant bastard, thought Charlie. I'll show him. Gathering her wits and her control, she lay back again and closed her eyes, determined to best him at his seductive game.

To her surprise she felt a tap on her raised knee.

"Hold this between your knees."

"What?" She looked down to see that Jordan was wedging the ladle between her knees, spreading them to the very edges of the tub.

"I..."

"I'm not touching you. But we never said anything about using what was at hand. Now just be a good girl and hold this between your knees. Or are you afraid you'll lose the bet?"

Charlie curled her lip. "Hah." Her knees widened and she felt the smooth wooden ladle spread her thighs wide.

Jordan smiled. "Better."

Charlie smirked.

Then she froze again as the washcloth was unceremoniously dragged across her breasts.

"Hoi. You're touching." Her eyes turned angrily to the man next to her, meeting his intense stare with hostility.

"No I'm not. The cloth is." He quirked up a corner of his mouth. "Can't take it? Give up?"

Charlie shut her mouth with a snap. "No."

"Good."

The washcloth dragged again, stimulating her nipples and making her gasp. As she did, her breasts rose from the newly lowered water, and Jordan moved quickly to blow on the damp skin.

She choked as the sensation jolted every nerve ending between her heart and her pussy.

"Feels good, doesn't it, love? A man's warm breath on those beautiful breasts. Breasts that were made for kissing and licking and sucking, and oh God how much I want to do all three. I want to hold them and squeeze them and bury my face between them. I want to do all sorts of wonderful things to your breasts, Charlie."

She tried to shift lower in the water, but couldn't manage to submerge herself as fully as she'd have liked.

Jordan's hand was now producing rhythmic waves in the water between her legs and the current beneath combined with the ripples on top were starting to really make her edgy.

Again and again the washcloth stroked her breasts, sometimes a light touch, then a rougher drag. Her nipples were now rigid and responded to each whiff of his breath as he spoke to her and allowed the warmth to tease her nipples.

She wanted to bury her hands in his silky hair and draw his face down to her breasts. She wanted more than a breath or a lap of the water, she wanted to be suckled and tongued and even nipped a little. She was beginning to want him to do "all sorts of wonderful things to her breasts".

She stifled a groan and kept her hands firmly clenched beneath the water at her sides.

"Did you know that a woman can peak just from having her breasts suckled, Charlie?"

Oh God, why didn't he shut up? His words and his voice and the visions he was creating were driving her mad. The way he kept repeating her name, softly, like a caress, was stirring her heart and her soul. She didn't want to be stirred like that.

"I wonder if you'd be one of those women. I want to find out very badly."

True to his word, Jordan was not touching her. His breath was brushing her body, and his voice was caressing her soul. But he had not, as yet, laid a hand on her.

Charlie was beginning to get very tense. She assumed it was anger, she'd never felt quite as irritated or edgy as she was right now.

"Of course, your breasts aren't the only place I want to explore, my sweet. There's so much more."

Charlie mentally groaned. She would *not* let go.

Or at least she didn't *think* she would.

Oh God, she was going mad.

* * * * *

Jordan knew he was succeeding. Just watching her nipples bud and harden and ripen before his eyes told him the story he wanted to hear. Charlie was responding to him, and responding wildly.

It was time to take this little experiment to the next level.

He pulled a washcloth from the bucket of cold water and laid it unceremoniously across her breasts.

"Aaagh. What the…" She jumped and her gray eyes opened, looking accusingly at him. "What are you doing?"

Jordan watched her reaction. "Just making sure you're still with me."

He removed the cold cloth and swished the warm water over her chillled nipples, observing the flush as the cold was replaced by warmth. His other hand kept up its slow undulation between her legs.

He knew the water would be lapping against her clit since the ladle was holding her legs wide enough apart that she would be exposed to the little current he was creating.

He moved his hand closer to her body.

Sure enough, there was a different, more viscous sensation around his fingers. Charlie's body was telling him that she was responding. Her cunt was ready for him.

And oh God his cock was more than ready for her.

"Your body wants me, Charlie." His hand increased its speed a little and encouraged firmer ripples against her clit.

She fidgeted very slightly.

"Your cunt is filling with sweet slippery honey. It wants my cock sliding slowly inside…my hard cock, which can fill that empty place right up. It will touch all those secret places inside you, Charlie, touch them, stroke them, press and fill them."

His hand maintained the increased pace, making sure that now the water was pushing itself against her body. Her nipples hardened even more under his gaze and her head tipped back a little as she became further aroused.

Jordan was spellbound by her response. Just watching her body as each different sensation caused a reaction was one of the most stimulating things he'd ever done. If his campaign succeeded and he got Charlie underneath him, fucking her would rank as one of the highlights of his life.

His hand trembled for a moment as the full implication spread through his mind. His cock was leaking small beads of cum just from playing with Charlie. Was he really ready to go the distance with this woman when she could rouse him to such extraordinary heights without a single touch of her body?

His rational mind chided him. This was simply a different and fun erotic experience. He might have been doing this with anyone. Hell, Elizabeth would certainly enjoy it.

Yes, said his conscience. But would *you* enjoy it so much?

Jordan mentally turned his back on that conversation and returned his attention to the woman who was now wriggling with arousal in the water.

It was nearly time to seal his success.

He reached for the bar of lavender soap and slipped it into the water above her body.

She gasped as he let it slide from her belly down over her clit into his waiting hand. Very carefully, so as not to touch her at all, he allowed the soap to press against her hot flesh.

She gasped, forgetting to stifle the sound.

"And now, Charlie, the moment has come. If we were naked together, your breasts would be pushed hard against my chest. You'd feel the heat of my body all over yours, from your shoulders to your toes. Your belly would feel empty, your legs would spread wide for me. You'd be hungry, needy, wanting my cock, Charlie."

She moaned, lost now in the images his words were creating.

"Perhaps we would be lying amidst my sheets, perhaps you'd be feeling the roughness of the carpet against your soft backside or the warmth of the fire on your breasts…"

Jordan slid the soap down over her swollen flesh and towards her cleft.

She sucked in a breath and tilted her hips slightly to give him greater access as he spread her cheeks with the soap.

He grinned, painfully, feeling every one of her responses echoed in his cock.

"Maybe we'd have decided to try fucking from behind, Charlie. What do you think? Would you like me to position myself behind you as you knelt on all fours? I could slide right into your hot wet pussy that way, and as I pushed in, you'd feel my balls against your thighs."

The soap continued its pressure, running over all the places Jordan mentioned. Charlie's sounds continued as her body began to pulse beneath the water.

"I could use one hand to fondle your nipples, Charlie. Touching and teasing them, in time with my cock as I pulled out and then thrust back in…"

The soap thrust against Charlie's clit. She grunted as her lips peeled back from her clenched teeth.

"The other hand would find your sweet clit. The spot where your world would begin and end. The spot that I want to make my very own, Charlie. I want to suck your clit, lick your clit, rub my face all over your clit. I want to have it jerk against my cock as you come with me so deep inside you neither of us knows where one begins and the other ends. I want your clit, Charlie. It's mine. The things I'll do to it will make you scream, and sob, and beg me for more. And I'll give you more. Each time you ask there'll be more. There'll be more even when you don't ask."

The soap was rubbing hard now, and Charlie's muscles were tensing. Her breath was coming in irregular gasps, her nipples solid, and her breasts flushed. She was seconds away.

"I want to fuck you Charlie, fuck you until the world ends for both of us." It burst from him, surprising him with the force and emotion of his words.

"Open your eyes. Charlie. Open your eyes. *Look at me…*"

Gray eyes opened wide and a second later, she grunted as her whole body spasmed beneath the water.

Jordan was helpless to resist. He dropped the soap and plunged his hand to her pussy, sliding a finger into her cunt to share her explosion.

Her eyes were stormy and brilliant, like thunderclouds slashed with lightning. Her pupils were dilated, there was sweat on her face, and her mouth was open in an "O" of surprise.

Her cunt clamped down on his finger for what seemed like an eternity, releasing it only to clamp down again.

He gingerly thumbed her clit, only to send her into more paroxyms of pleasure. She was incredible. And very, very tight.

He couldn't stop his other hand from leaving the tub and grabbing his cock. In time with Charlie's spasms, he squeezed himself hard, needing only a few quick touches to bring himself release.

Her gaze was unfocused, so lost was she in her orgasm. He probably could have come several times right in front of her and she'd never have noticed.

The water roiled as her body rode out the sensations, and Jordan gently withdrew his hand.

She moaned slightly as he disentangled his fingers from her cunt. "Please, Jordan…"

"Please what, my sweet?" Jordan dropped a light kiss on her forehead.

"Touch me there again…now…*please*…"

Cautiously, Jordan obeyed, slipping his hand back under the water. He eased the ladle away from between her legs as he followed her instructions only to find her thighs clamping his hand to her clit.

Amazingly, she orgasmed again, the instant he slid a finger into her cunt. He gently slid a second finger inside, stretching her slightly. As he moved them around he felt the spasms build once more.

She was incredible. It was as if he'd opened a door to her body that she'd never known existed. Now that he'd shown her what a climax was all about, her body was demanding its due.

Her third climax clearly drained her, and he felt her muscles weaken as the tremors finally subsided. The tension eased from her spine, and her nipples softened as he watched them.

She had closed her eyes once more against him, but Jordan knew that this time it was not to keep him out of her thoughts. It was to keep her thoughts away from him.

Rising, he stripped off his soaked breeches, and quickly rubbed himself down, wrapping the towel around his waist.

Within seconds he had Charlie out of the tub, and held tight against him. Weak as a kitten, her legs refused to support her weight, so he carried her over to the fireplace and grabbed towels on the way.

Efficiently, he balanced her against him and dried her off, whisking the towel roughly over her damp skin and bringing a moan to her lips as he touched her sensitive breasts.

His cock stirred, but he sternly told it to take a rest. He'd accomplished the first part of his strategy.

Patience would be called for in the next phase of his campaign.

Chapter 11

Charlie didn't know what to feel. What to say or what to do or what to think either.

She was warmly cuddled into a large and soft dressing gown, as was Jordan, who had manhandled them both quite efficiently into some semblance of dryness following their bathtime adventure.

She was now held firmly on Jordan's lap as he lazily ran his fingers through her tangled curls, straightening out the knots and spreading it over her shoulders to dry in the warmth of the fire.

Her muscles were languorously content, as if a pulse of energy had over stimulated them only to leave them relaxed and limp.

Her skin tingled, whether from her "blissful" experience or the brisk rub that Jordan had administered, she had no idea.

And her mind, for once, was adrift.

This was very unusual for Charlie, she reluctantly admitted. It seemed impossible for her to focus on the many things she should be doing. Chief amongst which was getting as far away from Jordan Lyndhurst as she could at the earliest possible moment.

Well, she probably would have to do that—but not right at this minute.

For once, she was going to allow herself the sensual pleasure of being cherished by a man who had brought her senses to life and her body to orgasm.

She quietly smiled. So *that* was what it was all about.

"That is a very enigmatic little grin," said Jordan, brushing a finger along her lips.

"Is it?"

"You know it is. Want to share the thought?"

Charlie tilted her head back and looked at him. Brown eyes stared back, golden lights catching the flicker of the fire and dancing in their depths.

"That was my first…my first experience with *that*, Jordan." Why she confessed that, she had no idea. But it seemed that the moment called for nothing less than complete honesty. "Thank you."

His arms tightened around her and he dropped a kiss on her head.

"The first of many, I hope. You are beautiful when you're aroused, Charlie. You're beautiful all the time, don't misunderstand me, but there's a special sort of beauty that comes from within when a woman is in the throes of her passion. You have it. Your eyes become stormy. Your cheeks glow…" His fingers traced her eyelids and ran over her cheeks, "your lips swell and redden, and your scent, aaah, Charlie, your scent."

He buried his face in her neck and drew a deep, dramatic breath, making her giggle.

"I could find you in a dark room even if I was blindfolded. Your scent is inside me now." He pulled back slightly. "And, if I'm not mistaken, *that*, Miss Charlie, was a real giggle."

Charlie looked at the fire pensively. "There hasn't been much to giggle about in my life."

"Tell me?"

The warmth of the fire and the warmth of Jordan's arms were working their magic, and Charlie felt many of her inhibitions melting along with her muscles.

She knew there were secrets that must remain hidden, but a part of her yearned to share others, ones that had burdened her for so long.

She sighed. "It's not an uncommon story, Jordan. You'd be bored within minutes."

Jordan shifted slightly and reached for his brandy decanter with his free hand, pouring two healthy glassfuls. He passed one to Charlie and took the other himself.

He clinked the snifters together. "Here's to you boring me, Charlie. It'll never happen, but you're welcome to try."

He grinned and took a swallow, waiting for her to begin.

Charlie swirled the liquor and let the fumes tickle her nose, then took a small sip. It burned, but warmed her as it spread through her system.

"I was married when I was very young to an older gentleman." There, the story had begun.

As if the brandy had loosened her memory and her tongue, more words began to flow.

"It was, of course, an arranged marriage. But the arrangements were such that I had no recourse but to wed. My father had been somewhat imprudent in his financial affairs, and I was the surety offered against his debts. It was either marry this man or lose everything we had."

Charlie took another sip of the brandy. She felt, rather than saw, Jordan's gaze fixed on her.

"My mother had died less than two years before, and this had hit both my father and I very hard. We were both lost without her, and my father especially. I don't think he ever really recovered from the loss."

There was so much she was not saying. Would he know?

Could Jordan possibly imagine the pain of losing one's mother to illness, only to subsequently lose one's father to a broken heart?

She sighed.

Jordan gently stroked her hair away from her face. "I'm sorry, Charlie." His touch brought her back to the moment and gave her the courage to continue.

"Well, the outcome was already decided. I married, left home, and became the new wife of…of this man."

Now she must be cautious. There must be no slip of the tongue, no whisper of a name. She felt that Jordan would want the entire story, so she would give him the entire story. The edited version of the entire story.

"As I mentioned, he was older. By some several decades, as it turned out. He had no heirs, and looked upon me as his last chance to breed some."

Jordan made a disgusted sound.

"It's not uncommon, Jordan. Let's be quite honest here, many marriages are arranged for just that purpose."

Jordan lowered his head in agreement. "That doesn't mean I have to admire the practice," he growled.

"True," acknowledged Charlie.

"I'm sorry, sweetheart, go on. You married him?"

"Yes." She bit her lip as she wondered how to deal with the rest of the story. "It is difficult to talk about, Jordan. I have not shared this with anyone except Matty, and I don't know why I feel I want to tell you now, but I do…"

Charlie turned in Jordan's lap and looked at him, knowing her gray eyes were probably asking too much of him.

God, could he ever understand?

* * * * *

Jordan's gut was cramped. He had horrible visions of Charlie being used sexually by a vicious old man. He knew she needed to share these things, but had no clue where he was going to find the strength to handle them.

He did know, unequivocally, that he'd kill anyone who hurt her. Without a second thought.

"Tell me, Charlie. It's all right. Just tell me." He hugged her again and urged her on.

Her voice was steady and low in the quiet room, accompanied by the regular ticking of the clock.

"My...my husband, it turned out, was impotent. No matter what he tried, whatever he made me do to him, or what devices he employed, he was unable to...to impregnate me."

"Ah." Jordan's mind whirled with visions of Charlie forced to her knees or worse. His teeth locked.

"This was, of course, a great tragedy for him. He had a mistress, who could, apparently, satisfy him. But such a union had never resulted in a child. He even..." She swallowed, "He even brought her into the bed with us, in the hopes that seeing the two of us together might bring him to the point of release within me."

She reached for her brandy and took a large gulp, as if washing a bad taste away from her mouth.

"It failed. Miserably. I bore the brunt of the blame from both of them for his failure. Then he had another idea."

Jordan could feel her body as it tightened on his lap. "You don't have to go on if you don't want to, love," he said, holding her close to him.

She wriggled a little and tucked her head under his chin. The movement caused a bolt of hot lightning to pierce a place deep in his body. Somewhere that nobody had ever touched before. He wanted to explore this new sensation, but she was speaking again, quietly, against his chest.

"His desire for an heir was desperate to the point of madness, I think. He kept talking about 'a child of my body' inheriting his legacy, and before long the expression triggered the idea that *my* producing a child was sufficient."

She took a deep breath.

"He had his valet attempt to succeed where he had failed."

"Dear God." Jordan tried to be horrified, but in point of fact, it was not an astoundingly surprising tale. Such things had been hinted at many times in the past where large legacies were at stake.

"His valet was a big and uncouth man, and he seemed to take great pride in the fact that he'd, as he put it, 'tupped the Master's bitch'. The worst part was that I was not very willing to participate. My...my husband held me down as his valet did his work for him. He made me sort of lie on his lap while his valet...did...things...It hurt."

Her voice tapered off and the clock ticked for a minute or so into the silence.

"Anyway," Charlie's voice regained its normal level of control. Her moment of weakness had clearly passed. "Within a few weeks, he died. I managed to come to London, learned that I had inherited the Crescent, and made a new life for myself. And there you have it. The rather uninteresting life story of Char...Charlie."

Jordan held his breath, fighting to control his anger and the nausea that overcame him at the thought of Charlie being so abused. No wonder she had developed such an intimidating level of self-control. And no wonder she'd succumbed to shock after encountering Ponsonby's violent attack. Several things now made sense to Jordan, and the knowledge of what she'd suffered pained him more than he could have imagined.

"Where does Mistress Matty fit in?" he asked, more to give himself time to recover than from any great desire to know.

"Dear Matty," smiled Charlie. "She was going to be my maid when I made my come-out, my mother had been training her for just that purpose. But then, after mother died, we became closer than just maid and mistress, and I fought tooth and nail to have her accompany me as my companion after my marriage. "

Jordan felt calm enough to reach for his brandy. His teeth still chattered slightly against the crystal.

"So she was there, thank God, to help me through the worst of it, and it was she who got me to London after the...after he died. I just wanted to disappear. It turned out that everybody thought I was dead too, so we decided to leave it that way. It worked out very nicely."

"And Mistress Matty's burns?"

Charlie raised her head. "You noticed them? Yes, of course." She turned away from him. "There was a fire. Matty managed to escape but was burned during her flight."

"Rumor has it that you were burned too, Charlie." Jordan made the statement quietly, with no emotion.

"I have a scar, yes, Jordan. I'm surprised you didn't see it earlier."

Jordan coughed. "If it wasn't on your breasts or any of those places driving me crazy, I probably wouldn't have noticed if you'd had the flag of the House of Hanover painted somewhere." He grinned apologetically.

Charlie moved to get off his lap.

"Whoa, where are you going?" He held her tight.

"I want to show you." She slid from his arms and turned her back on him, undoing the tie at her waist.

With one hand she pushed the fabric behind her, holding it away from the smooth sweep of her left buttock.

There, into the soft white flesh, was burned a brand. The letter "C", in the medieval illuminated style.

"My dear God." Jordan was aghast.

"It doesn't hurt now. I like to pretend it's more like a tattoo. Rather like those sailors who come home from wonderful foreign lands with marks on their bodies. I saw some once at the Crescent."

Jordan's eyes had never left the mark on her sweet bottom. Obeying some inner impulse, he leaned forward and ran his tongue gently over the scar. Then he pressed a kiss on it, and lowered his head even more, taking a small nip from the fleshy part of her cheek.

Her shiver was reward enough.

"Why, Charlie? Why did that animal brand you?"

She covered herself and took her seat in his arms again. It was a natural act of trust that told Jordan more than all the life stories she could have rolled out for him.

Another little part inside his body flickered to life.

"I believe he felt it was important to make me understand that I belonged to him. I was his property as much as the cattle he branded for his dairy farm or the sheep he raised for their wool. He wanted me to know that he could do with me as he pleased. Or have done to me whatever he pleased. I was not, in the early days of our marriage, very compliant with his wishes."

Charlie's eyes were downcast modestly as she made this announcement, and Jordan's lips kicked up.

"Bit of a handful, were you?"

A delightful grin spread over her features, bringing a quite unsuspected dimple to one cheek and a matching smile to Jordan's face. He was entranced.

"Well, I wouldn't like to agree too much, but I certainly didn't understand the concept of having a 'place' and staying in it."

Jordan laughed, holding her close. This was one extraordinary woman. He felt her laugh with him, and noticed the yawn that followed.

They'd had no dinner, only brandy, but it was now going on for nine o'clock, and he had no doubt in his mind that his Charlie was exhausted.

"Time to tuck you into bed, Charlie."

She tensed in his arms.

"Alone, my sweet. Not by my choice, but because I think you still need to rest. And if I were with you, near that delectable body of yours, neither of us would rest. At all. Not only for this night, but for many nights to come..." *In fact, for the rest of our lives...*

The words dashed through Jordan's mind and brought him up short. He frowned as Charlie quietly slid from his arms and allowed him to help her back to her bed.

The room had been tidied, the covers turned down, and a single candle burned.

"Thank you Jordan." Her words were sleepy, and her eyes warm as she looked at him. "For everything."

"It was my pleasure, Charlie. And we're not done yet. Not by a long shot."

He just touched her lips with his, and then blew out the candle.

She was asleep before the flame died.

Chapter 12

Over the next few days, life settled into a sort of routine for Charlie, as she remained at Calver House.

There had been a couple of odd incidents reported against guests of the Crescent, and one girl was convinced she had been followed while running some errands. There were enough unanswered questions to make Jordan uneasy and absolutely positive that keeping Charlie under wraps was a good idea. Matty was in complete agreement with his position.

Charlie had been given free rein within her suite, and had set up her desk to resemble a small office. She kept quiet and busy, and had few visitors, except Matty and Jeffreys, her newfound friend.

As for Jordan, since the night he'd shown her what passion between a man and a woman could be about, he'd stayed scrupulously correct in his behavior and they'd not been alone for a moment.

Charlie couldn't decide whether to be pleased or sorry. Although she did privately admit to herself that she was rather relieved. The tranquil period allowed her to regain a measure of her self-possession, and to overcome her regrets that she'd shared so much of her intimate thoughts and feelings with him.

However, she was aware that a degree of calmness had settled over her mind and, to be honest, her heart. As if by releasing some of her memories, she had shed the burden of disgust that she had carried for so long.

Confident that she'd betrayed nothing of a personal nature, she was able to respond politely and appropriately to Jordan when he made his occasional visits, and to chat comfortably with Matty during the afternoons when the older woman made her daily reports and brought any new paperwork over.

Charlie and Jeffreys had immediately found an unexpected common ground—business. While Jeffreys had approached his master's guest with a certain amount of caution and a great deal of curiosity, Charlie had immediately set him at his ease and begun to daintily pick his brains. By the end of their first hour together, both announced themselves wiser for the discussion.

Jeffreys' admiration for Charlie's uncanny financial acumen grew as he listened to her questions and watched her consider the answers. Charlie's interest in the subject and her willingness to learn increased his burgeoning belief that this woman would have been a force to be reckoned with if she'd been allowed to take a seat on the Exchange. As it was, both parties benefited enormously from their times together, and both looked forward to the chance to discuss financial matters that were of mutual interest.

By Saturday, however, Charlie was getting itchy feet. It was time for her to get back to the Crescent, back to her real work, and out of Jordan Lyndhurst's realm of influence.

"Just another few days, Charlie, that's all we're asking." Matty sat next to the window, enjoying the sunshine.

Charlie paced the floor. "This is becoming frustrating."

"In what way, love? This is a charming house, you're in a perfect suite, you have everything you need?"

"Did you know that these were the Earl's rooms, Matty? Jordan put me in his own suite?"

"Well, I rather guessed as much, but what does it matter? It's not as if you'll be here forever. Just a few more days."

Charlie felt an unusual thump around her heart at Matty's words. She paced again.

As her steps took her back and forth, her sense of discomfort grew. She was terribly afraid that she didn't want to leave.

That she wanted to be near Jordan Lyndhurst as much as possible. With as few clothes between them as possible.

The words he'd used to seduce her into her climax haunted her on a nightly basis, and she was tired of waking up trembling, aching and alone.

She was ready to experience some more bliss.

Her eyes wandered to the paperwork that lay scattered across her desk. Matty was chatting about something or other, but Charlie's mind refused to pay attention to anything but the growing notion that she was developing feelings for the Earl of Calverton. Feelings that she had no business with, feelings that were as inappropriate as they were risky.

Feelings that might make her act like the whore the world thought her to be.

She silently chided herself for that last thought. Jordan had never intimated that he thought her to be any less than a lady, even when he was goading her at their first meeting. His manners had been exemplary, and his behavior—well, certainly not that of a man and a prostitute.

In fact, she could be forgiven for thinking he might cherish a certain amount of tender emotion towards her. After all, he had spent much time caring for her, and then there was the cuddling before the fire, and the talking, and all the time his hand had run through her hair, soothing, gentling...

Her loins began to ache and she could feel herself growing damp between her legs. This would never *ever* do.

Jordan Lyndhurst, the Seventh Earl of Calverton, was off limits. For at least a hundred and fifty reasons, but most of all because of who she was now. Madam Charlie of the Crescent.

Any liaison between two such people would be extraordinarily scandalous and damaging to Jordan. For her part, notoriety like that might well help her business, but at what price?

Was she willing to risk a broken heart and a permanently destroyed reputation for the chance at more "bliss"? Could she countenance becoming his mistress and sharing his bed, but nothing more?

At that moment, Jordan walked into the room to tell Matty that the carriage was ready.

Charlie looked at him, so strong, so handsome, so much a man.

Did she have the courage to submit to her desires? To pull him down to her and beg him to do with her whatever he wanted? Did she have the courage to admit to herself that she desperately wanted him, to know his arms and his body? Intimately? Was it just possible that he was the one man who could really make her "let go"?

* * * * *

Jordan marched into the room for what he was now coming to regard as his daily dose of torture.

Surely the Spanish Inquisition could have devised no worse punishment than to be in the same room with Madam Charlie and not touch her, strip her and take her. His cock was in a state of permanent arousal, riding had become exquisitely uncomfortable, and he was afraid that if he didn't do something soon he was going to be pushed into lunacy by unsatisfied masculine need. He wondered if there was a ward at Bedlam specifically for men who suffered from unrequited lust. He wouldn't have been surprised.

For lust was certainly all it was, he constantly reminded himself.

No matter that he'd never had the urge to hold a woman tight for hours before.

No matter that he'd never been so aware of a woman's scent before.

No matter that he'd crept in and embarrassed himself by switching pillows, just so that he could sleep with the fragrance of her hair filling his nose all night.

No matter that every time he walked in to his suite and saw her again, his breath caught in his lungs and his heart gave an odd little stutter.

None of that mattered a whit. It was all lust. He wanted her naked, underneath him, and screaming. Clamping that hot, tight cunt around him until she milked his brains out along with his seed.

It was simple lust.

And tonight was the night he was going to do something about it. To finally complete his campaign.

If all remained quiet at the Crescent then he could no longer, in all conscience, keep Charlie at Calver House. This might be his last chance for action, and he was damned if he was going to waste it. Once seduced, fucked, and his, perhaps he could get his mind off her and back onto the business of being an Earl, where it belonged and where he still had huge amounts to do.

He'd rather enjoy having her for a mistress, he thought. Provided she'd agree. Of course they'd have to be quite discreet, but he was an ex-soldier. Cunning was his middle name.

Well, all right. Actually it was Edward, after his father, but Jordan knew that should he succeed in persuading Charlie to become his mistress, he would have no problem in continuing the liaison in a private and confidential fashion. Unlike many in the Ton, he did not believe in flaunting his sexual conquests.

Charlie had no notion that she'd revealed much more about herself than she'd intended when she unburdened herself to him in front of the fire.

He now knew, for example, that she'd been intended for a come-out. This indicated that she was certainly a member of the aristocracy, and probably from the country, as most debutantes of her age would have been noticed, surveyed and catalogued by the fashionable London Ladies as they moved from the cradle to the altar.

Clearly she had not been in the public eye, or her marriage would have made headlines, again bringing her notoriety. The fact that she was able to mingle with the Ton within the walls of the Crescent and had never had anyone regard her as anything other than Madam Charlie, told him she was not from London, and had never been to town in any other capacity.

Consequently, he'd tallied up his "clue" list, handed it over to Jeffreys, and was even now awaiting the answer to his questions. Who had married a young woman some three or perhaps as much as four years ago? Who had died shortly thereafter? He had to be older, probably titled, and not from London.

There had to be records somewhere, and Jordan had confidence that Jeffreys would be able to root them out even though they still had no last name. There couldn't have been too many Charlottes that fit the criteria he'd so carefully assembled. The man was amazingly efficient when presented with a challenge, reminding Jordan of a terrier with a bone.

Before too long, they'd solve some of the mysteries that still surrounded this unusual woman. Within days perhaps, he might know all the other things she *hadn't* told him while she was curled so comfortably in his arms. She'd shared some difficult experiences with him, and perhaps explained some of her behavior, but Jordan had a gut feeling that there was more involved.

He wanted to know. More than that, he needed to know. What he couldn't fathom was *why* he was obsessed with these unanswered questions.

With that thought in mind, he watched Charlie as she bade farewell to Matty, hugging the older woman and smiling at her in her usual innocent style.

She had no notion that her smile crept into his breeches, and her dimple — on the rare occasions it peeped out — made his balls clench.

Perhaps that lack of awareness was part of her charm.

She may have been ignorant of her effect on him, but he could tell that he had an effect on her. He grinned inwardly as he noticed her obviously "not" looking at him.

He politely bowed to Matty and gave her into his valet's capable hands.

He suppressed a smile as Charlie's step quickened and she hurriedly put the desk between them.

"May I take it all is well at the Crescent?" he asked politely.

"Indeed. Matty has handled everything in an amazingly competent fashion. I find myself hardly needed." Her response was calm, her eyes controlled, and the little pulse at the base of her neck was fluttering madly.

"You are always needed, Charlie," he murmured. "In fact, I find I need you myself."

Charlie raised an eyebrow, not letting any emotion into her expression.

Jordan saw a tiny muscle move in her cheek.

He smiled at her and moved towards the door. "I'm here to ask if you'd care to join me for a game of chess later this evening? I have to attend an annoying business dinner, but it will be concluded by ten at the latest. I find that at present I have no interest in pursuing some of the more mundane Saturday night pursuits. A quiet game or two of chess would be a pleasure for me. Might I ask that you grant me your company?"

Charlie allowed her eyes to meet his. For a second, he could have sworn he saw them heat up and turn stormy. But then it was as if a curtain fell and the calm tranquility that was her usual expression returned.

"It would be my pleasure, my Lord. A game of chess is small recompense for the kindnesses you have shown me. I trust my skill will not disappoint you."

"On the contrary, Charlie. I have to trust that my skill won't disappoint *you*."

Knowing he'd given her plenty to chew over, Jordan bowed and left, wondering if he could possibly survive the next few hours. He reminded himself to check and see if he had a pair of evening breeches that would conceal the fact that he had a raging erection, which he fully intended to take care of this very night.

* * * * *

The light shower that had greeted Jordan when he left his house that evening had turned into a soaking downpour by the time he returned, necessitating a much-needed change of clothing.

"Arthur, please ask Miss Charlie to join me in the Book Room in half an hour? She's expecting the invitation," said Jordan as he ripped his wet clothes off and dumped them in a pile on the floor.

"Yes, Colonel." Arthur sighed and picked up the wet clothing.

"Dammit, where's my favorite shirt?"

"Next to your favorite breeches, sir," responded Arthur dryly. "May I suggest a towel before you dress?"

Arthur regally extended a towel for his wet master's convenience.

"Don't get on your high horse with me, man. Remember I've seen you roaring drunk with your pants on the floor and two women on your lap." Jordan's muttered warning came from the depths of the towel he was violently rubbing across his hair.

Arthur sighed. "I do remember that night fondly. And you, if memory serves me correctly, were entertaining the other two."

Jordan coughed. "Yes, well. Perhaps we should both strive to purge our memories of that little incident."

"Will you and Miss Charlie be requiring anything further from the servants this evening?"

Jordan cocked a suspicious eyebrow at his valet. The question had been just a *little* too smoothly phrased.

Arthur looked urbane. "A natural question, Colonel. The staff will be happy to retire early for the evening once you signify your needs have been met. I, myself, will ensure the house is secure and take to my own rooms as well."

Having thus been informed that his staff was leaving the coast clear for him to play with his "guest", Jordan shook his head. "One of these days, servants will rise up and conquer the world. The aristocracy will find themselves out of a job."

"And a better world it will be, too, Sir."

Jordan slipped his shirt on, and left the neck open, waving away jacket and vest.

"I'm not 'at home' this evening. To anyone. Not that I'm expecting company, but I'm damned if I see why I should have to sit uncomfortably by my own fire in the privacy of my own house. Charlie won't mind."

Perhaps Charlie would even like seeing his chest. Good lord, where had that thought come from? Perhaps the same place that was telling him to just leave all his clothes off and save time.

He gave himself a mental shake and grinned at Arthur. "You've placed everything in the Book Room as I asked?"

"Indeed, Sir. I believe you'll find everything to your satisfaction." Arthur paused. "It is to be hoped that Miss Charlie does too."

Jordan cocked an eyebrow at his valet. "You know, Arthur, I believe I liked you better as my permanently drunk batman. Once you sobered up you developed a very nasty streak of sarcasm from somewhere."

"Perhaps I learned it from you, Sir." Unfazed, Arthur cleared up the detritus left by Jordan's hurried change.

"Now, if you will permit me, I will summon Miss Charlie and ask her to join you? I assume you would prefer not to wait *too* long?"

The formally polite phrase was accompanied by a pointed look at Jordan's crotch where the beginnings of a healthy erection were already distorting the soft fabric of his breeches.

"Arthur, you are a devil sent to plague me. I'd be offended if I didn't know that you could outgun me in just about every battlefield *and* every bedroom I've ever been in!" Jordan chuckled ruefully.

"I am glad your present case of lust hasn't blinded you to some fundamental truths." Arthur took the compliment as his due. "Subject to future developments, I am considering broadening my relationship with Miss Charlie's duenna, Mistress Matty."

Jordan tipped his head. "Oh *really?*"

Arthur shot him a disapproving glance. "Yes, *really.* Mistress Matty is a charming lady, of great intelligence and vast personal appeal. She has a ready sense of humor, a good head on her shoulders, and although others might find her scars unpleasant, I happen to think they add a touch of piquancy to her character."

Jordan's eyebrows rose. "Piquancy? Did I hear you say 'piquancy'? What did I tell you about reading those dreadful Fanny Burney novels?"

Arthur sniffed. "I might have known a young whippersnapper such as yourself, begging your pardon, my Lord, would scoff at my assessment of the lady's charms."

Jordan laughed. "Tread carefully, my friend, but follow your heart."

"As you intend to, Colonel?"

The question brought Jordan up short. Was that what he was doing? Following his heart?

Chapter 13

"Thank you for joining me this evening."

Jordan spoke calmly as he ushered Charlie into the Book Room. Her head swiveled as she surveyed the massive racks of books that towered to the ornate ceiling and gave the room its name.

Several candles flickered in wall sconces, and the curtains were drawn tight against the rain that hissed against the windowpanes. It was not a large room, but certainly gave the impression of being well cared for and well used.

"How lovely," she smiled.

"I like it. Would you care for a little sherry, or perhaps port?"

He led the way to a small table where glasses and decanters stood.

"Thank you. Sherry would be nice."

The candlelight sparked crystal rainbows from the delicate glass as Charlie raised her sherry to her lips.

Jordan's eyes followed her every move.

"Your business meeting was concluded successfully?" The question was polite and impartial.

"Yes. Dull as dishwater, but necessary. Some investments are now secured, and others perhaps to be considered. I had to go, but I'm glad I'm home."

A pleasant fire crackled and popped in the large hearth and Charlie moved toward it, drawn perhaps by the lure of the two high backed chairs that had been arranged in front of it.

"I see you are ready for our match, Sir," she said lightly, running one finger along the side of the table.

"Indeed, I am, Charlie. Playing with you will be a very great pleasure, I'm sure."

The finger halted in its progress over the shiny chessboard.

"I trust you will not be disappointed."

"Never with you."

The answer was firm, and brought Charlie's head up quickly. Their eyes met for a second or two, then he was seating her across from him and reaching for a black and a white pawn.

With hands behind him, Jordan mingled the pawns, bringing his hands around him again, each closed around a different pawn.

"Ladies' choice. Would you care to select your color?"

Charlie raised her hand and lightly touched the back of his left hand.

Jordan opened his fist and revealed the white pawn.

"The lady plays white. The opening gambit is yours, Charlie."

Charlie nodded in agreement.

Jordan took his seat opposite her and the two players bent to their game.

The white pawn made the customary opening move and was parried by an equally customary response from black.

Charlie bent towards the table slightly as she considered her next move. A white knight joined the fray.

Jordan narrowed his eyes, thought for a few moments, and then moved another pawn.

Charlie countered with an additional pawn, starting slightly as a log settled in the fireplace. The rain pattered against the windows, punctuating the sound.

Jordan slid his pawn diagonally across and claimed hers. "You have some experience with this game, I take it, Charlie."

"I do indeed, my Lord. My father taught me at a young age, and I have always enjoyed the challenge."

"You certainly indicate your willingness to sacrifice the small things in your pursuit of the greater goal."

Charlie pressed her elbows inwards a little, deepening the valley between her breasts. "I hope I will always know which stratagem to use to achieve victory, my Lord."

Jordan's gaze fell to the soft mounds that were revealed by the low neckline of her gown.

He shifted on his chair.

Charlie allowed her knight to remove the offending black pawn and brought a surprised look to Jordan's face.

"I see you also believe in aggressive play?"

Charlie held the pawn in both hands, rolling it backwards and forwards as if warming it between her palms. She licked her lips, leaving a sheen of moisture behind. "Can such moves be termed aggressive? Is not the object to win, whatever the stratagem employed?"

"It would seem that you have placed my pawn in jeopardy," said Jordan, leaning back in his chair and allowing his shirt to separate across his chest. "You are quite a daring woman. *Especially* when you set out to win."

Charlie's eyes jerked away from the spectacle of Jordan's solid muscles reflecting the golden firelight. Her throat moved as she swallowed silently.

Jordan's hand stretched across the table and touched the top of her knight, circling, scraping with his nail, and finally flicking.

She leaned forward, bringing her breasts closer to that finger.

Her nipples hardened beneath their light covering, standing out proudly through the muslin. "I was taught that only the victory counts, my Lord. No sacrifice is too great."

Jordan smiled and moved his knight into play. "We are well partnered here, then. See how my moves so closely follow yours? Perhaps even match? Are we fated to follow each other in the game...of chess? To move together, in concert, two minds as one?"

Charlie brought her hand to the board and her fingers caressed the tall figure of her rook.

Up and down they went, sometimes circling, sometimes holding, idly playing as she considered her next move.

Jordan shifted in his chair once again.

"Are you comfortable, my Lord? Is your chair perhaps too low?"

Charlie's question pierced the silence of the room and brought one of Jordan's eyebrows up. "I think it is more a case of my anticipation being very high. The thought of mastering you has me very much...aroused..."

"Mastering me?"

"At chess, of course." Jordan picked up his queen and raised it to his lips. "The thought of taking that final move, Charlie..." He rolled the piece over his lips and down to his chin, "The mere suggestion that I may well triumph over your strategies this evening has me tied up in knots."

"And if you should win, my Lord," Charlie brought her other knight into play. "We have not discussed the prize, I believe."

Jordan stared at the board.

"It is your move, my Lord."

Jordan raised his head and looked at her. He carefully replaced the queen on the board. "If I win, Charlie, I believe I shall claim as my prize...a kiss?"

"A kiss, my Lord?"

"A kiss, Charlie. Freely given. Is that fair?"

Charlie's answer was swift and decisive. "Agreed."

Jordan moved a black pawn forward one small space with a hand that shook very slightly. "And if you should be so fortunate as capture my king, Charlie? What would you wish to claim as your prize?"

His eyes roved across her body, as a bead of perspiration rolled down between her breasts. He licked his lips and spread his legs wide beneath the table, just brushing her thigh with his knee.

Her indrawn breath could barely be heard over the sound of their clothes as they rustled against each other in the stillness of the room.

"What shall I claim?"

"That was my question, yes."

Charlie's gaze remained fixed on the board as she danced her fingertips over the pieces. Her thigh moved against Jordan's beneath the table, pressing very slightly, and making the pulse in his neck beat faster. He watched as she countered with yet another pawn.

"It is an interesting question. There is much I would like to claim."

He drew in a ragged breath. "You have but to ask."

Charlie's gaze remained fixed on the board. "It is your move."

Jordan ran a hand through his hair and stared at the game. He grabbed a bishop and roughly slid it forward. "I'm waiting…"

"And I'm thinking." Charlie leaned forward even more, allowing Jordan to enjoy her breasts and the sight of her running a hapless pawn over the skin beneath her neck and down towards her cleavage.

"What are you thinking?" His words were almost harsh now, as harsh as the sound of his breathing. His feet locked around one of her legs and pulled it towards him under the table. She looked up at him.

"What are you thinking?" he repeated, moving her leg back and forth with his own.

"I'm thinking that if I move this pawn here…"

Jordan's hand stayed her move. "No more moves until you tell me what you will claim at the end of the game should you win."

His tone brooked no argument.

Charlie sat motionless, leg between his, wrist in his grip.

She took a deep breath, forcing her nipples against the taut fabric of her bodice. "If I win, I claim this night with you."

Silence fell within the room. Even the fire refused to crackle, as if it was shocked by what it had just heard.

Slowly, without releasing her wrist, Jordan rose from his chair. One hand swept the board to the floor, sending chess pieces every which way.

The other drew her towards him until she was pressed against his body.

"You win."

* * * * *

Jordan's mouth crushed hers in a kiss that sent her mind into oblivion and her already aroused body into heaven.

His arms pulled her even closer and she automatically slid her hands to his shoulders and around his neck, helping him plaster their flesh together.

Charlie was almost incapable of thought. His lips were doing everything she had imagined they would. Firm, warm, demanding, they caressed and teased and then parted to allow his tongue to tantalize the corners of her mouth.

She gasped for air and he followed the breath inside her mouth. She realized for the first time the wonderful feeling of a man cherishing her tender tissues, learning the different textures of her tongue, sliding across her teeth and teasing her with little touches and curls.

Without conscious thought she followed his lead, imitating his intrusion by slipping her own tongue into his mouth and tasting him.

Warm, sweet, with undertones of sherry, Jordan's flavor had an intoxication all its own and it was going right to her knees.

She felt his arms slip down and within seconds she was whisked off her feet and up against his body.

"Are you sure?" he asked roughly, tearing his mouth from hers to voice the question.

She had no chance to answer before he was hungrily kissing her again, eating her lips, sucking her tongue, squeezing her body with his hands and holding her against him with a grip of iron.

Her arms banded his neck and she returned his embrace fiercely.

"I'm sure," she choked as she wrenched herself free to draw a breath.

"Good." Jordan strode from the room, and almost ran up the stairs to the second floor with Charlie in his arms.

The house was dark and quiet, and within moments the door was locked and he was lowering her to her feet next to the bed.

"I want you. I've never wanted anyone as badly." Jordan's words were harsh, but honest, as were his eyes.

"I know." Charlie stared back at him. She'd made a decision this evening. She would not go back on it.

"Why tonight?" Jordan brushed his hands over her breasts, smiling a little as the nipples leapt to attention beneath his fingers. "Why now, Charlie?"

Charlie ran her own hands over Jordan's firm chest and daringly pushed his shirt apart. He obligingly shrugged it off and tossed it into some shadowed corner. She obeyed an inner urge and leaned forward, running her tongue over the flat disk of his nipple.

She heard him gasp and it sent a tremor through her, just accepting the knowledge that she could cause that kind of reaction was an accomplishment in itself.

She raised her eyes to Jordan's, seeing the gold flecks flashing with desire for her. "Because I want you too, Jordan. Because I want your hands on me. I want to know bliss again, but I want to know the real thing this time. Because for the first time I can ever remember, I want to be touched by a man — by you. Because I want to know what it's like to make love rather than to have sex."

She allowed her gaze to wander over his body. "Because I want to touch you and learn about you, and have you touch me. Because I can't stop myself from wondering what it's like to have a man inside me making me feel wonderful instead of…instead of…well, I suppose I want to see if together we can wipe out the past, Jordan."

He took her hand from his chest and slid it between them, allowing her to feel his cock as it pushed against his breeches. She curled her hand around it, wonderingly, and squeezed a little, smiling as he drew in a sharp breath.

"I don't know if I can wipe away your memories, Charlie. But I can damn well make sure you have some new ones."

His hands slipped behind her and her dress fell to her waist.

"I can kiss these beauties…" His lips dropped to her nipples and he ran his tongue around one, making her gasp. "And suckle them too," he moved to the other breast, suckling gently on its rigid tip. "And so much more, Charlie love," He pulled his mouth from her and pressed her naked breasts to his body letting her sensitized nipples feel the rasp of his hair and the heat of his body.

It was her turn to explore and without hesitation she reached for the front of his breeches.

"I think it's time we dispensed with these, Jordan," she muttered, struggling with the tapes. "Damn things…"

Charlie's hands dived between the opening, hungry for the touch of his cock, and with a groan he ripped his breeches away and fell into her palms.

"Oh Jordan," she breathed.

He was so hard and hot and wonderful to feel. His skin was smooth in places, rough in others, and she found her fingers fascinated by the difference in textures she was discovering.

She touched the little drop of moisture that welled from a tiny slit on the head, and raised her eyes as his hand gripped her wrist.

"You will lose me to my desire too soon if you keep that up, Charlie. Let's get lost together."

He slipped his hands beneath her rumpled clothes and pushed everything down over her hips to the floor.

She stood naked before him, feeling the heat crashing from his body in waves to break over hers.

For a moment neither touched, just letting their senses loose and basking in the enormity of this moment.

Charlie could smell him, feel his warmth, and almost absorb his yearning through her skin. She had no idea that she could be aware of a man on so many different levels, each causing a response within her that only added fuel to the fire.

"Charlie, touch me."

The husky whisper touched Charlie's ears and heart at the same time. It was a plea, an encouragement, a prayer and a demand.

She touched.

She took his cock in her hands and rubbed it over her belly, wanting to experience him on some level different to any conventional thinking.

She moved closer to him, forcing him to push himself up between them, and her hand slid behind him to grasp one firm buttock.

She pressed their bodies together, sandwiching Jordan's cock against her softness.

His groan pleased her.

His hands on her backside pleased her even more, and when he started to knead and grasp and slip his fingers up and down her cleft, she couldn't stay still. Her hips began to move against his hardness before her and his hands behind her.

"Jordan," she breathed, as he tilted her slightly and aligned her clit with his balls.

"Open your legs, Charlie."

His hands pulled her cheeks apart and his finger slid towards her tight little rosebud. The millions of nerve endings sent shudders of pleasure through her as Jordan gently caressed them.

Reaching down, he gathered her juices and smoothed them up and around her taut ring of muscles, stroking with a touch as light as a feather. Charlie felt her body beginning to ignite and her hips to move more forcefully against him.

Her knees began to buckle and she knew she could not hold together much longer.

She didn't have to. Within a few seconds of her legs starting to tremble, Jordan had toppled her onto the coverlet behind them.

His body was all over her, hard, hot, moving, touching, nipping, caressing, driving her insane.

She twisted and turned, unable to get closer to him but aware that she had to or die trying.

Jordan slid his hand down her belly while he suckled forcefully on a breast.

She knew she was making some kinds of sounds, but was helpless to control them. Then he found her clit and the noises became a shout of pleasure.

"God, Jordan," she sobbed.

"Like that, do you?" His answer was husky, and took him away from her breast for all of five seconds.

"Yesssss..." she answered, tossing her head back and closing her eyes. "Oh *yesssss...*"

His hand slipped into her swollen and wet folds, exploring, stroking, finding places that made her writhe and places that made her sigh.

He teased and fluttered, sometimes leaving and inserting one or two fingers inside her, then returning to play with her clit some more.

His head moved from her breast to nibble on her lips.

"Ah, Charlie. I can't get enough of you," Jordan's voice was hoarse as he returned hungrily to her nipples.

Her hips wriggled and heaved beneath him, and he pulled away from her breasts and slid down the bed. With no further ado he wrenched her thighs wide and buried his face against her pussy, lapping and tonguing her flesh and bringing a choke of shock and pleasure from her throat.

It was amazing, drove all rational thought from her head, and turned her into a wild thing.

She raised her hips, pushing herself against his face, seeking his tongue, his lips, offering all she had, all she was, for his pleasure.

But still it was not enough.

"Jordan, don't wait..." She gasped out the words, head turning frantically on the pillow.

Jordan obeyed.

He rose above her, taking his weight on both hands.

"Charlie. Open your eyes. Look at me, Charlie."

She was helpless to refuse him anything at this point, even though she wanted to hide from every distraction and focus her attention on what he was doing to her.

His cock brushed her cunt, prodding, parting, encouraging her. "Look at *me*, Charlie. This is your new memory coming—right—up—"

In three forceful thrusts he'd entered her.

In three swift moves he'd filled her body, and pierced her soul.

He stilled within her.

Her eyes opened wide, focused on his, seeing his brown eyes darken to near black as his body claimed hers. A bead of sweat trembled on his temple, and the muscles in his shoulders were standing out.

"God. Move Jordan, please, *move*…"

She spread her legs as widely as she could, as if to devour the man whose cock was buried to the hilt inside her.

She thrust towards him and with a great gasp he thrust back, pounding her mercilessly with his hips and his cock, tenderness forgotten, seduction a thing of the past.

This was no gentle, mannered lovemaking. This was primeval, needy fucking, and Charlie was in ecstasy.

Her body was answering each and every demand with one of its own. When he thrust in she pushed back. His hands lowered to her buttocks as he slid his legs off the side of the bed, pulling her with him and never missing a stroke.

Standing, he was able to increase the force of his relentless possession, gripping her hard with his hands and helping her impale herself on his hammering cock.

It was raw, it was almost violent, and it was everything Charlie had ever imagined it could be.

A strange tightening began to steal her breath and her eyes found Jordan's.

"Jordan…I'm…it's…"

"Yes, I know..." His words trembled as his body kept up its ceaseless rhythm of plunder and withdrawal. One hand quickly found her clit and her lips pulled away from her teeth in a feral snarl.

Hands twisted in the linens, and legs now locked tight around Jordan, Charlie waited for the rising wave to crest, relishing each increasing moment of tension, each muscle that tightened, and each touch of Jordan's body against hers.

Finally, the wait was over.

She came fiercely, silently, and for what seemed like years.

* * * * *

Jordan wanted to howl as he watched the woman on his bed jerk and spasm around his cock.

He slowed his rhythm, holding back his own orgasm by force of will alone. He remembered the time he'd touched her, how she'd begged him for more within seconds. He wondered if tonight would be the same.

Her muscles relaxed a little around him and he slid deeply inside her once again.

She was silky, wet, and hotter than anything he'd ever experienced. Her cunt was clutching him still, and he felt as if he could never ever withdraw from where he was right this second.

Her body fit his.

She trembled, opening her eyes and fixing him with her stormy gray gaze. As he'd hoped, one word came from her mouth.

"More."

Some primitive instinct roared with pleasure inside Jordan's mind. His woman wanted more from him. By God, she'd have it.

He quickly slid from her, ignoring her little cry of protest.

It was soon muffled by the bedding as he flipped her onto her stomach and allowed her legs to hang down over the side of the bed.

He settled himself between her thighs and pressed back into her hot pussy before she'd had chance to catch her breath.

This time, his strokes were slower, and coupled with the pressure of his hands as he ran them from buttocks to shoulders and back again.

She flipped her hair away from her body, giving him access to her naked skin.

He leant forward, pressing himself into her buttocks and her spine, keeping his driving rhythm, and rubbing his flesh against hers.

She sighed, and then moaned, raising her buttocks slightly to push against him, demanding, encouraging, enjoying and just plain loving.

Amazed at his own control, Jordan settled down to play. It was almost as if his cock knew this woman was special. That she deserved something more than a quick fuck, no matter how satisfactory it was. This woman was going to have a night full of incredible memories if he and his cock had anything to say about it.

He slipped one hand beneath her, gently massaging her pussy and tenderly stroking her clit. She was soaked with her own juices, thighs damp with warm honey, skin moistened with sweat. Jordan knew it was a combination of both of their scents that filled his nostrils, he was sweating too.

He straightened slightly and looked down at where their bodies were joined. His cock was sliding in and out of her body with ease, shining where she was bathing him with her liquids. Her buttocks were perfect, smooth and rounded, and even the brand seemed erotic and stimulating to him.

He gently covered it with his hand, smiling as she pushed back against him, as if anxious to increase their contact in any way she could.

He eased her cheeks farther apart and moistened a finger in her honey. Her tight little anus, wrinkled and rosy, was begging for his touch.

She writhed and grunted as he began his delicate teasing, never once losing the thrusting beat of his penetration.

Her breathing grew choppy as his finger pressed against her.

"Jordan...what..."

"Hush love. Let me play with you."

He felt her relax beneath his hands and another little piece of his heart cracked at the trust she was placing in him.

He began to increase his speed, matching it to the now-rhythmic pressure of his finger against her cleft.

She moaned again, responding wildly to his movements.

Within seconds his finger broached her muscles and she gasped as his finger sank into her darkness.

He slid an arm beneath her and pulled her buttocks even further towards him, all but lifting her off the bed.

His pounding hips slapped against her buttocks as his finger moved in her virgin anus, gently teasing the nerve endings he knew were there.

He felt her tighten, he thought she might actually have stopped breathing, and then she exploded.

This time, her scream was deafening.

Every muscle in her body cramped tight. Jordan's finger was squeezed and his cock felt like he'd been caught in a living clamp.

He gasped, unable to comprehend the strength of her body as it orgasmed around his.

Her cunt pulled, pressed, and savagely squeezed his cock, sending his mind into orbit and his body into the most massive orgasm he could ever remember.

He thrust deeply into her body, as deep as he could go, pulling his hands away from her buttocks and driving his cock to where it wanted to be.

He swore he could feel her womb reaching out for his soul as her cunt rippled up and down his cock and every single organ in his body yelled out in release.

He exploded into her, filling her, swamping her with his come, drowning her womb, her cunt and flooding her tissues with his hot seed.

It was a moment unlike any he'd ever experienced. For a few seconds he wondered if death was imminent as his vision disappeared into a blur, his heart completely stopped, and his existence funneled down to one small eye at the tip of his cock.

As his climax passed and his body decided to hang on to life, Jordan allowed his tortured muscles the luxury of relaxation.

He made to move away but a groan from Charlie kept him where he was.

"Don't move, please. Not for a moment or two."

Jordan attempted a grin. "Ah, Charlie," he whispered, leaning his body fully along her back and carefully letting her take his weight against her. "I'm not going anywhere."

Charlie made a sound, which to Jordan strongly resembled a purr.

His next words surprised the hell out of him. "I just want to hold you next to my heart."

Chapter 14

Something was pounding, thrumming, and rousing Charlie back to a level of consciousness from a sound sleep.

She turned beneath the covers to find herself alone, but there were voices in the room.

Memories flooded back. Memories of passion, of hot bodies and sweat and the smell of sex and desire. Her muscles ached slightly, but it was a wonderful ache, and she smiled as she recalled Jordan's whispered words.

He'd eased them both beneath the rumpled covers, and pulled her tight to him, against his heart as he'd promised.

There, with her body relaxing and her mind humming, she'd fallen asleep against the steady drumbeat of his pulse.

Now, it seemed, something had awoken them. Something or someone...

She felt Jordan's presence next to the bed and opened her eyes to see him light a candle.

"Charlie love," he said softly.

"I'm awake, Jordan. What is it?"

His face was in shadows but his touch gentle as he stroked her tangled hair away from her face.

"We have a problem, sweetheart. There's been a fire at the Crescent."

Charlie felt her heart stop.

She shot up in the bed, heedless of her nakedness and grabbed Jordan's shoulders.

"How bad? Who was hurt? Is everybody all right? What about Matty? Jordan, can you get me there? I must go..."

She pushed him aside and flew from the bed, nearly tripping over her own feet.

"Whoa, Charlie, easy now. Firstly no one has been hurt."

She frantically grappled with her robe, but the arms were inside out and she couldn't quite work them back to the way they were supposed to be.

Her hands shook and her vision blurred. "A fire. Oh God, Jordan, a damned fire…"

His hands fell solidly on her shoulders.

"Charlie, listen to me. Listen, dammit…" He turned her forcefully and grabbed her chin, making her look at him. "Everyone is all right. Little damage was done because it was caught before it went very far. Matty is fine, the girls are fine and you are not to worry. Now…" His touch relaxed on her shoulders, and she felt her breath as it returned to her lungs. "Are you listening?"

She nodded distractedly. "But I should be…"

Jordan growled. "What you should be is in this robe and downstairs with me in about five minutes. Elizabeth Wentworth brought the news over along with a message from Matty. She'll want to deliver it to you. Can you do that, Charlie? Put this robe on, and then come down to the breakfast parlor? I have to grab some clothes and I'll meet you there. All right?"

He gave her a little shake then pressed a hard kiss on her trembling lips. "Don't worry, love. It'll be all right."

As Charlie made her way downstairs she wondered a little hysterically if anything would ever be all right again. She'd grabbed her own robe, fastening it tightly to her neck, and had dragged a brush through her tangled hair, blushing as she remembered how it got that way.

Her thighs were still sticky from Jordan's passion, and her body pulsed with fulfilled pleasure. But her heart was aching for another reason—the belief that she was responsible for what had happened to the Crescent.

True to his word, Jordan was waiting for her. But he was waiting next to Lady Elizabeth Wentworth who looked as beautiful in the daylight as she had the first time Charlie had seen her at the Crescent. Looking at the picture the couple made together, Charlie's heart sank. At that moment, she faced the reality of her situation, the reality of Jordan's situation, and the inevitable end of their affair.

There could be no future for a Madam from a brothel and an Earl.

Squaring her shoulders, she entered quietly.

"Lady Elizabeth?"

"Oh, you *are* here. I didn't believe it at first, but your friend, Mistress Matty, was so insistent. How can you be here and no one know?"

Elizabeth's bright blue eyes danced curiously from Jordan to Charlie, neither of whom betrayed by a flicker that they had been roused from a tumble of sex-soaked bedding. "I apologize, Madam Charlie, I should have introduced myself, but I guessed you'd probably want to read this first."

She held out a parchment to Charlie, who calmly took it and retired to the side of the room to read it.

"Elizabeth, stop staring, sit down and tell me exactly what happened. And please remember," Jordan's voice was stern and uncompromising, "that you are not entertaining a gaggle of young women at Almacks. Dramatics and embellishments will not be appreciated. The simple, unvarnished facts, if you please."

Elizabeth sighed. "Jordan, you are a sweetie, but you do remind me of my father sometimes. Thank God I have no interest in you as a suitor. I think I'd probably shoot you long before we ever tied the knot."

Charlie was immersed in her note, and refused to allow Elizabeth's words to disturb her outward calm. Inwardly, of course, she was heaving an enormous sigh of relief at the thought that at least she hadn't slept with a man who had committed himself to marriage. She refolded her note and moved back to the couple by the fire.

"Indeed, Lady Elizabeth, please do tell us what happened. Now that I am reassured there is no injury to anyone involved, I can set my mind to restoring the Crescent and finding those responsible."

Charlie kept her tone calm and polite, and felt secure that her cloak of imperturbability was once again firmly in place. Then she glanced at Jordan, only to see a burning gaze sweeping her from head to toes.

In spite of her control, she blushed.

Elizabeth watched the byplay with interest, but refrained from comment. "Well, there's not an enormous amount to tell."

Charlie seated herself as she watched Elizabeth relate the adventures of the evening. She drew a measure of comfort from the fact that Jordan casually moved to take a position behind her, leaning protectively on the back of her chair.

"A small group of us had decided to visit the Crescent this evening. Tony, of course, who loves the Billiard Room, and Pomeroy wanted to try your smoked herring, Madam Charlie. It's really excellent, you know, especially with that delectable sauce…"

"Elizabeth? You're rambling…" Jordan's brows drew together.

Charlie turned slightly. "Please, Jordan. Let Lady Elizabeth tell the story in her own way. " She turned back to the woman. "I'm sorry. Thank you for the compliment on the herring, but we are understandably anxious to get to the part about the fire?"

Elizabeth continued. "Well, it was just gone one o'clock and I was thinking I might have time to drop in at the Devonshire's rout, when I saw an odd looking man peering in one of the lower windows. One of the *back* lower windows. You know the ones I mean?"

Charlie nodded, recalling the windows that looked over the small garden. At night, they were dark, although the drapes were seldom closed. The garden was very private, and inaccessible to guests. She frowned.

"Well, seeing his face like that really made me jump, as you can imagine. I was about to mention it to someone, when I saw him pull his hand back and throw an object. He threw it right through the window, breaking the glass—shattering it, actually. It landed about five feet from me and promptly exploded."

Elizabeth said this so calmly, it took Charlie a moment or two to fully register the meaning of her words. When she did, she all but erupted from her chair and ran to the other woman's side.

"My poor girl. Are you all right? Were you injured at all?" She stared worriedly into Elizabeth's face as she noticed the tumbled hairdo and detected a slight stench of smoke.

Elizabeth grinned down at her. "There's no need to act like my duenna, Charlie. I'm fine. Well, I did catch a bit of it, but ever such a nice man stepped on it and put it out." She held out the hem of her gown where a large chunk of charred and blackened silk bore mute witness to the truth of her casual statement.

Charlie paled, and Jordan's mouth thinned.

"Actually," continued Elizabeth with a wicked giggle, "the man who was stomping on it ended up tugging on my gown, *very* hard. He didn't realize how hard until he looked up and found my breasts staring him in the face."

Jordan sighed.

Charlie's eyes widened. "Lady Elizabeth. That's terrible. I'm deeply sorry such a thing had to happen in my house. Did you find out his name? He should be severely chastised."

"Whatever for?" Elizabeth's brows rose as a grin crossed her face. "He was a bit taken aback for a second or two, but then he smiled and..." She leaned towards Charlie, turning her shoulder on Jordan. "Do you know what he did?"

Mutely, Charlie shook her head.

"He dropped a kiss on one of them, and said 'Ma'am, I think your dress is extinguished, but the fire has spread to my breeches.' Wasn't that delightful?" Elizabeth giggled.

"God, Elizabeth," exhaled Jordan, running a hand through his hair. "You have no decorum whatsoever, do you?"

"Well, Jordan, for heaven's sake don't be so prissy. There was smoke everywhere, people screaming and running and fussing like the world was ending. And here was one man with the presence of mind to do what was necessary and still have a bit of fun into the bargain." Her blue eyes lowered to her lap. "I do wish I knew who he was, however. I didn't get his name."

She turned excitedly towards Charlie.

"Oh Charlie. Perhaps you could find out for me...perhaps he's a member or something, perhaps you know him..."

Charlie absently patted Elizabeth's hand. "I'll see what I can do, Elizabeth. But we have a slightly bigger problem than the identity of your ill-mannered gentleman."

"We do?"

"We do indeed." Jordan was looking at Charlie and for a second she could read his thoughts as if they were her own. In fact they could have been, since they were both very attuned to the potential dangers of this situation.

"Here's the thing, Elizabeth," said Jordan. "We now are in no doubt that someone is after Charlie, and by default, the Crescent." He raised his hand to forestall Elizabeth's questions. "Later. You can discuss all that later. But here's the new wrinkle. You have seen this perpetrator. You got a good look at him, didn't you?"

Elizabeth nodded. "Nasty looking piece of work. Odd moustache."

"You see you are now a witness. And someone who could very easily send that man to the gallows."

Elizabeth sagged a little as the import of that statement sank home. "Oh hell. Now he'll be after me too."

Jordan looked at Charlie. "She may be flighty and indecorous, but no one ever accused her of being unintelligent."

Charlie frowned at Jordan and returned her attention to Elizabeth. "We must ensure your safety at all costs, Elizabeth."

Elizabeth pulled her bottom lip between her teeth and chewed on it absently.

"I suppose I could retire to the country for a few days, Mama and Papa are still down there…"

"And the rest of the world would immediately know where you'd gone. Right. Clever. Go exactly where you'd be expected to go."

Elizabeth flashed a glance of dislike at Jordan. "Well, Mr. Genius. Do you have a better idea?"

"Actually," said Jordan, looking from Elizabeth to Charlie, "I think I do."

* * * * *

Elizabeth settled back in the carriage and looked over at her companion. "Whatever else you can say about him, you have to admit that Jordan is extraordinarily competent when it comes to getting things accomplished. It's probably the soldier in him."

"Indeed."

The polite response irked Elizabeth, who was not known for her reticence or her patience. She looked out the window at the early light of day, hardly able to believe that Jordan Lyndhurst had managed to get them both changed, packed, and bundled into his carriage to be sent to Calverton Chase without further delay. He'd even managed to arrange for half a dozen outriders to accompany them.

Neither girl had slept a wink, yet neither would confess to being tired now. Elizabeth knew she was too tense to even think about closing her eyes, and she could only guess at Charlie's state of mind.

For that woman had, unquestionably, the best self-control she'd ever seen.

Elizabeth allowed herself a small grin at the thought of the special tincture she'd grabbed from her dresser drawer in the fifteen minutes Jordan had allowed her to pack. An admirer had brought it from Paris where it was apparently all the rage, having been part and parcel of Napoleon's pack trains when they returned from their Egyptian campaign.

The tea made from this tincture, it was rumored, did delightful things to one's inhibitions. Elizabeth couldn't wait to try it out, and thought that Charlie would probably be a perfect trial subject. Along with herself of course.

It was her curse. She had long ago come to terms with it. The endless quest to feel, to experience, to *know*. Especially about herself and her body. She was still a virgin, technically, anyway, but she enjoyed climaxing, whether she was alone, or whether she permitted another the privilege of assisting her.

Actually, other than Jordan, only Ryan Penderly had had that honor, and he wasn't terribly good at it.

A slight frown crossed her brow.

"Problems, Elizabeth?" Charlie had noticed her expression.

"Always, Charlie. Always." She smiled back, hoping that a bond of friendship might well develop. Elizabeth was too attractive to have many loyal friends amongst her contemporaries, and although devoted to her own hedonistic investigations, she occasionally missed the companionship that another woman could offer.

"You are far too young and far, far too lovely to be plagued with problems," wryly answered Charlie.

"Hah. That's 'Hah' to both those statements, Charlie. For an intelligent businesswoman, you certainly have some silly notions. Firstly, age hasn't a damned thing to do with troubles, and I'm sure you know that only too well, running a place like the Crescent. Secondly," she held up two fingers, "being attractive means that men fuss over me while they're trying to ascertain if I'm worth anything in the dowry department, and other girls stick to me like glue in the hopes that they'll get some of my leavings in the way of eligible bachelors. All their mothers either love me or hate me. "

She sighed loudly. "God, I hate it so much. Such a stupid game."

"What do you *want*, Elizabeth?"

The question made Elizabeth sit back and think. It was a simple question, but the answer was complex, incomplete and a little disturbing. For the truth of the matter was, Elizabeth wasn't sure she knew.

"Well, perhaps it's easier to start by making sure I know what I *don't* want..." Her blue eyes gazed out of the carriage window, seeing little of the passing countryside.

Charlie remained silent, offering patience and room for thought. Elizabeth was grateful.

"I don't want to be married off like some clause in a business contract. That I'm certain about." She nodded her head decisively.

"Is that likely to happen?"

"Fortunately, no. My family has enough money and assets to make me a prize on the Marriage Mart, but they have no need of titles, and Mother has been very supportive of my taking my time before deciding to settle down. I have a suspicion she's not going to allow me to repeat her mistakes..." Elizabeth's mouth pursed as she thought of her mother's crusade for the downfallen woman and her father's attempt to keep her mother busy by making sure there were plenty of them.

"I also don't want to be courted for what I have. I want to be loved for who I am. And who I can be with the right man."

"That's an interestingly sophisticated viewpoint."

Elizabeth smiled her pleasure. "Thank you. I knew you'd understand. I think there is much that we share, Charlie. A sense of independence, a curiosity, an interest in the world and its ways. Would you agree?"

"In some respects, perhaps," answered Charlie cautiously.

"You see, you are immersed in becoming completely independent. You have your own business, and you use your own sexuality to further your financial goals. Oh don't mistake me, please..." She held up a hand. "I knew right away that you are simply the owner of the Crescent. No one who looks like you and behaves like you could ever be one of its workers."

"You think not?"

"Absolutely. Why do you imagine so many members of the Ton now come openly to the Crescent? They come because you are there, Charlie. Your personality is as elegant and regal as any at Carlton House, more so, in fact. You welcome your guests as correctly as Sally Jersey, and you're about as approachable as Mrs. Drummond-Burrell."

Charlie wrinkled her nose at Elizabeth's comparison of her to two of the leading Patronesses behind the phenomenon of Almacks.

"You make people feel that the Crescent is only one step lower in the scheme of things than, let's say, Cavendish Square, and you make them feel a damn sight more comfortable than Caro Lamb ever did. Let's face it, Charlie, you're a lady, through and through. Regardless of where you are or what you do, you'll always be a lady."

Charlie's expression warmed slightly as she gave Elizabeth a little, but genuine, smile.

"You're too kind."

"Not at all. I'm just being honest here. Plus, of course, I fully intend to pick your brains about some of the activities at the Crescent. A girl can't know too much before she finally gives her body to a man. And I want to know all of it. How to please him, how to make sure he pleases me, what kinds of things we can do together. All that wonderful information that girls like me aren't supposed to know."

Charlie laughed, surprising both of them. "And you think *I* know all that?" Her amusement was evident.

"Well of course, my dear Charlie. You couldn't go to bed with Jordan Lyndhurst and not learn *something*."

Charlie's mouth shut with a snap, but before she could reproach Elizabeth for her comments, the other girl intervened.

"Don't even bother, Charlie. You two only have to be in the same room to strike sparks off each other. I swear Jordan would have stripped you and taken you right in front of me the other night if matters hadn't been so serious. He was in a bad way."

She grinned across the carriage.

"This does, of course, bring up a couple of differences between us. I doubt that you're a virgin. And you're in love with Jordan Lyndhurst. So what I want to know is, what's it *really* like to make love to a man?"

Chapter 15

Charlie was spared having to answer Elizabeth's totally inappropriate question by the sound of hooves pounding alongside the carriage. Within moments the vehicle slowed, and Jordan had entered, tossing his riding gloves next to Elizabeth and seating himself comfortably next to Charlie.

"Well, ladies, I hope you've been well entertained with each other? We should be there in just a couple of hours now."

The scent of fresh air and horses rose from his jacket, and Charlie had a difficult time resisting the urge to bury her nose in his chest and inhale. Mixed with Jordan's own male scent, the fragrance was doing dreadful things to her body. Dreadfully wonderful things.

She gazed at his hands, resting on his knee, and tried to focus away from her newly-awakened awareness of him.

Her attempts failed dismally — she could only think of what those hands had done to her in the darkness of their bed. She had to work very hard to wrench her attention back to the conversation.

"…So I was able to catch up with you after all. Arthur, of course, is way behind with the other carriage, he's never been one for neck-or-nothing riding."

Charlie turned her head and permitted herself the pleasure of looking at him.

"Are you convinced this is the right course of action, my Lord?"

Jordan grinned. "Since you've been calling me Jordan for quite some time now, and in front of Elizabeth too, it's a bit silly going all formal on me, don't you think?"

Charlie colored and turned away.

"Charlie, love, Elizabeth is a dear friend. I trust her, and I like her. I hope you do too."

"Indeed I do. I just..."

Elizabeth leaned forward and patted Charlie's hand. "I understand, Charlie. You're a private person. Anyone can see that. Just because I tend towards being a bit blatant at times..."

Jordan hooted with laughter. "Calling you merely blatant is like saying the Tower of London is a big stone house."

Elizabeth frowned at him and promptly ignored him, returning her attention to Charlie. "He can be an annoying nuisance at times, Charlie, but you can trust Jordan and I hope you can trust me too. I'd like to think we could be friends, you and I..."

Charlie looked up and met blue eyes, smiling and honest. They stared into hers, asking for her faith that they shared something, some indefinable values or beliefs that united them as women and as friends.

She felt her lips curl, and her hand moved to clasp Elizabeth's. "You are the very devil, aren't you?" she grinned.

Elizabeth took that as a huge compliment. "Yes. And only a very smart woman such as yourself would recognize it."

Jordan sighed loudly. "Oh God, we're in for it now."

Elizabeth turned on him, but before she could unleash a tirade, Jordan seized Charlie's hand and held it tight, refusing to let her withdraw it.

"Charlie, I want you to know you'll be safe at Calverton Chase." He tightened his clasp and his voice took on a serious note.

"I am sworn to protect both you and Elizabeth, and I have set various kinds of security measures in motion that will be awaiting us when we arrive. A messenger was dispatched before first light with instructions."

Jordan's voice was calm now, but very intense. "I am going to ask that you both remain within the house as much as possible. There will be guards set around the property at various points, but it will be difficult, if not impossible to protect you both if you wander off willy-nilly."

Charlie inclined her head, agreeing. She saw the rationale of Jordan's words even if Elizabeth pouted a little at them.

"The house is quite new, you both know I've rebuilt a good portion of it recently. This means that the workmanship is excellent, the locks fresh and tight, and the windows well secured. This is no longer a pile of rubble with a couple of rats for tenants, but a solidly built house. It will be much easier to guard than something older which might not have withstood the ravages of time."

Charlie stirred, longing to ask a question, but afraid that her words might reveal too much.

As if he sensed her needs, Jordan turned to her and raised an eyebrow. "Questions?"

"Your staff, Jordan. Have they been with you long?"

"Years, Charlie. I had a small house of my own long before I found out I'd inherited the Chase. My servants had kept it running smoothly while I was away on the Continent, but they were only too happy to leave and move out here, where they felt the surroundings did more justice to their elevated notions of themselves."

He snickered. "Then they saw the place."

"Bad?" Charlie hid her emotions, remembering her last glimpse of Calverton Chase — a glowing pile of embers shooting sparks into a dark sky.

"Almost total ruin. It took about six months to clear the debris and get an idea of what was left in the way of foundations. The fire, of course, had claimed much of it, but all the servants had fled following the disaster, and it had been pretty much ravaged by weather, creatures, and the occasional looter. Not that there was much left to loot."

Charlie remembered the fine silver plate and several valuable pieces of jade. Someone had benefited from the fire. She wondered who.

"So all my staff are mine, I trust them, they've been with me since I was in short coats, practically. A fact which they remind me of on a daily basis when I'm here. There are a couple of local lads helping with the livestock, but I know just about everyone by name."

Elizabeth giggled. "You have to admit, there's nothing more lowering than to have your maid look at you and remind you about something very embarrassing you did when you were four."

Jordan laughed and agreed.

Charlie let the conversation drift over her as she gazed out of the window and wondered how much of the Chase she'd remember.

Her time there was blurred now, deliberately, she supposed.

As a young bride, she'd had no visitors. Partially from the well-meaning desire to allow newlyweds some privacy, but also partially because her husband was not well-liked in the area.

So it was very unlikely that she'd meet anyone she knew or who might remember her from the six short months she'd been in residence.

The fact that the servants were all Lyndhurst people was an enormous comfort. Charlie had hated the Calverton staff.

They'd been snobbish, sarcastic, cruel, and had delighted in tormenting a young girl who had proved herself unable to breed an heir for their master. She tried to feel sorry for those who had perished in the flames, but all she could remember was the foul breath of Johnny Dobbs as he'd pushed himself into her, grinning and muttering all kinds of disgusting things.

She shivered.

Jordan's hand tightened on hers. "All right, sweetheart?" he asked softly, under cover of the noise within the carriage.

Charlie glanced over at Elizabeth to notice her resting against the corner cushions with her eyes closed. The lace at her breast fell regularly and she appeared to be asleep.

Daringly, she allowed herself to squeeze Jordan's hand back.

He pulled her across the seat and settled her against his body, draping an arm around her shoulders and turning her so that she could lean against him.

"Try to rest, love. It'll be a while yet. Then we'll be there and you'll be safe, and you and I..."

His tongue flicked out and just brushed her ear. She shivered again, this time from the flame that he'd fanned deep in her belly.

"...You and I will find some more ways to have fun. And I don't think chess will be involved..."

* * * * *

It was with a strange mixture of pride and trepidation that Jordan Lyndhurst, the Seventh Earl, returned to Calverton Chase with two women, one of whom was becoming more important to him as each and every minute passed.

He knew the house looked well, his workers and his architects had performed admirably. He desperately wanted Charlie to like it, and yet he himself had no great attachment to it. He hadn't grown up here, knew few if any of the locals, and didn't care too much for the property. It was a project to Jordan. One upon which he'd lavished his usual time and attention, but a project nevertheless.

It had never become "home".

That is, until the moment he ushered Charlie across the threshold.

Seeing her standing there, chatting comfortably with Mrs. Hughes, the world suddenly shifted slightly on its axis. She looked *right*. She looked like she was completely at her ease in such surroundings. In fact, she looked like she was born to be in such surroundings.

She looked at home.

She looked like *his* home. His anchor. His missing piece. The indefinable something that he'd been searching for without even knowing it.

He swallowed, hard. This was a bit too much to handle all at once.

"So, Master Jordan, you finally brought home a nice young lady." Mrs. Hughes beamed at Charlie.

Jordan wondered how she knew. Why Charlie and not Elizabeth? Equally lovely, equally adept at handling introductions. How did Mrs. Hughes know? He made a note to ask her at the earliest possible opportunity.

"*Two* nice young ladies, Hughie," teased Jordan. "I take it you got my message?"

Mrs. Hughes sighed. "Such terrible goings on. Yes, we did get word, and I've prepared rooms for you all." She shot a direct and rather intimidating look at Jordan who met it blandly. "Miss Elizabeth will have the guest suite at the top of the stairs, Miss Charlotte will have the Rose Rooms further down the passage, and you, of course, will have the Earl's suite."

Jordan smiled. Bless her for not mentioning that the Rose Rooms were destined for the future Countess and adjoined the Earl's suite. His heart quickened and his cock stirred.

"Miss Charlotte" turned inquiring eyes on Jordan. She'd accepted his suggestion of a suitable name without demur, knowing that "Charlie" was rather unusual and might be spoken about unwisely in the vicinity of unwelcome ears.

She didn't know that he'd deliberately chosen that name, of course. He wanted her comfortable, and also knew that hearing her own name would elicit a natural reaction, again something that he wanted.

The world was going to be kept in complete ignorance of Charlie and Elizabeth's whereabouts, if Jordan Lyndhurst had anything to say about it.

"Let me show you ladies to your rooms..." He offered elbows to the girls and led them upstairs, while Mrs. Hughes bustled off to prepare tea and refreshments for the weary travelers.

"Here you are Elizabeth, what do you think?" Jordan swung a large door wide onto a sunny room with floor-to-ceiling windows overlooking a long stretch of lawn.

"Oh Jordan, perfect. This is quite lovely." Elizabeth danced in, smoothing the soft gold velvet of the couch, and opening the desk to see its secrets. "May I write letters?"

"I think you should. Your parents must be informed of what has transpired, although I'd encourage you not to let them know where you are, of course. Just tell them you're safe and protected."

Elizabeth nodded. "They'll understand. And I know they're busy, so it will probably be a relief to them not to have to bother with my goings on for a while."

Something in her tone caught Jordan's ear, and Charlie obviously heard it as well. She beat him to the punch, following Elizabeth into the room and giving her a big hug. "We love your 'goings-on', Elizabeth. They make you who you are."

She grinned, and allowed her dimple out for an airing. "In fact, I think I might ask you to teach me some of them."

Jordan snorted and rolled his eyes. "Oh lord. I don't think so, Charlie..."

Elizabeth smiled wickedly at both of them. "Well, I think when it comes to 'goings-on' you two could probably teach me..."

Charlie blushed and Jordan decided it was time to get out of the room. Quickly.

"Rest, Elizabeth. Write your letters, unpack—your baggage should be here soon. We'll meet downstairs in an hour or so for lunch and have a strategy session... there are some areas we must touch upon for the safety of both of you."

Jordan led Charlie from the room and closed the door behind them, leaving Elizabeth to her unpacking. Without a word, he turned and led her down the corridor, all the way to the end.

"These are the Earl's rooms, Charlie. Mine by default, I suppose."

He showed Charlie into a brand new suite, elegant and smelling slightly of paint.

"And my rooms?"

"This way..." He walked across his study, into his bedroom and past the huge four-poster bed. A soft carpet in tones of deep maroon cushioned his steps.

Detailed carving outlined a doorway at the far end and Jordan turned the handle.

"These, my love, are your rooms. Right next to mine."

He smiled and gestured for her to precede him.

* * * * *

She was next door to his bedroom. Charlie's heart was in her throat somewhere as she took in the significance of their sleeping arrangements. Overwhelming her was a sense of joy. He wanted her still. He wanted her near to him in the night. They could come and go as they pleased, and the household would be none the wiser.

Another little voice said "so what?" but Charlie ignored it. She was too happy at this moment to allow any kind of doubts to cast shadows across her pleasure.

She stepped into a room full of sunlight and flowers. Or so it seemed at first. Her bedroom also featured a four-poster bed, but a light and dainty one. The hangings were embroidered with large damask roses, and the coverlet matched. The carpet had the same muted tones of rose and green and Jordan opened the far door showing her a sitting room decorated in the same tones.

There were no unpleasant memories filling these rooms. They'd been swept out along with the damaged plaster and replaced with light and color. Gone were the murky and shadowed corners that had lurked in her mind for so long. These rooms, and this one in particular, was brand new.

It was elegant, delightful, and her eyes filled with tears.

Jordan was before her in an instant. "What, love? You don't like it?"

"J...J...Jordan." Her voice caught, in a moment that was so completely out of character for her, she wondered if she was losing her mind. All she wanted to do was to throw herself into his arms and stay there forever.

"It's beautiful. So very beautiful..." she whispered the words as she raised her eyes to his face. She saw it soften from its worried lines and watched as his eyes warmed into something other than concern.

That "something" was echoed between her thighs.

"Jordan," she breathed, reaching out a hand towards him in a vague gesture, not sure what she was asking, but knowing that he had the answer.

He did.

His lips were on hers before she had finished her thought, sweeping her mind clear and rousing her body to fever pitch within seconds.

Hands scrambled to unhook, untie and untangle, and she heard him sigh as her breasts sprang free of her bodice into his hands.

"Jordan...the door..."

With a muttered curse, Jordan left her breasts, rushed across the room, slammed the door shut and locked it, and shed his own shirt and jacket on the way back. His heat was pressed against her before she realized he had returned.

His hands slipped down and relieved her of her gown and undergarments, just as hers were freeing his cock from his breeches.

"Jordan…I want…"

"What do you want, love? Ask. Anything…" mumbled Jordan from her breasts, obviously forgetting the old dictum about not speaking with his mouth full.

"I want to know you."

A quick laugh greeted this statement. "Well, sweetheart, I don't know how we're going to manage that. We've already been introduced, we've been naked together, and I've been inside you. I'd hazard a guess that you know me pretty well…"

"That's not what I mean." Charlie pulled away from him and ran her eyes over his body. She delicately teased a flat nipple, loving the way it beaded beneath her fingers.

"I want to go exploring. To take the Grand Tour. Of Jordan Lyndhurst."

Jordan's expression was beyond price. She bit her lip against the laugh that wanted to erupt as he stared at her like she was Father Christmas, the Duke of Wellington and his Fairy Godmother all rolled into one.

She took advantage of his stunned state by turning and pushing him down onto the bed.

"Let's get you out of these first," she said, turning to place his booted foot between her knees.

Jordan cleared his throat. Roughly.

Knowing what he was seeing as she bent over and clasped his boot, Charlie was abashed at her own daring. But it was as if she'd left her scruples and her inhibitions behind in London. Here she was free to obey her inner urges. And my goodness, she was finding she had plenty of those.

His boot pressed hard against her buttocks as she freed one foot and repeated the action with the other, feeling his bare foot against her cheeks as he pushed her away from him.

"So beautiful, Charlie. Your bottom is a work of art."

She chuckled as she tugged his other boot off and dropped it with a thump. "Jordan, bottoms aren't beautiful."

"Yours is. Trust me on that."

She moved between his legs and helped him slide out of his breeches, loving the way his cock thrust towards her like a lodestone to North.

Finally, she had him naked. She pushed him onto his back, encouraged him to scoot back onto the bed, and eased herself up to kneel beside him.

She licked her lips.

Now she could play.

* * * * *

Jordan's world disappeared as his attention became focused on the woman touching him.

Her expression was full of interest and fascination as she ran her hands through his hair and onto his shoulders. He loved the little curl to her lips as she bent and dropped a featherlight kiss on his mouth and followed it with little licking touches to his chin and neck.

Every now and again her breasts would brush his body, and he had to fight the urge to reach up and pull her hard against him. It was difficult, because he could sense her excitement and matched it with his own.

He could also smell her scent and knew she was getting hot and wet someplace he wanted to explore himself. Very badly.

But she'd asked for a chance to learn about him, and by God he'd give it to her. If he happened to expire from pleasure during the experience, well, he'd die a happy man.

"Aaahh…" A gasp of laughter was surprised out of him as she brushed the sensitive spot just beneath his armpit.

She grinned. "Jordan, you're ticklish. I'd never have guessed."

Jordan bit his lip and willed himself not to react. "Not very much. And I'll wager I can find your ticklish spots in less than ten seconds."

She laughed aloud, tracing his muscles with her fingertips. "You probably could. That's one wager I'm not accepting. I'm too busy on my voyage of discovery."

She leaned forward and delicately suckled his nipple, swirling it with her tongue and bringing a moan of delight to his throat.

"God, Charlie, I love it when you do that."

She pulled back with a final loving lick. "I never knew men could be so sensitive there." She smoothed the length of his torso with her hands, half in a caress half in a massage.

Jordan sighed with pleasure. "Men are sensitive everywhere, Charlie," he chuckled. "Anything you do to us weaklings, we'll respond to."

Charlie swept down to his navel, slithering down the bed a little.

Jordan's voice became rougher as her hands dipped into the little well and tickled the flesh of his abdomen.

"Things like that..." He swallowed as her tongue followed her fingertips. "When you do something like that, it makes me want to...ooooh," he groaned.

She'd slipped her hands to the very edge of his pubic hair and her breasts were brushing his flesh. He could feel the taut nipples as they pressed against him. Her tongue lapped at his navel then traveled south, making every nerve ending flicker. His cock was harder than a tree trunk and felt about the same size. He prayed it didn't bounce against her head and kill her.

"It makes you want to what, Jordan?" she asked, blowing gently on the skin her tongue had moistened.

Jordan's hips fidgeted.

"It...it...you make me want to return the favor. I want my tongue on you, Charlie. Everywhere..."

His voice failed him as she reached her destination and took his cock in her hands. He was so sensitive to her that he could feel the breath as it blew from her nostrils while she ran her fingers over him, learning him, feeling him, looking at him.

He was lost. "God, Charlie," he muttered, his head arching back a little as her hand explored his ridges and veins, gently smoothing, caressing and adding a little squeeze now and again for good measure.

"Do you like this, Jordan? Is it pleasant for you?"

Jordan could only grunt. Her lips had closed over his cock and the rest of his mind had gone off someplace else. What was left had just achieved the ultimate bliss.

Cautiously she slid her mouth over him, moving her tongue a little, licking and tasting and discovering textures and nooks and crannies he never knew he had.

Women had performed this service for him before, many times. He was a soldier and this was accepted as the safest way to get pleasure from the women they met in their campaigns. Jordan had never had the desire to contract any of the virulent poxes that were rampant in any army, so this was how he'd achieved his release.

But this was a totally new feeling. This was something that transcended the physical act. This was a blending, a giving, a sharing, that was unique in his experience. The way Charlie's tongue loved him was soft and warm and wanting, and he felt he needed every little move she gave him.

He raised his head slightly to watch her as she moved on his body, her golden hair swept back and teasing the skin of his thighs.

Her cheeks moved as she sucked, setting up her own rhythm that tugged at his heart as well as his balls.

Clearly, she was a newcomer to this kind of fun, her movements were a little awkward and hesitant, but Jordan wouldn't have had it any other way. It was so much more than just the touch of her mouth on his cock. It was her wish to taste him, to touch him, and to learn his pleasures that reached deep inside him. She was sucking on the one place no one had ever even neared before.

His heart.

Intrepid and adventurous, she moved a hand between his legs and found his balls. She cupped them gently, as if they were the most fragile treasure in existence. Jordan couldn't argue, because at this moment they were.

She found the little spot beneath the head that made him writhe and moan.

"Charlieeee…" he hissed, gritting his teeth and hanging on to his control for dear life.

"Jordan, let go," she breathed, blowing air over his wet cock and making it tremble. "I want you to let go. I watched as you came in Jane's hand at the Crescent, and I wanted it to be me that made you come. Let it be me this time, Jordan. Give me that experience. Please…"

She didn't have to ask twice.

As soon as her lips slid back over his cock, she allowed her hand to grasp the base and slipped her other hand behind his balls to that wonderfully sensitive spot that raised every hair on his body and sent his muscles into spasm.

"God, I'm going to…I can't hold on…"

He knew he was going to lose this battle. Charlie had asked nicely, and although his mind was telling him that she was a lady and he shouldn't be doing this, the rest of him was screaming for release and plunging down towards his cock in readiness.

She moved her head more quickly, more sure now of her movements. It was all over for Jordan.

Seconds later he felt his buttocks tighten, his legs went rigid and it was as if a bolt of lightning traveled down his spine, through his balls and up his cock, making it explode in the warmth of Charlie's mouth.

She hummed as he came, spurting long and deep into her throat. She held him tight, squeezing a little as if milking every last drop.

Exhausted, he flopped onto the bed.

"Oh my God. Charlie. Oh my God."

His wits had clearly gone wandering. A woman gave him one of the greatest pleasures that he had ever experienced and that was the best he could come up with. He sighed.

"I take it you enjoyed that," she was beside him with a very wicked smile on her face.

Her eyes narrowed and she leaned over and gently kissed him, letting him taste himself on her lips. "Now you know what *you* taste like," she breathed. "It's nice. A little salty, quite unique. And you feel so wonderful, Jordan. That was a moment I'll always treasure. Holding you as you came. It was magic."

Jordan Lyndhurst was lost. He looked into her gray eyes and saw the genuine pleasure and honesty shining from within. At that moment he knew he'd fallen in love.

The battle was over, the campaign finished. He'd taken his objectives with great success, and when the dust settled, he had to admit defeat.

He'd been rolled up, foot and guns. His adversary, with a combination of cunning, intelligence, sensuality and affection, had routed him decisively and taken a prisoner.

She now had his heart.

Chapter 16

Charlie sensed it was late when she awoke the next morning.

The sun was shining through the half drawn drapes, and Jordan's side of the bed was empty and cold.

After they'd recovered from their sensual games the day before, events had swirled around Charlie at record speed. Elizabeth too, had professed herself at a loss to fully comprehend Jordan's security arrangements.

But he'd been a whirlwind, organizing his staff and his extra guards to within an inch of their lives.

Elizabeth had been required to describe the man from the Crescent several times, and even tried to draw him at Jordan's insistence.

Unfortunately, she could not claim much talent in the field of portraiture and so the effort was abandoned.

Charlie had not been able to stop herself from glancing around her as she realized that she was once again at Calverton Chase.

She also spent considerable time wondering why she didn't feel more uncomfortable returning to this place which held so many dreadful memories.

But it didn't take long for her to understand that the Calverton Chase of her past had gone up in smoke.

The dark and dreary rooms that had figured largely in her nightmares were gone. The main staircase was about the only thing that looked vaguely similar to her memories, and even that was glowing with beeswax and had a lovely Aubusson stretching its entire length. Many of the rebuilt rooms were still empty and Jordan made no bones about the fact that any monies he'd inherited had gone into construction. It was his opinion that future generations could worry about the color of the curtains, his duty was to see that there were good solid windows from which to hang them.

In truth, Charlie could see nothing of the Calverton Chase that had haunted her for so long and another weight slipped unnoticed from her shoulders.

A small furor had been occasioned in the middle of the afternoon when a cloud of dust announced a rider approaching at great speed.

Jordan sent the girls into the library and waited at the door himself. A dueling pistol was unobtrusively lying on a small shadowed table within arm's reach.

Charlie and Elizabeth had snorted with disgust at such cavalier treatment, and peeped cautiously from the room, anxious to see who had arrived.

Loud voices accompanied by Jordan's laughter assured them that all was well, and they left the room in a hurry to rush to the front door.

There, on the steps, Charlie saw Jordan being hugged by a Viking. Well, someone who fit the description of what she always imagined a Viking would look like.

Very tall, well muscled and with a shock of light blonde hair, the man was laughing and slapping Jordan on the back. Hard.

Charlie winced for him.

She noticed the uniform. This must be one of Jordan's old comrades in arms.

Elizabeth was very still beside her. "That's him, Charlie..." she whispered.

"Hmm? That's who?"

"That's the man who kissed my breast."

Charlie jumped, and realized Elizabeth was hanging on to her arm with a grip like death.

"I'd never forget that hair or those eyes," Elizabeth's voice trailed off as she stared at the man at the bottom of the steps. "Whatever do you think he's doing here? And I don't remember him in uniform…"

The men turned and saw the two girls standing arm-in-arm in the doorway.

Jordan's gaze blistered Charlie and for a second it seemed he'd forgotten where he was.

But a sound from his companion recalled his attention and together they moved up the long flight of stairs.

"Look who's here…" said Jordan, grinning from ear to ear.

"Oh I'm looking," muttered Elizabeth, sotto voce.

"Charlie, Elizabeth, this is Lieutenant General Sir Spencer Marchwood. Spence, may I present Miss Charlotte, and Lady Elizabeth Wentworth."

"Ladies, it's a rare day when the sun is outshone, but I must conclude that this is indeed a rare day."

Sir Spencer bowed gracefully, and Charlie wondered if he was on Wellington's staff, all of whom were renowned for their smooth manners and gracious address. Sir Spencer oozed charm, but it was tempered by the rather wicked curve to his lips as he raised Elizabeth's hand.

"To kiss this hand sends chills up my spine, Lady Elizabeth. Your skin is amazingly soft against my lips." He paused and stared down into her eyes. "As I remember."

Even Charlie shivered and Elizabeth was rendered mute. Good heavens, the man was good.

Jordan cleared his throat. "Inside please, ladies. Spence has news."

The rest of the afternoon had passed with talk of Wellington's great victory near a small town in Belgium.

Spencer had apparently been on his way to rejoin his regiment, but was unable to reach Brussels in time. So he'd turned back from the coast as soon as the first dispatches arrived, and heard the rumors that linked trouble with Jordan Lyndhurst.

"After all, I couldn't let one of the old brigade handle this sort of thing by himself. He'd mess it up for sure."

Jordan sighed. "So there are mutterings about this business. Damnation, I hoped we'd kept it quiet. That doesn't mean the entire brigade is going to arrive on my doorstep within a few hours, does it?"

"Wouldn't hurt to have the extra help," muttered Arthur as he brought in a tray burdened with glasses of fresh ale and a pot of tea.

"Arthur, you old sod. Still plowing the local fields?"

Arthur accomplished the amazing feat of glancing down his nose at the man who towered over him by at least twelve inches. "Still keeping your brains in your breeches, Sir Spencer?"

Jordan chuckled. "Don't even try to out-Arthur Arthur, Spence. You'll never succeed. Now, let me tell you what's been going on and you can tell us about...what was the name? Waterloo?"

Apparently, talk of war was both arduous and lengthy, because long before the men had finished, Elizabeth and Charlie found themselves drooping before the fire. Dinner had been very informal, and dominated by reminiscences of friends, sighs over losses, and laughter at bygone escapades.

All of which were quite fascinating to the gentlemen, but palled after a while on their female companions.

Both men stood politely when Charlie and Elizabeth announced they were retiring for the evening.

Jordan had flashed a hot look at Charlie, and Spencer had very obviously stripped the clothes off Elizabeth with his eyes.

Both girls had retired, blushing, to giggle their way upstairs to their rooms.

Charlie had tried to stay awake, but Jordan was a long time coming, and sleep had claimed her before he'd come upstairs.

She'd vaguely felt him pull her into his arms, and had turned to hear the solid thump of his heart beneath her ear.

She'd slept, content, knowing he was there.

But now it was morning, and he was up and gone. Time for her to face the day and whatever it might bring.

It brought Elizabeth.

* * * * *

"Well *finally*," said an exasperated voice. Charlie pulled herself up on her pillow to see Elizabeth waving away a servant and bringing Charlie's morning repast in all by herself.

"I've had all night to think about him, and I've come to a decision." She plopped the tray down on the table next to the bed with a thump, and landed on the bed next to Charlie, crossing her legs Indian-style and tugging up her skirts in a very inelegant way.

"I want Spencer Marchwood."

Charlie closed her eyes. "I think I'd like my tea first please. And pass that toast too. Have you had anything?"

"Yes, I've eaten. Although that crumpet looks quite fresh. You don't mind?" Charlie vaguely waved her hand as Elizabeth commandeered the crumpet, slathered butter on it and devoured it with relish.

"So," said Charlie, allowing her eyes to finally focus on her companion. "You want Spencer Marchwood."

"Yes."

"Define 'want'."

"Well, I want him in my bed. On top of me. Taking my virginity. I think he'll do an excellent job of it. What do you think?"

Charlie coughed as a huge crumb lodged behind her windpipe. It took several sips of restorative tea to get her voice working again.

"Elizabeth, this isn't something you should be casual about. This is something you should save for your husband. And I thought you said Ryan Penderly was the victim—er—candidate for that job."

Elizabeth quirked a brow at Charlie. "You haven't seen Ryan Penderly. He's nice. *Nice*, Charlie." Her lips curled. "He deserves a nice wife, nice children. I thought at first that that would be me, but the more time passes, I am realizing that I'm *not* nice." She sighed and put down the remains of her crumpet.

"I want more, Charlie. I want excitement. I want stars and bugles and fireworks. I want to *feel*. You asked me a little while ago what I wanted. Well, now I know. I want to feel Spencer Marchwood. When his lips touched my skin it was like a fire or what they say that electricity machine makes. A tingle, an almost painful sensation that shoots down to some very private places..."

Elizabeth gazed at Charlie. "Do you understand anything of what I'm talking about?"

Charlie looked back at her. "Oh yes. Oh yes indeed I do."

"Well, then. Believe me when I tell you that I have met many men...I couldn't be a member of the Ton and not have them run past me like bidders at an auction." Her lips pouted in distaste. "Not one of them ever made me feel like he does, Charlie. Not one."

"Not one of them ever kissed your breast, either," reminded Charlie.

"True. But the thing is, the same feeling happened yesterday when he kissed my hand." She waved at her bodice and colored slightly. "He touched me and *things* started happening. I could feel my breasts...it was most unusual..."

Charlie smiled comfortingly. "Not really. It was arousal, Elizabeth. This man arouses you. Sexually. That's a good thing. Ordinarily, he'd speak with your parents and you two could further your acquaintance..."

"But that's just it, Charlie. I don't want that. I simply want to know what lies between us. What the potential is for our mutual pleasure. I *don't* want to think about heirs and bloodlines and dowries. Why can't I just enjoy him all by myself? Why does it have to affect the future of the nation? I just want to fuck him, for heaven's sake."

Charlie's eyebrows rose. "Well, that's calling a spade a spade, isn't it?"

"I'm tired of mealy mouthed chits who flutter around and look like they're going to faint if someone so much as mentions a body part in their hearing." Elizabeth nodded her head assertively. "I'm not like that."

"No, that's absolutely certain," agreed Charlie with a grin. "So do you want me to hold him down while you strip him and play with him?"

The question caught Elizabeth off guard and she stopped, stunned, before going off into peals of laughter.

"Oh lord, Charlie, you're wonderful. I'm *so* glad I know you." It took a few moments for the merriment to die down. "No, I don't think we need go that far, besides, Jordan would never permit you to touch another man while he's around. Even a blind man could sense that." She chuckled. "I always wondered what Jordan would be like when he found his woman. Now I know. He's really rather sweet."

Charlie's heart missed a couple of beats. "His woman?"

"Unquestionably. I've known Jordan Lyndhurst and his family for many years, Charlie. We played together — well, I should say I played with his younger sister. I've never seen Jordan look at a woman the way he looks at you. It's special, possessive and passionate and, oh I don't know. It's just unique. You'd better love him back, Charlie, because I'd hate to see Jordan hurt."

Elizabeth shot a very pointed look at Charlie.

Charlie's heart started up again, strong and solid. "How could I not love him?"

The simple question hung there between the girls for a few moments. Then Elizabeth leaned forward and hugged Charlie tight for a few seconds. "I'm so glad."

She pulled back and swiped the last piece of toast. "Come on, hurry up and get dressed. I need to talk to you about something I brought with me that I'm dying to try out. Meet me in the breakfast room when you're ready?"

Charlie smiled and nodded, and steadied the tray as Elizabeth slid from the bed and left the room in a rush.

Alone with her thoughts, Charlie stared at her teacup.

"I love him." She said the words out loud, as if trying them on for size. "I'm in love with Jordan Lyndhurst."

They got easier the more she said them.

Now all she had to do was work out whether this was the best thing that could ever have happened to her in her entire life.

Or maybe the worst.

* * * * *

It was late afternoon by the time they all met again in the small parlor for tea.

Charlie and Elizabeth had spent the morning gossiping, chattering and muttering over something like two young girls in the schoolroom.

It had warmed Jordan's heart to see Charlie so carefree.

He'd wanted to slip into her welcoming heat so badly last night when he'd finally staggered to bed, but he knew he was tired, she was tired, and he'd allowed Spencer to talk him into far too much brandy.

So with a rueful smile to himself, he'd cuddled her against him, and had slept like a log with her weight nestled next to his heart.

He realized he couldn't imagine spending his nights any other way.

Now all he had to do was formulate a new campaign to handle all the obstructions that life was doubtless going to throw their way. Prime amongst which was Charlie's own very obvious hesitation about the possibilities of a relationship between a brothel-owner and an Earl.

Jordan sighed. He was going to have to put in some thought on that one.

Spencer, too, had given him food for thought.

The brandy had mellowed both men, and not long after the women departed, cravats had been discarded, jackets tossed aside, and long legs hooked comfortably over the arms of chairs.

"I can't say I'm not thrilled to find Lady Elizabeth here, Jordan."

Jordan had narrowed his eyes. "It was you who saved her that night at the Crescent, wasn't it?"

Unabashed, Spencer had continued staring into the fire. "Yes. It was all rather a muddle, a lot of screaming, some smoke. Elizabeth was the only one who didn't panic, but she never realized her gown was burning. I had no notion how rough I was until I saw her body." Then he'd glanced up. "I truly meant no insult to the lady, Jordan. But my God, man, what breasts." His cock stirred at the memory. "Yes, I know," he said addressing his manhood. "But you can bloody well go back to sleep."

Jordan had chuckled ruefully. "Elizabeth is a law unto herself, Spence. But you're a good man and I'm in no position to throw stones. I trust you with Elizabeth, wherever the dance takes you. She's a handful, mind you, but perhaps you might be the man to keep her in line. Just don't compromise her or hurt her, all right?"

Spencer had sighed. "I'm just a little bit afraid of that woman, Jordan. And if you ever repeat that I shall be forced to call you out and rid the world of your troublesome presence."

Jordan knew that Spence was skilled in many areas, but marksmanship wasn't one of them. He'd chuckled. "Why are you afraid of Elizabeth?"

For a moment the room had fallen silent, the ticking of the clock and the crackling of the fire loud in the stillness that followed Jordan's question.

"Because when I touched her and looked into her eyes, I...I felt something. A shiver up my spine, like someone walking over my grave. She's trouble, Jordan. And I'm running headlong into it."

Jordan's shoulders had shrugged off the sense of inevitability. "It comes to us all, old friend. It comes to us all."

Looking at the girls seated across from him now, in the waning afternoon light, Jordan realized how prophetic his words had been. The "trouble" Spencer had described last night had come to Jordan and settled in his soul. Its name was Charlie.

And he couldn't be happier.

Well, he thought he couldn't. But then Charlie smiled at him, and watched him. Oh lord, she'd asked him something. He was so lost in his thoughts he'd not heard a word she said.

"I'm so sorry, ladies. My mind was elsewhere." Like between your legs, Charlie. "What was that again?"

Charlie grinned at him, letting him know she had a pretty good idea where his mind had been, and liked it there. A lot.

Jordan shifted uncomfortably, and offered a prayer of thanksgiving when Elizabeth took pity on him.

"Jordan, Charlie and I want to prepare a special dinner this evening. Sir Spencer has told us something about his trip to Egypt, and Charlie has admitted to some fascination with the Middle Eastern stories she's heard. So we thought it would be fun to dine ' à l'Egypte' this evening. What do you think?"

"Depends," answered Jordan carefully. "What does that entail?"

"Well, some very big cushions for us all to sit on. Not in the dining room, obviously. We can use those low tables in the back parlor. It's got a nice soft carpet too. We must be barefoot, of course, and you gentlemen will be excused from cravats and such, find something close to an Arabian robe, will you? We girls will dress suitably too." Elizabeth's enthusiasm was infectious.

"I'm sure Jordan and I can come up with something suitable, Elizabeth. And I, for one, can't wait to see you as harem girls..." Spencer wiggled his eyebrows suggestively.

"Harem? Oh I don't think so, Sir Spencer. Charlie and I would never settle for anything but the top wife's job. We will be desert warrior women. None of your perfumed houris for us, right Charlie?"

"Um, right," agreed Charlie, helpless against Elizabeth's determination.

"Good. It's settled then. Oh and I have a special tea I'm going to prepare. It does come straight from Egypt. Paul Faremont brought it for me from Paris—it's all the rage there, I've heard. Some kind of stimulant tincture, nothing harmful, but very much in keeping with our theme for tonight."

She grabbed Charlie's hand. "Come on, there's lots to do."

Charlie looked at Jordan and threw him a quick smile. "And I suppose I have 'lots to do' along with you," she said as she hurried along behind Elizabeth. "We'll see you both later."

Jordan grinned as he watched the flurry of gowns bustle from the room. "Life is never dull with those two around," he muttered.

"Any news from London?"

Jordan instantly sobered. "Not a word. I've men tracing down our would-be assassin and it looks like they may have discovered his whereabouts. I'm hopeful that a messenger will show up perhaps as early as tomorrow to let me know the situation."

"Well, we're safe enough here. Nice job on the perimeter, by the way."

Jordan smiled at the military compliment. He knew it was warranted. He had posted men at unlikely spots around the grounds, with instructions to vary their positions randomly throughout the night. He knew the foolishness of having regular patrols.

The house was locked and guarded, and the stables secured. Several of the stablehands had professed themselves willing and able to help, and a couple of men from the village had arrived offering their assistance.

They were amply staffed, well protected, and Jordan knew he'd done all he could for the time being.

"What do you know about this stuff from Paris Elizabeth was talking about? Ever heard of it?"

Spencer leaned back in his chair and raised his eyebrow. "Oh yes. Indeed. You haven't?"

"No. Buried down here at Calverton, I sort of lost touch with what was the rage in Paris. Not much call for that when you're trying to decide where to rebuild a wing."

"True," laughed Spencer. "Well, if it's the stuff I'm thinking of, then Napoleon's troops brought it back with them after the campaign in Egypt. It's an herb, not harmful at all, but it sort of relaxes one. I tried it once, not bad."

"We're not talking opium or anything here, I trust?" Jordan raised one eyebrow.

"God no. Not even laudanum. No, this stuff doesn't even leave you with a headache, although I have to admit it made me hungry as the very devil. And making it into a tea weakens it too. I have heard that some sect of Assassins uses it in its native form as part of their rituals, but that's just hearsay. Probably Elizabeth has herself a bottle full of dandelion juice, and doesn't know the difference."

Jordan shuddered and stood, stretching his arms behind his head. "Oh well. Anything to keep them happy and stop them worrying about our problems. I suppose we'd better go and cobble up something in the way of a costume."

Spencer grinned and rose from his chair. "Of course if it's the real stuff, it will keep us *all* happy."

On that rather enigmatic note, he followed Jordan from the room.

Chapter 17

Charlie leaned back on her heels and surveyed the room. She and Elizabeth had worked quite hard for the last couple of hours getting it to match Elizabeth's vision of an Egyptian bower. Or harem. Or whatever it was that Egyptians had in their homes.

At this point, Charlie wasn't quite sure they'd succeeded.

Candles were burning in several branches around the room, and many yards of almost transparent silk caught the flickering beams of light. The silk had softened the traditional lines of the room, and, along with the fragrant herbs that Mrs. Hughes had donated to the evening's entertainment, the room now possessed an aura of mystery.

Enormous pillows had been found in one of the attics, and Elizabeth had hastily thrown soft blankets over them to cover the rather worn brocade. The fact that the occasional feather sneaked from several small holes simply added to the ambience of the occasion. At least that's what Elizabeth said as she blew on one of them and allowed it to twirl its way to the floor.

Charlie shivered a little and moved to bank up the fire.

She wondered for the seventeenth time why she'd gone along with this plan, especially as she glanced down at herself. She couldn't help blushing.

"You're doing it again," chided Elizabeth.

"Doing what?"

"Blushing. Thinking you're indecently attired."

"Well, for heaven's sake, Elizabeth. Why would I think that? I am wearing several yards of sheer silk and a pair of scandalous pantaloons. Nothing else. What could possibly be indecent about that? Other than the fact that I'm convinced you can see right through it, and I miss my chemise. Oh and pantaloons…well. There you are."

Elizabeth giggled. "And very decadent you look too, Charlie. Of course, the blonde hair does rather kill the illusion of a Middle Eastern woman, but never mind, we do make a nice contrast to each other."

Charlie couldn't argue that point. Her gold hair had been left free for the evening, according to Elizabeth's instructions. Another thing that made her a little uncomfortable. It was rare to see a woman with her hair loose anywhere other than her boudoir.

But next to Elizabeth's exotic looks, Charlie knew she would have looked ridiculous in her regular attire.

Elizabeth's midnight black hair hung in a curtain down to her buttocks. Charlie admitted that it was probably a sin to try and twist those locks into a fashionable style every day. This was how they should always be seen.

Both girls had fashioned draped costumes from the silk they'd found on their earlier scouting expedition, Charlie's was a dark blue and Elizabeth's was blood red.

Their breasts were covered with soft drapes, and they'd wrapped soft folds of the stuff into skirts that were fastened low on their hips. Every now and then a little glimpse of white skin appeared between the silks.

Elizabeth had rummaged through an old jewelry box and grabbed the most unlikely items. A large and very heavy collar that looked Elizabethan and was probably metal was now busily rusting around Charlie's slim hips, while Elizabeth was sporting an enormous and very fake looking teardrop ruby between her eyes.

They looked exotic, and, Charlie had to confess, quite sensual. Elizabeth had revealed another secret when she'd dragged Charlie into her room and demanded she try her cosmetics.

Charlie, who had never so much as wiped rouge on her cheeks, was fascinated. She'd allowed her girls at the Crescent color on their cheeks and eyes, but had never considered it for herself. An hour later, she had eyes bigger than she'd thought possible, and a delicate touch of pink on her cheeks.

Elizabeth was certainly a fount of surprises.

She was also a fount of nerves, and Charlie could see her hand tremble as she straightened the fringe of one of the exotic shawls that she'd spread over the low table.

"You don't have to do anything you don't want to, Elizabeth."

Charlie touched the other girl on the shoulder in reassurance.

"I know, Charlie. I know. But I do want this. I want it so much I ache with the wanting. Suppose I get it wrong..." She turned agonized eyes towards Charlie, who tried valiantly to hide her smile.

"My dear girl, there's nothing to get wrong. Your body will tell you what it wants when the time comes. Your heart and mind knows that Spencer is your choice, let your body follow and trust it to guide you well."

Elizabeth sighed.

The door opened, and two exotically garbed gentlemen walked in.

Charlie and Elizabeth gaped.

* * * * *

For Jordan, walking into the room and seeing Charlie on the floor dressed in some flimsy silks was a moment that would remain etched in his mind forever. It was as if someone had rummaged around in his deepest desires and brought one of them to life.

The fact that he was wearing little more than a sheet with a hole cut in it and an old bathrobe with its arms removed mattered not one whit.

He'd slit the sheet down to his navel, in the hopes that his Charlie would like what she saw. He knew she liked to play with his chest...might as well show off the toys.

Spencer had gone one step further, manufacturing a headdress with a piece of fabric and some cord. With blond hair covered, this tall man looked the very essence of desert barbarian. The toy scimitar he'd stuck into his belt didn't hurt, either.

Jordan mentally pouted. He'd wanted to carry the sword and there had only been one of them. Damn.

However, he felt redeemed when Charlie seemed unable to take her eyes off him.

His cock stirred and he immediately recognized the advantages of the loose garment he'd fabricated. There was much to be said for the Arabian style of dress, not the least of which was that it served to hide a nice healthy arousal. For a while, anyway.

Roused from their shock, the girls led their sheiks to the pillows, settling them in what was supposed to be a subservient slave girl fashion.

Elizabeth's orders about where to sit, what to eat first, and a hearty slap to Spence's hand which was about to crawl up her skirt rather destroyed the slave girl image, but the illusion was still one of magical decadence.

The burning bundles of sage around the room infused the air with a sweet tang, and Elizabeth carefully poured her special tea.

She'd procured some small oriental cups without handles, so she gingerly presented each person with their beverage using both hands.

They settled onto the pillows with muttered laughter and fidgets, finding a comfortable position and sipping the tea.

Spence's eyebrows rose at the first taste and he shot a quick glance at Jordan.

Jordan read his friend clearly. This was the good stuff.

"I'm impressed, Elizabeth. Not only is your tincture genuine, it's very tasty indeed."

Elizabeth raised her nose. "I'm worth nothing short of the best, Sir Spencer. I am surprised you doubted the gift I received..."

Charlie silently sipped her tea, as Jordan watched. He'd decided the brew was acceptable. It tasted a bit like new mown grass, with a few herbs thrown in, but he could tolerate it.

He drained his cup and made no demur when Elizabeth refilled it, as she did for the others.

They casually nibbled on the trays of foods that the servants had prepared. Although Spence had said that to be quite genuine they should all be eating lamb stew from the same bowl and with nothing but their fingers, no one had felt like taking the illusion quite that far.

So instead, they enjoyed the simple meal of cheeses and fresh bread and fruits that Jordan's kitchen staff had prepared.

Jordan smiled as Charlie, entering her role as slave girl with enthusiasm, fed him a grape.

A shiver of desire crossed his flesh and he hardened even more beneath his robe. He watched Charlie closely and saw her nipples beading under their light shielding of silk.

Spencer was also enjoying the feast, persuading Elizabeth to offer him a piece of fruit with her lips. Which led to the inevitable — a quickly snatched kiss.

Only Jordan was at the right angle to see Spence's hand brush Elizabeth's breast as he leaned in for his food.

The sexual tension in the room was rising along with the scent from the incense.

Charlie reached for a peach and bit into it, allowing the juice to spill over her lips and onto her chin.

It was a challenge Jordan couldn't refuse. He pulled her pillow close and brought his face to hers.

"Allow me to be your napkin, Charlie," he breathed as he put a hand to her head.

He slid his fingers through her golden hair, cupping the back of her head easily in his hand, while his tongue gently licked away the traces of juice from her mouth and chin.

She moaned slightly and wriggled.

Beside him, Spencer was having the time of his life with Elizabeth. He was balancing grapes on her shoulders and nibbling them off her, laughing when they fell into her lap.

Within seconds she'd been pushed onto her back, a large pillow beneath her, and Spencer was searching for a lost grape in her cleavage. With his mouth.

Elizabeth's laughter rang around the room as she encouraged him.

"Charlie," said Jordan, just for the pleasure of hearing her name. "I love your hair like this..." He raised his hand and let the softness fall through his fingers.

"I like it when you do that, Jordan," answered Charlie, closing her eyes and obviously enjoying the feeling.

"You do?"

She nodded her agreement, smiling as a gasp from Elizabeth echoed around the room. Spencer must be doing something she liked too.

"I'm glad you like it, Charlie. What else do I do that you like..." His tongue was circling her ear now, flicking in and out, tasting, teasing, and making her breath come faster. He knew he was getting harder by the second, and he fancied he could scent Charlie's arousal over the incense.

Just the thought of that arousal made him slightly delirious.

He leaned over behind Charlie and snuffed out a branch of candles, one by one, with his fingers, leaving their side of the table shrouded in shadows.

Part of his mind noted Spence easing Elizabeth into a darkened area between two large sofas across the room.

He grinned. The two old campaigners had the same thought in mind. *I'm not going anywhere right this moment, but I'm damned if I'm going to let anyone else watch.* He'd never let Charlie or Elizabeth know, but he and Spence had played this routine a couple of times before in drunken revelries. A soldier's wages seldom allowed for privacy and neither had been monks.

This time, however, it was Charlie. And she deserved the best. He eased her pillow backwards, along with his, until they reached the far side of the room.

In spite of the shadows, he could see the gleam in Charlie's eyes and the quick twinkle of her teeth as she smiled at him.

He laid her down onto her back, letting her hair spill over the pillow.

"Jordan," she whispered. "Jordan, my love."

"I'm here, sweetheart." Her words touched him and his head spun with a heady mix of joy and desire.

"Jordan, touch me." She reached for his shoulder and ran her fingers down his arm until she found his hand.

She brought it to the silks over her breast and held him against her.

"Show me how, love. Show me what pleases you..." He gave her breast a little squeeze, and then moved his hand away, pulling the silk along with it. The folds of dark fabric dropped away from her, framing the paleness of her breasts with a swath of darkness.

"I...I..." she stuttered, clearly unsure of what to do.

"Touch yourself, Charlie. Let me see the way you like it, show me how to bring you pleasure."

He leaned back a little and shrugged off his robe, letting the sheet slide up and over his bare knees.

He brushed her skin with his naked thigh.

She gasped at the contact.

"It's all right, Charlie. Go ahead, touch yourself. No one can see but me. I want to watch you, sweetheart. It's exciting. I love looking at you, your softness, knowing it's all for me…"

Charlie's tongue licked her lips and her eyelids lowered as her hand tentatively hovered over one bared breast.

"Charlie…love. For me, do it for me…"

His voice was seducing her as sure as his hands and his eyes and his lips would have done if they'd been on her body.

Charlie was melting beneath the seductive onslaught of his words.

Her mind was reeling, spinning, and unrestrained for once by conventions, concerns, inhibitions or protocol.

She felt liberated, at peace, and free for the first time in her life to let go. It was a heady experience and knowing Jordan was so near and so ready added a little extra jam to the pudding.

She felt more than saw him lay beside her, propping his head on one bent arm and pulling his silly sheet away from himself so that he could rest his cock against her silk covered thigh.

She giggled. That sheet had been so funny, and yet so sensual. She'd wanted to run her tongue down the cut to his navel. Maybe she would. In a minute or two.

Right now, he was waiting for her to touch herself. Oh God.

Hesitantly she lowered her hand to her breast, hearing an indrawn breath from beside her.

She rubbed her palm over her nipple, fascinated at how it immediately hardened and protruded from her breast.

Her hips moved in response to the sensual signals they were receiving and she jumped as Jordan's teeth nipped her shoulder gently.

"Now the other one, can't play favorites, Charlie," came a soft tease from the man beside her. "Here, let's get rid of this," he tugged the silk away from her altogether, leaving a pile of rumpled softness beneath her and her upper body naked to his gaze.

His cock lay hot against her, burning its way to her skin. She could feel it move as she reached to fondle her other breast.

Again, she rotated her palm gently against the nipple, abrading it to its aroused peak.

"You like that, do you? That circling motion...like this..." Jordan imitated her movements.

Her natural reticence having vanished, Charlie responded wildly. "It's different when you do it, Jordan. Your hands on me, oh God, they feel like heaven itself."

"How about my tongue, Charlie? How does it feel when my tongue does it?"

He leaned in and pressed his hot chest against her bare skin, letting his tongue firmly rub the pointed nubbins that were now jutting high from her body.

"Exquisite," she sighed, reaching to the back of his head and holding him against her, encouraging him to suckle and play, while she enjoyed the heat that spread throughout her body.

"Where else, Charlie? Show me other places you like touched. Now is the time to tell me these things. Let me know your secrets, your desires, your fantasies." His lips pulled and tugged a nipple, stretching it away from her. "Let me make them all come true."

"Oh God, just keep doing that, and you will," she sighed, somehow able to feel every little bump on his tongue as he bathed her breasts.

"Just a minute, let's loosen ourselves up here, shall we?"

With military precision, Jordan had her skirt unpinned and unwrapped in under five seconds, taking a deep breath as it fell away exposing her pantaloons.

"Oh my. What have we here?"

Charlie let a little giggle escape. "They're Elizabeth's. Shocking, aren't they? But she says pretty soon everyone will be wearing them."

"I think she may be right," said Jordan, running a hand up the slick fabric and spreading it apart where it split between her legs.

He slid his hand into the opening and cupped her mound.

Charlie moaned, loving the warmth from his hand as it spread over her loins and through her flesh deep into her womb.

"This is mine, Charlie. My pussy. No one else's. I can never allow anyone to see or to touch this. As soon as I put my cock inside you I knew you were made for me. We fit so well, love. And you're so hot for me...feel your juices, Charlie?"

His hand was working magic between her thighs, and Charlie gasped as he smeared moisture on her sensitive skin. Then he brought his hand back up and rubbed the dampness onto her breast.

He bent his head and licked her honey away. "Dear God, Charlie, you taste so good..."

Charlie was floating. Her body was becoming lighter than the air around her, all its focus on each sensation Jordan was creating with his tongue and his lips and his heat. His voice was the cloud on which she was lying, his hands were the instruments of her passion, and she wondered if Heaven could be anywhere near as wonderful.

She'd forgotten that Spencer and Elizabeth were entertaining each other scant yards away from where she lay. For her, the world had narrowed to this little spot, tucked behind a couple of large chairs and next to a wall. A small dark cavern where a man was bringing her to a peak of sensation she'd never have believed possible.

Strangely, she felt no sense of urgency to have him bury himself inside her. Her body was weeping for him, but her mind was content to let him take it step by step. To follow each of his movements and directions, and to analyze, examine and enjoy every single one.

Her breasts felt marvelous, swollen and sensual, alive to the least breath of air created by Jordan's movements.

She could feel the warmth of her own tongue as it flicked over her lips, and she daringly licked Jordan's shoulder when he brought it near.

He tasted slightly salty, and just like Jordan. Her favorite flavor.

Every single iota of her awareness was focused on her own body, and its responses. And the wonderful things Jordan was doing to it.

She felt him undo the tapes that held her pantaloons in place, and it was almost a relief as he drew them down and away from her. She wriggled free of the silks and sprawled naked, wantonly spreading her thighs in invitation.

A rustle and a thump followed by searing heat told her that Jordan was naked too. He was pressed to her side, rubbing himself against her, like a cat scenting its territory.

"God you feel good," he moaned, letting his cock press into her flesh.

"So do you," she answered, reaching for his body, wanting to touch him, feel him, any part of him.

"Now, back to my lesson," said Jordan, pulling away a little and bringing a sigh of disappointment to her lips.

"Do you want to be touched...here?" Jordan had taken her hand and placed it on her mound.

In spite of her amazingly relaxed state, Charlie still felt a blush heat her cheeks.

"It's all right love, show me. I want to see you, to watch you, to learn from you. Feel what it does to me when you do." He pulled Charlie's free hand to her side and curled her fingers around his cock.

"Now go ahead, show me what you like."

Slowly Charlie did his bidding, feeling a little embarrassed, rather sensual and very aroused.

She slipped her fingers across her pussy and let them spread the lips beneath apart. She could feel her own moisture and the sensation of the air on her hot damp skin left her breathless.

Jordan's cock jumped within the confines of her fingers and the movement gave her strength to go on. He really did enjoy watching.

She reached down a little further and spread her juices around, much as Jordan had done earlier. She was unsure of what to do next, but let her body direct her actions. A sense of doing something wrong vaguely niggled in the back of her mind, but she remembered hearing her girls talk about pleasuring themselves. Just because she'd never done it didn't mean it was forbidden.

Her questing hand found a certain spot, one that made her shiver when she brushed against it.

She shivered a whole lot more when Jordan's tongue pushed her hand aside and took over.

"Is that a good spot? Right there…" His tongue thrust into her folds flicking and fluttering against her clit. "That's your clit, Charlie. I can feel it growing harder." His tongue continued its movements, and now he was leaning against her, holding her still as her hips tried to buck him off.

She held onto his cock for dear life, feeling its hardness within her grasp.

"Jordan," she gasped. "I can't take that, it's too…too…"

"Too what, love?"

"Too much," she sighed as he pulled his mouth away.

"Too much for here, that's for sure…" muttered Jordan.

His warmth receded but before Charlie had chance to protest, she was being pulled, naked, into his arms. He stood with her clasped to his chest.

"We need our own room, sweetheart. Hang on."

In a few long strides, Jordan was out of the door and across the hall into his study. The door slammed behind him, and he snicked the lock. The only light in the room was from the fire, which burned brightly letting Charlie see his eyes. The pupils were almost black, and a bead of sweat was running down the side of his face.

She thought she'd never seen anything more magnificent. Slowly he released her, letting her naked body slide down against his sheet. As soon as her feet reached the ground, he let the sheet fall completely away from his hips, leaving them both naked.

He spun her, pressing her back against the heavy oak door.

"God Charlie, I want to fuck you. I want to fuck you until there's no life left in either of us. I want to spend my whole life with my cock deep in your sweet cunt. I don't want to be apart from you. Ever."

Charlie pushed her breasts against his chest, as desperate as he now for their joining.

She rubbed from side to side a little, letting his hairs abrade her nipples. She couldn't stop the moan from seeping quietly from her throat.

His cock pressed against her belly and she lifted onto tiptoe, using Jordan's shoulders to steady herself.

"Lift your leg, darling. Put it behind me."

She did as she was bid. Jordan's hands slid downwards and cupped her buttocks and he lifted her, positioning her for his cock.

"I can't wait any more for this Charlie. Let me fuck you. Please, fuck me..." Jordan's need tumbled out in words Charlie could scarcely follow.

His cock was thrusting, seeking, and at last finding her heat.

The door was hard against her back, and Jordan was hot against her front. She was in heaven as he thrust into her, filling her, completing her, making her whole.

Jordan's gasp of pleasure was echoed by her own shout of joy.

"Jordan," she yelled, unable to keep her emotion inside. "Jordan, yesss…"

She really was floating now, her weight held firmly by his hands around her buttocks. She raised the other leg and locked her ankles behind him.

Her position opened her widely to his touch and when he began to move she thought she'd die.

His body buffeted her clit and her pussy as his tempo increased, and her breath came and went in sobbing gasps timed to each of his thrusts.

It seemed to last forever, moments of indescribable bliss as Jordan's cock plunged deep and then withdrew, taking her ever higher into a plane of pleasure that seemed endless.

Jordan too, seemed tireless. His movements were strong and passionate and his groans of delight excited her even more.

He dropped his head to watch as his clock slid in and out of her cunt, shining with their combined juices and rigid with arousal.

She watched too, finding it erotic and unbelievably sensual.

This mating, this joining, was the foundation of so much that was beautiful between two people. She realized that in a moment of personal and blinding enlightenment.

This was how it should be. No pain, no anger, no fear, just two people loving and giving their bodies to each other for the sheer and simple pleasure of *this*.

Jordan withdrew with a shudder and raised his gaze to Charlie's face. "I have to come now," he said, quietly.

His words seemed to resound within Charlie's womb, because her whole body tensed, waiting for his final thrust.

"I'll come with you," she promised.

"Yes you will," he answered, adjusting her weight on to one hand and slipping the other between them.

He pressed her clit from beneath, hard, as he thrust into her one final time.

Charlie's buttocks hardened in his hand, and she could feel her whole body grow taut and tremble.

And for both of them, the world ended in an explosion of sensation and light that seemed to continue for an infinite number of lifetimes.

They both cried out.

They both shuddered in endless tremors of pleasure as their bodies released their stored sexual energies.

And they both held tight to each other as their weakened muscles deposited them in a heap on the carpet.

Chapter 18

They were sprawled on the couch in his study. Jordan couldn't for the life of him remember how they got there, his mind had blanked out after an orgasm to end all orgasms.

But there they were, warm and snuggled together beneath one of the soft blankets he liked to keep here for cold evenings.

Charlie's bottom was tucked against his groin and he found the sensation to be delightful.

And, amazingly, arousing. His cock stirred as the clock struck twice. He felt clear headed, wonderful, satisfied and lusty all at once. He grinned. This truly must be Heaven. If it wasn't, he wasn't going.

Charlie stirred in his arms, moaning a little and pressing herself against him.

"Mmm, Jordan," she muttered as he held her close and cupped a breast.

"Mmm, Charlie," he echoed, licking her ear.

"More, Jordan..." she mumbled, turning towards him and opening her eyes.

"More?"

"Oh yes. I have a lifetime to catch up on. More, Jordan."

Never one to turn down a lady's request, Jordan kissed her, hard and long, surprising himself by the rapidity of his new arousal. It hadn't been more than an hour or so since he'd fucked himself stupid inside her and now he wanted her again.

"What do you want, Charlie?"

"I want you, Jordan. In me, on me, everywhere, anywhere..." she whispered against his lips. "I want it all."

That was a tall order.

She was getting slicker by the second as his lips nibbled hers and his hands wandered caressingly over her body. He pulled her close, pressing their lower bodies together and cupping her cheeks.

She nestled her bottom into his hands and moaned as his fingers pulled her cheeks apart slightly.

"God Jordan, that feels good," she said, pushing herself into his grip even harder.

"Turn over, my love," said Jordan, reaching for a pillow and stuffing it beneath her hips.

Her bottom wiggled at him provocatively.

"Spread your legs a little," he ordered, slipping between them and running his cock up her cleft and back to her cunt.

She groaned. "God that's wonderful." Her hips wriggled.

Jordan reached beneath her and caught her honey in his hands, sliding it up and around and between her cheeks and especially around her ring of tight anal muscles.

"I won't hurt you, love, all right?"

"You could never hurt me, Jordan," she answered, widening her legs even more.

Jordan was getting harder by the second. She seemed to want this, to know his intrusion into her dark and secret place. To be touched where no one had ever touched her.

He continued to spread the slickness around, listening to her moans and smelling her womanly fragrance as she soaked his hand and the pillow and his cock. When he could moisten her no more he raised up slightly and touched her anus with the tip of his cock.

A bead of his own come slipped from him and added to her slippery state.

She sighed with pleasure.

"Just relax for me, my darling," he said, wondering if she knew this was a first for him too. "Let it all go, just feel me here, pressing against you."

He replaced his cock with his fingers, knowing that to plunge into her would hurt her. That was not his goal.

Gently he allowed one finger to press past her muscles and into her body. She jumped and sighed as he eased inside.

Then he added another finger, stretching, moving a little, encouraging her to take him.

He slid his other hand beneath her and teased her clit, letting the twin movements of his fingers increase her arousal.

She panted and gasped and thrust against his hands, demanding, needing, wanting all he had to give.

Her muscles were so tight around his fingers that Jordan realized he couldn't dare breach her there. This was a time for exquisite pleasure, not remembered pain. She'd had enough of that.

He adjusted his position slightly.

With one hand still teasing her anus and the other playing with her clit, he carefully slid his cock into the burning heat of her cunt, filling her just about every way he knew how.

Her buttocks pressed into him and his balls touched the back of her thighs. She moaned with pleasure.

Her own hands slid beneath her as she felt for her nipples and unashamedly added to her own sensations by playing, pulling and squeezing them.

Jordan was rocked by his own arousal. Seeing her like this, vulnerable, exposed, aroused, hiding nothing of her responses to everything he was doing to her, was the most erotic moment he could remember.

No woman had ever brought this kind of emotion to his mind, his heart or his loins before.

Neither had any woman ever used her body to tell him of her feelings the way Charlie was right at this moment.

Her sounds and her movements told him how much she loved the feel of his fingers in her, his cock in her, and his balls slapping loud against her flesh.

Madam Charlie

He moved his fingers deeper into her anus, hearing her moan and almost feeling his own cock as it thrust into her cunt.

His mind reeled as his orgasm neared, and Charlie's whole body tensed in readiness for his seed.

"Now, Charlie, now..." he yelled, throwing his head back and pumping into her so hard he should have blown her eyeballs halfway across the room.

Her body went into spasm, clamping and releasing, clamping and releasing, and driving him higher and higher. Every muscle below her waist was grabbing onto whatever part of his body she could hold.

He figured he'd have bruises on his fingers and his cock when this was all over, but by God it was worth it. He shook and shivered and finally his cock released his seed, pouring the hot spurts into Charlie's body in an endless stream. Filling her with his life. His future. His soul.

He sobbed and felt a tear trickle down over his face.

Dear lord, could he survive a lifetime of lovemaking like this? But more importantly, how could he ever survive without it?

* * * * *

Dawn was coming. Charlie could feel it, even though the light had not yet percolated through the heavy curtains that shielded the windows of Jordan's study.

The man beside her slumbered peacefully. Exhausted, probably, too, grinned Charlie to herself. He'd ridden her hard and wonderfully, giving her a night that would remain her most favorite memory for the rest of her life.

She moved carefully, wondering how her body had survived.

Easing off the couch, she winced as a couple of places twinged a little, but overall she felt amazingly well. She was clear-headed, alert, and slightly stiff, but surprisingly all in one piece.

Turning, she gently tucked the thick blanket over Jordan's shoulders. He snuffled and buried his face in the pillow.

Charlie grabbed another blanket, wrapped it around herself and quietly slipped from the room.

She needed to wash, dress and perhaps find some clothes for Elizabeth and Spencer. Wherever they were.

If their night had been anything like Charlie's, those two might even now be upside down on the grand staircase. Or on top of the stables. With Elizabeth's enthusiasm and Spencer's obvious skill, the sky was probably the limit for them.

Charlie grinned again, feeling extraordinarily happy.

The hall was deserted and the corridor empty, and she was in her room within seconds.

The water in the ewer was cold, but refreshing, and she felt quite restored as she bathed her stickiness away.

Her hands paused as she passed a cloth over her pussy. Her cheeks blushed as she remembered some of the things she'd done and let Jordan do.

Let him do?

Hah, she snorted to herself. She'd encouraged him every step of the way.

She knew without a doubt that she was head over heels in love with Jordan Lyndhurst, the Seventh Earl of Calverton. What she didn't know was exactly what she was going to do about it.

She sighed as she slipped into her chemise and buttoned her morning robe tightly. Something *would* have to be done about it, but perhaps she might steal another day of pleasure before the issue had to be faced. Before she had to finally reveal the truth about her identity to him.

She was afraid that once she did that, her idyll would be over. All that she'd have left would be her memories.

She prayed that she could cram a few more into this day.

With an armful of clothes she left her room and started down the corridor, to be brought up short by the sight of a figure leaving Jordan's rooms.

Arthur perhaps?

No, he was moving too stealthily through the shadowed corridor, almost like a shadow himself.

Then she smelt it.

Smoke.

For an awful second she froze, paralyzed by that smell, the sounds and memories of the first fire she'd experienced here returning to swamp her consciousness.

She gasped and turned to run, heading for the staircase, praying that her legs would hold her up.

She got to the top step when she felt a hand seize her robe and drag her to a halt.

She finally found her lungs and screamed at the top of her voice.

"*Jordan...FIRE!*"

A voice behind her hissed in her ear as she was pulled against a rough coat.

"Fucking bitch. Why are you never where you're supposed to be?"

She struggled against the man's hold, dropping clothes over the steps and writhing and tugging, trying her best to get a punch or an elbow to connect with her attacker.

She brought her head back and whacked it against his chin, surprising a shout from him and sending stars across her vision.

"That's it, you whore..."

A solid thud clipped her behind the ear and she saw the stairs rise up to meet her.

She took a step only to have her foot catch in the tangle of clothes that had fallen around her.

She slipped and fell, rolling, tumbling, bumping on the Aubusson carpet and finally onto the marble floor of the hall.

Somebody was shouting her name, but she couldn't quite hear…then everything went dark.

* * * * *

For Jordan, it seemed as if his entire world had ended. He was standing practically naked in his own hall watching as Charlie tumbled down the stairs to land in a heap on the cold marble floor.

And following her down was a man with a large pistol.

Before Jordan could do more than shout her name, the man was straddling her, aiming the gun at her head.

Charlie didn't move.

Jordan's heart stopped dead in his chest, and he raised his eyes to the man standing over her.

A red film clouded his vision for a moment.

"Who the fuck are you?"

A high pitched giggle was his answer. "Don't you wish you knew?"

Across the hall a door opened and Spencer erupted through, followed by Elizabeth.

Within seconds, Elizabeth had been pushed back through the door and Spencer was standing alone, alert, ready for a word or an action from Jordan. Both men were as near naked as you can get when wearing only a blanket, and neither were armed.

Jordan felt completely helpless and furious, and scared to death. Charlie still hadn't moved. His heart was thudding madly. He refused to believe she was anything other than unconscious.

"What's going on Jordan?" asked Spencer quietly.

"I don't know. This man just pushed Charlie down the stairs. I'm trying to find out why."

"Charlie? Oh that's her name now, is it?" The man waved his gun around then pointed it back down at the woman between his legs.

"I liked Charlotte better. Actually I liked Lady Charlotte. It made sticking my cock into her cunt so much more exciting."

At that second the wheels in Jordan's mind clicked into place and he knew who the man was.

"So you were the valet to her late husband, were you? The one who was going to help the line continue?"

Jordan tried to get the man's attention away from Charlie and Spencer and on to himself. He knew that a moment's glance towards him would allow Spence to move a little, and again a little more, until they were both in a position where one would have a chance against him.

It didn't work. The man remained fixated on Charlie. So did his weapon.

"Oh yes, that was me. And you should be shaking my hand and thanking me for failing, shouldn't you, *my Lord*?"

The emphasis on the last two words was lost on Jordan. His attention was splintering in several different directions, seeking solutions, discarding ideas, working furiously to plan his response.

"She's got a hot little body, don't she, my Lord? I really liked fucking her, you know? Pity she used to scream a lot, though. Occasionally he used to let me gag her, but most of the time he liked to hear the noise."

He nudged her with his toe, making Jordan's blood boil. But, experienced soldier that he was, he knew his anger would only cloud his judgment. With a great effort he sat on his fury and encouraged the man to talk. Perhaps that was the way to distract him.

"O'course she was kind of pale and yellow, all that hair. We mostly liked 'em dark and fiery like that Maria. Now there was a hot little taint for our pleasure. She could suck the brass off a poker, she could. Got the master all uppity and ready, but he'd lose it afore he could stick it in this one."

Charlie moaned slightly, and Jordan felt the life flood back into his body. She was alive. She might be badly hurt, but she was alive.

"What's your name?"

"What's my name? Well, hell, my Lord, you should be askin' *her* name." The man giggled again. His weapon never moved an inch, still pointing straight at Charlie's head.

"Still being a bloody nuisance, too, that's what she is. Never where she's supposed to be."

Jordan frowned. "I don't understand."

Spencer moved an inch or so to the side.

"I wouldn't bother, Mister. My finger on this trigger can put her brains all over this nice new marble floor long afore you can get to me. And that's where the pleasure will be for me, you see."

His eyes glittered madly as he stared around at the men and back to Charlie.

Jordan shook his head slightly at Spence, letting him know not to make a bad situation worse. Clearly this man had something to get off his chest.

"You plan to kill her, do you?" said Jordan calmly.

"Oh yes. I tried before, you know. But it all went wrong." He blinked for a moment as if to clear his vision. Jordan breathed in, but the man's head came back up before he could move.

"I loved that old man. He was like a father to me. Taught me stuff. Like how to read and write, and he let me share his pleasures. It wasn't his fault he was old and died in the furrow, as they say. He just wanted an heir. And he'd given me so much, it was my bounden duty to help him. It was *her* fault..." His voice hardened and his hand shook.

Jordan's breath left his body as he watched the man's finger tremble on the trigger.

"When it looked like it wasn't working, we figured it was time to get rid of her. Or at least I did. I knew he was going to get her into his bed that night, and he always went for his brandy right before he fucked her. So I knew if a fire broke out when she was alone, he'd be off the hook. He'd be free. We could try again..."

Tears were running down the man's face as Jordan and Spencer listened to his horrible tale. Charlie was still beneath him, but Jordan had been keeping his eye on her and could have sworn he saw her move slightly.

"But she wasn't there. She wasn't bloody there. He'd forgotten, my master, that we were going to do it that night. He'd taken Maria instead. I didn't know. I started the fire in his dressing room. I didn't mean to kill them. I loved him. It was her fault."

This time he kicked Charlie, who grunted when his boot hit her ribs.

"Her. All her. You ask who I am, well, I'm Johnny Dobbs. And I can tell you who she is, *my Lord*. This bitch, the one you've been sticking your cock into all night, this woman is Lady Charlotte Calver. The *Dowager* Countess of Calverton."

He looked at Jordan, grinning madly through the tears pouring down his cheeks. "Funny isn't it? You've been fucking Philip Calverton's widow!"

Suddenly a loud noise rang out and the expression on Dobbs' face changed to one of surprise.

He looked down at himself and seemed amazed to see a small circle of blood appearing on his chest. It grew larger. He looked up at Jordan and waved his hand. "All her fault..."

He staggered, and Charlie immediately rolled away, moving like a blur across the floor.

Dobbs stumbled, falling to one knee. With another look of astonishment at Jordan, he fell forward onto his face and lay still.

The blood pooled beneath him, bright scarlet against the black and white marble.

Jordan ignored him, running to Charlie, falling on his knees beside her and grabbing her to his chest. He clutched her more tightly than he'd ever held anything in his life. She groaned and raised a hand to her head.

"You're alive, Charlie, God, you're alive." Jordan Lyndhurst held his woman to his heart and did something he'd never done in his life. He sobbed.

Chapter 19

The pandemonium that had broken out in the hall remained rather a blur for Charlie. Her ribs hurt and she had a massive headache, so she had only been vaguely aware of Spencer rushing to the rear of the hall and pulling a naked Elizabeth out of the shadows.

A very nude Elizabeth holding a large dueling pistol.

It seemed she'd lost no time in rushing out the windows of the small parlor and breaking into Jordan's library, where the intrepid woman, still stark naked, had primed and loaded one of the several prize dueling pistols kept in a display case there.

To the amazement of all of them, she'd then crept back into the hall, unseen by anyone and calmly shot Dobbs from behind.

As Spencer drew her forward and covered her with one of the robes he'd snagged from the stairs, she'd stumbled against him on her way over to Charlie.

"My God, Charlie, are you alright?" she'd asked.

Charlie remembered managing a weak smile from the closeness of Jordan's arms. "Thanks to you, Elizabeth, thanks to you," she'd whispered.

Jordan had been unable to speak, simply holding her tight and wiping his tears on her hair.

Spence had gone to check on Dobbs.

"He's dead."

Elizabeth had paled and turned, and promptly vomited.

At that point, a shout had alerted everyone to the smoke in the upstairs corridor, but Charlie remembered little more since Jordan had picked her up off the floor and carried her away from the noise.

She'd fainted again in his arms.

That had been several hours ago.

Now the fire had been extinguished with minimal damage, Elizabeth was tucked up in her bed, with Spencer standing guard over her like an aggressive guard dog, and she herself was bathed, dressed and sitting in Jordan's study. On the same couch where they'd shared such passion not more than twelve hours before. She'd overcome his arguments, fought his orders and ignored his demands.

Her headache had lessened to a dull throb, her ribs hurt a little, and she had a few bruises to show for her tumble, but all in all she was remarkably lucky to be all in one piece.

What was really hurting was her heart.

The truth had come out in the worst possible way. Now Jordan Lyndhurst knew who she was and it was time for them to part. There could be no other course of action.

Jordan quietly entered the room and took a seat behind his desk.

Charlie appreciated the gesture. Keeping space between them would make this difficult conversation easier.

"You are well?" His voice was steady and showed none of the emotion he'd released when he'd held her tight earlier.

"Thank you, yes. A few bumps and bruises, that sort of thing. I'm really very lucky."

"Thanks to Elizabeth. Truly an intrepid young woman." Jordan's mouth twitched into a grin.

Charlie couldn't help but smile back. "Indeed she is. I wanted to pop in and see her, but Sir Spencer is prowling the corridor, absolutely forbidding anyone to disturb her rest."

"He's quite the possessive martinet where she's concerned. I doubt that she'll get the chance to do any more naked target shooting if he has any say in the matter."

Charlie paled at his words as they brought the memories back.

"Charlie, we must talk."

"I know. Let me start, please, by saying I'm sorry that you had to find out who I was in that terrible way." She stared down at her lap and found she'd laced her fingers together tightly. She forced them apart and struggled for her control.

"Why didn't you tell me?"

"Tell you? How could I, Jordan? I was supposed to be dead. The world believed that Philip Calverton and his bride died that night. The bride being me. I didn't want anything more to do with the name of Calverton."

"Even me?"

"Especially you. You were a very real threat to my secrets. Then when fate threw us together..."

"And we found passion together."

"Yes," she swallowed and failed to meet his eyes, "when that happened, I was truly in a muddle."

She stood and paced the room nervously. "It was one thing for you to have an affair with...with a Madam from a brothel. It was another for you to have an affair with your step—something or other. The Dowager Countess of Calverton sleeping with the current Earl? Can you just imagine what the Ton would do with that little tidbit of information? It would ruin you, Jordan."

She stared from the window, blindly, not seeing the sunshine as it swept the green lawns.

"I would have told you. At some point, I would have told you. It wasn't because I didn't trust you that I didn't say anything. Never think that. It was because..."

"Because?"

"Because I was...I was happy. For once in my life I'd found someone who made me happy in so many ways I can't even begin to count them. And I was greedy. I wanted more days of pleasure, of joy. Something to keep me warm and remember when I'm old and gray. So I put off telling you, Jordan. Even when you brought us here, I couldn't tell you. There were no servants from before, everything was new. I had no idea that

Dobbs was still working in the stables, biding his time. And you never knew his name, did you?"

Sighing, Jordan shook his head. "No. If I had, perhaps something would have clicked before this morning, but it didn't."

"I am glad of one thing, however." She turned and faced Jordan, resting against the low windowsill. "At least I know I didn't kill Philip Calverton."

Jordan frowned. "Of course you didn't. The fire did. There is no question of that…"

Charlie closed her eyes against the love that shone from his gaze. She couldn't permit herself the luxury of enjoying it. The pain of leaving it would be too great.

"I went to his room that night, Jordan. I knew he wanted to try again and I was unwilling. So I dawdled. I even sent Maria a message, supposedly from Philip. I hoped that if she were there, they wouldn't want me. But they did. And when I got there, she was…she was—well, let's just say she was pleasuring him. And I got sick to my stomach, and knocked a candle over on my way to find a chamber pot."

She opened her eyes again, not realizing that the pain of years was reflected in their gray depths for Jordan to see.

"I thought it was my candle that had started the fire, Jordan. All these years, I lived with the knowledge that I had probably killed my husband and his mistress."

* * * * *

Jordan's mind was in turmoil. The woman he loved beyond life itself was not who he thought she was, but was in fact the widow of a very distant relative. Although her existence did not negate his inheritance, it certainly complicated it. His heart went out to Charlie as she revealed her innermost fears. What must it have been like to live with such guilt?

It certainly explained her regal and unapproachable demeanor and her rigid self-control.

"Matty was here at the time, I take it?" he asked, more for something to say than a need to know.

"Yes. She managed to get me out when we realized how much of Calverton was on fire. It was a poorly kept house, Jordan. There was much disrepair and it went up like a tinderbox. A piece of burning wood fell on Matty as we left, and that's what gave her the scars. In spite of that, she'd taken…"

"Taken what, Charlie?"

"She'd always said I was too good for Calverton," Charlie attempted a small smile. "She said I should have been married to a nice man and have had several children. So as we were running from the fire, she grabbed a couple of the pieces of jewelry I'd brought with me. And thanks to her foresightedness, we had enough to buy the Crescent."

"Buy the Crescent? You didn't inherit it?"

"No. It belonged to Matty's cousin. I wanted Matty to have it, but she said no, she'd rather stay as she was. I didn't want anyone to know where I was or who I was, so for some time I dressed as a boy. I was simply Charlie, errand boy from the Crescent. It was actually fun."

Jordan stared at her as if learning her features all over again. How could she make him understand?

"I don't know if I can explain how wonderful it was to be free, Jordan. Free from a marriage that was more torture than anything else, but also free from any of the restrictions that our society places on a woman. As Charlie, I could go anywhere, do anything, say anything, and learn whatever I wanted. It was that kind of freedom that was so attractive."

She sighed and resumed pacing. "I was able to go about the city unnoticed. I could go to the Exchange and indulge my interest in business. Gentlemen are always happy to show off their expertise to an up and coming lad. If I'd gone as a woman, I'd have been given tea and shown the door."

Jordan nodded in silent agreement.

"I got to know the girls too. Oh they guessed my secret, but they realized I had no other choice. They didn't know who I was, of course, just that I was hiding out and being useful. I took the money we got for my jewelry and started investing it. Turns out I have a talent for investments, because by the time Anne fell ill and we knew the Crescent came up for sale, I had more than enough to buy her out. I think she was happy to let it go, knowing it would come to me."

"And you began to improve the lot of the girls working for you."

Charlie jumped a little at his words. "You've been doing your research."

"Indeed."

She shrugged. "Someone had to make a start. I just knew that none of my girls would ever suffer what I suffered if I could possibly avoid it. It wasn't much but it helped me sleep better."

"And now?"

There it was. The big question. Hanging in the air between them like a cloud of smog on a winter's day in London.

"Now? Now I don't know what to do."

Jordan stood and approached her.

Charlie backed away not wanting him near her. Not yet wanting to know the pain that leaving him was going to bring her.

"May I make a suggestion?"

"No."

"No?"

"No. Jordan, this…this whatever it is we've had between us. It has to end. Here and now."

Silence fell as Jordan watched her, toying with a quill pen from the set on his desk.

She couldn't meet his eyes.

"Why?" His question ricocheted off the bookcases. "Because you don't care for me?"

She snorted. "Don't be stupid. That has nothing to do with it."

She turned away from him and missed the smile that lit up his features.

Charlie continued, voice level, hands twisting together. "It has everything to do with who we are. And we have to face up to who we are. No more hiding. Not for us, anyway."

She turned back and pulled her dignity into place, becoming the impenetrable and elegant woman of the Crescent.

"I was the Countess of Calverton, married to and widow of Philip, the Sixth Earl, and your...whatever he was. Third cousin twice removed. Or something." She waved away the annoying details.

"I am also Madam Charlie, owner and proprietor of the Crescent, a house of pleasure. You are Colonel Jordan Lyndhurst, war hero and now the Seventh Earl of Calverton. Any future for the two of us is impossible."

"Impossible?"

"Yes. Completely. It would finish you socially to be known as the man who slept with his predecessor's widow. It might also ruin you socially were your association with Madam Charlie to emerge. Although not quite so badly. For some reason the Ton takes such matters more lightly."

She paused for breath.

"While my business would probably profit were word of our association to become public, it would only be because men would be lining up to take your place once our liaison concluded. I will not have that."

Jordan's jaw had tightened at her speech and the quill between his fingers snapped in two.

"I see you would dislike it also," she added wryly. "Therefore, I must leave, Jordan. I have made arrangements to return to the Crescent shortly, as soon as my belongings are packed. The sooner I go, the sooner you can clean up this business with Dobbs. The authorities will want some explanation of his death, but I'm sure you and Sir Spencer will be able to keep Elizabeth out of it and satisfy all concerned."

She crossed to the door, trying to keep her head high and her tears at bay. She couldn't, however, look at Jordan.

"I must thank you for your complete and amazing devotion to my protection. You said you'd keep me safe and you did. For that, I owe you more than I can ever repay. The best thing I can do for you now is to leave, and ask that you forget me. Your future and mine lie along different paths."

She risked a look at him as a tap sounded on the door.

Arthur quietly poked his head in. "Beg pardon, Sir. Lady Charlotte's carriage is ready for her."

Jordan nodded and Arthur withdrew.

"Charlie." His voice stopped her in her tracks. "I love you."

A sob escaped from her throat. "Don't, Jordan. For the love of God don't make this harder." She closed her eyes as the tears flooded them.

"Why not? You're leaving me. I don't want you to go for some stupid reasons of appearance or reputation."

"They're not stupid and you know it. I have no other choice. Do you think I *want* to leave you?"

"I don't know, Charlie. What do you want?"

There it was, that aggravating question she'd asked Elizabeth some lifetimes ago.

She gathered every ounce of her courage in her hands and walked across the room to Jordan, head held high, tears kept at bay by sheer willpower.

"What I want is for you to be happy, Jordan. What I want is for you to know that you've made me a new person. Someone who is free from many of her burdens, someone who's left her shadows behind. Someone who now has memories enough to last a lifetime. And they're good ones, Jordan, thanks to you."

She reached her hand out and brushed his cheek, watching his sherry brown eyes burn as they devoured her face.

"I want you to know that I've never loved anyone before you, Jordan, and I'll never love anyone again. That's why I have to leave."

She leaned forward and brushed her lips softly against his.

Turning, she left the room and within moments was settled in her carriage.

"Goodbye, Lady Charlotte, have a safe journey," said Arthur as he swung the carriage door closed.

"Thank you Arthur. It's been a pleasure knowing you."

Arthur grinned at her.

She supposed he was happy to see the back of her. The horses pulled the carriage away, and Charlie glanced out of the window. This time she wasn't leaving a pile of burning rubble.

She was leaving her soul.

* * * * *

Jordan sat in his empty study and listened as the horses rolled away down the gravel driveway of Calverton Chase and took Charlie away from him, back to London.

His lips tightened at the emptiness he felt, not only in the room but in his heart.

He wanted her. Beside him now, right at this moment, and for the rest of their lives. Somehow he had to make it happen.

She'd left him for all the right reasons and many of the wrong ones.

Society, he knew, would lacerate both of them were their familial relationship to become public knowledge. While there were absolutely no blood ties between them, the merest whisper of anything resembling incest would finish them both.

He grimaced as he recalled the unpleasantly titillating rumors that were already circulating about Byron and his sister, following the birth of her daughter last year.

He had no illusions that his fame was as widespread as the poet's, nor that his own reputation was as sullied with scandal, but the fact remained that he was engaged in a sexual liaison with the widow of the Earl from whom he'd inherited his title.

The Ton wouldn't care about relationships. The Ton would simply invent their own to suit their jaded and gossipy needs.

No, drastic measures were called for in this situation, and Jordan knew it was time for him to make some major decisions about the course of his life.

A life that included Charlie. He'd never believed that a woman could become so important to him that his entire existence would need to be reorganized for her. And yet there was not a question in his mind that he was about to do exactly that.

A life without Charlie was unimaginable. Even now he was feeling the pain of her departure. She'd been gone ten minutes and he was lonely. In a new and unpleasant kind of way. As if someone had taken his arm or his leg away, by mistake.

The door opened, interrupting his confusing ruminations, and Arthur popped his head in.

"You'll be wanting me to pack then, will you?"

Jordan sighed. The man was uncanny at times.

"Arthur, you'll be the death of me yet. Would you find Spence and ask him to spare me five minutes? Tie him up and use a sword if you have to in order to pry him away from Elizabeth, but I need to ask his advice. And come back with him yourself. I need to run a few ideas through your brilliant mind as well."

Arthur snorted. "About time, if you ask me."

Jordan raised one eyebrow at his unfazed valet. "Really?"

"Yes, *really*. I've been watching you tomcatting around for nigh on ten years, hoping that you'd find that one woman what would satisfy more than just that..." Arthur waved his hand scornfully at Jordan's cock. "It looks like now's the time."

Jordan grinned at him. "You think so, do you?"

"I do indeed, Colonel. And in my humble opinion, she's a good choice."

"Arthur, you are truly a man of great perspicacity."

"I've always thought so," Arthur agreed, modestly.

"And there's not a humble bone in your body."

"Well, of course not. I'm your valet, aren't I? We served together, didn't we? We've fucked through some of the best whorehouses in Europe together, haven't we?"

Jordan shook his head and laughed. "Those days are long gone, my friend. A new adventure awaits us both. Are we up to it, do you think?"

Arthur drew himself up to his full height. He was about level with Jordan's chin. "*Nothing* is beyond the 'Fighting 95th'."

The motto of their old battalion fired Jordan's soul. "Then let's get cracking. Get Spence for me and pull out the trunks. We're taking a trip."

Chapter 20

The noise in London was overwhelming.

Why hadn't she ever noticed how loud everything was? Charlie stood at the window of her room in the Crescent and watched the people in the street as they celebrated the downfall of England's archenemy, and sang the praises of England's newest hero.

In fact, the capital was drowning in good cheer. The name of Wellington was responsible for many a hangover, because just the sound of the Duke's name was sufficient to cause a toast to be drunk. Many times.

The grand spectacles of the "Amazing Victory at Waterloo" were springing up all over the place. Drury Lane was going patriotic, Vauxhall rushing national pride displays of fireworks into production for every single night since the news broke, and no one, it seemed, could get enough of the mighty Union Jack.

England's flag could be seen on everything from the Tower of London flagpole, to Lady Jersey's hat, to the common streetwalker's bodice.

Yes, it was a wonderful time to be British.

Unless you had a broken heart.

Charlie had returned to a Crescent bedecked with flags and a bunch of residents who were excited about the Victory, thrilled to see her back, and busy as always with their own lives.

Within hours, it was as if she'd never left.

Never traveled to Calverton Chase or been assaulted one final time by Johnny Dobbs.

Never met Elizabeth or Spencer Marchwood.

Never lain beneath Jordan Lyndhurst and given him her body, her heart and her soul.

It seemed that only Matty could sense the desolation that lurked beneath her calm exterior. "We had a message that you were coming home, dearie. The Colonel made sure we'd know when to expect you. His rider got here about an hour ago," she'd said as she welcomed Charlie with a big hug and a tea tray.

"And don't you worry your head about Ponsonby and his man. They were found two days ago—dead. The authorities say it was an argument between them. We got the message probably about the same time as Calverton did, but with all that was going on, I don't expect you heard," she added, shepherding Charlie upstairs and fussing over her.

"So I didn't need to flee to Calverton Chase after all," she sighed, wondering at the strange way Fate had of arranging people's lives.

"Well, I'm glad you did, sweeting, you needed the break. And you needed to lay some old ghosts too. And now you're home."

Charlie sighed again.

"You just get comfortable and enjoy your tea. I have a couple of matters to attend to downstairs, and then we'll have a nice cose, just you and me." Matty hugged Charlie again and bustled off, leaving her alone with her tea.

She stared at the pot.

Suddenly a great sob erupted from her lungs, and without further ado, the tears fell.

For the first time in many years, Charlie cried as if her world was ending. Perhaps it was, she thought to herself through her grief and her pain.

For what would her world be like without Jordan in it?

She sprawled on her bed, soaking her pillow with her tears. Letting the ache in her heart fuel her agony, and the ache in her ribs add to her pain.

Never had she let her emotions loose in this way, in spite of the punishing and abusive treatment she'd received at the hands of her husband. She'd never given in to tears. Not like this.

This was an almost unbearable, wrenching kind of pain, one that was torn from the very depths of her being. She had found her mate and had given him up. Lost him, left him, unable to be with him.

A part of her was dying inside, and oh God it hurt so badly.

She had finally fallen asleep on her soaked linens.

Now it was late afternoon, and her new, post-Jordan life, was about to begin.

She went through the motions of dressing for the evening, and tried to listen as Matty prattled on about recent events she'd missed, how business was going along, who was doing what to whom, and with whom, and how everyone was all agog to see the Victory celebrations.

She assumed her role as Madam Charlie with ease and dignity, having erased all traces of her earlier sorrow. Some may have wondered at the almost unnatural calm she displayed, but many put it down to the "rest" she'd enjoyed while visiting friends in the country.

Yes, Madam Charlie was back at the Crescent, Wellington had defeated Napoleon, and the world was as it should be.

All except for one shattered heart.

* * * * *

"So you see, Madam Charlie, it'll be just the most wonderful thing…" Three hopeful faces stared at Charlie two days after her return to the Crescent.

"Just about everyone is going to see the Parade and the grand assembly of the military in the Park…"

The request was but one of many Charlie had received over the past hours. Everyone, it seemed, wanted to honor the fighting forces that had performed so bravely and suffered such terrible losses on a small Belgian battlefield.

The celebrations were in full swing, and Charlie admitted to herself that her girls were right. It was a once-in-a-lifetime occasion and would be "the most wonderful thing"...

She made her decision quickly. "Very well. Pass the word amongst the girls. The Crescent is closed for the next two days."

Clapping her hands over her ears to deaden the sound of their screams of delight, Charlie gave them a wan smile and turned towards her office. Only there could she be guaranteed some peace and quiet in which to — to what? Yearn for Jordan?

Moon over a man like a silly maid in the throes of her first love affair?

Angry at herself, Charlie stalked in, closed the door firmly behind her and pulled some paperwork across the surface of her desk.

She had all of five minutes uninterrupted quiet.

"So you're going to close up shop for a couple of days?" Matty peeked her head around the door without ceremony.

"Yes."

"Good idea. Smart business move, too. Attendance has been down a lot since all this fussing about Waterloo began."

"Yes."

"Give the girls a rest, and the customers will start missing them when they find out we've closed for a day or two."

"Yes."

"You all right?"

"Yes."

Matty frowned. "So will you be coming in to see the Celebrations tonight?"

"No."

"But," she hesitated. "Oh well, suit yourself. All this moping around is a bit silly, though, don't you think? If you want the man that bad, go get him."

Charlie raised her head and glared at Matty.

Unimpressed, Matty shrugged. "So what do I know about the matter? Just that you're sitting there looking like a wet weekend, day after day. You've lost interest in the Crescent, Charlie, and that's not good. Perhaps you should use this little break to consider your priorities."

With a snap, Matty shut the door behind her, leaving Charlie with a desk full of paperwork and a heart full of pain.

It hadn't gone away by that night when the Crescent emptied into silence and the residents departed in a chattering flock to join their fellow citizens in merriment.

Charlie drifted through the rooms, noting their unusual state of tidiness. Indeed, business had been off.

Understandable, given the excitement that had poured through the streets of London since the victory had been announced. But what wasn't understandable was Charlie's lack of interest in whether business was up or down.

That was inexcusable.

Moving quietly up the stairs to her room, Charlie wondered if Matty was right. Perhaps it was time for her to leave and move on.

She slipped from her dress, lost in thought. Perhaps she could move to one of the inns she'd set up for her girls. But they already had people in place who were running them. They'd only end up resenting Charlie if she went to live there.

For one of the few times in her recent years she regretted not tucking something away for herself. A little cottage in some remote corner of Cornwall might be nice. Or perhaps the Outer Hebrides.

About as far away from Jordan Lyndhurst as she could get.

Somewhere far enough away from the rest of the world to allow her to enjoy her memories in peace. Without pain, without tears, and without this awful longing that suffused each and every part of her body as she remembered his touch.

And she remembered his touch every waking moment of her day.

Her breasts hardened beneath her chemise, and she stood there, eyes closed, focused on the sensation.

Then she slipped the light garment over her head and let it drop to the floor. She was naked, exposed to the air, and letting her memories wash over her like the firelight flickering from the hearth.

She hadn't lit any candles, so the corners of the room were dark. Dark like her thoughts, her emotions, and her needs.

She sucked in a fractured breath as her pussy ached in memory of Jordan and his wondrous fingers. Her breasts swelled and her nipples budded at the recollection of his mouth and tongue, and her juices slicked from her cunt as she remembered how it felt to be filled with Jordan Lyndhurst.

She yearned for his cock, hard and hot, plunging into her and showing her another universe of sensation and pleasure.

She yearned for the sight of his eyes darkening with passion as he climaxed within her and drowning her womb with his seed.

Her hand slid across her belly and into her short curls as she ached for the feel of his body against hers.

Daringly, she slid her fingers between her folds of soft flesh, stroking that which Jordan had loved so cleverly with his tongue.

She fondled her hardened nipples, all the while wishing for the one who could make them beg for his lips.

Tears began to fall as she stimulated herself even further, heedless now of her surroundings.

"Oh Jordan, Jordan," she sobbed, slicking her hand through her juices, and cupping and squeezing her breasts.

So involved was she that it seemed like another pair of hands was working her body.

Another hand plunged deep within her, stretching her, smearing her hot honey over her thighs, and teasing a spot inside her until she writhed in pleasure.

Another rough hand cupped her breast, lifting it, weighing it, pressing it against her.

Suddenly, a hard cock pressed into her buttocks, a hot body plastered itself down her back and the fingers thrust deep inside her.

"Charlie. My love. My heart. Did you think I would let you go?"

Charlie gasped, wanting to turn, wanting to scream but not being able to find her voice.

He was there. Behind her, loving her, arousing her to fever pitch in a way which told her he knew her body so well.

"Jordan," she moaned, leaning back into his embrace. "Why are you here? I can't stand the pain of leaving you again..." She gasped as his fingers played inside her and touched a particularly sensitive spot.

"No questions, Charlie. Not right at this moment. I'm just going to love you, make you feel, make you laugh and sigh and shout out my name. I just want to do what I always want to do. I'm going to bury myself deep inside you, Charlie, and it's going to be the most wonderful thing for us. Because we're making love as well. That's what's different about us, sweetheart. That's what's so special. Anyone can fuck. We make love."

Charlie felt herself loosen and flood his fingers with her moisture as her body responded to his words.

She wanted him, more than she wanted air to breathe. She wanted his lips on hers, his hands all over her and his cock thrust into her cunt where it belonged.

She turned and jumped on him, hungrily plastering her mouth to his, gnawing at his lips, and demanding entrance.

He permitted her tongue to venture inside, teasing it with his, flicking, withdrawing, tantalizing her with his mouth, while his hands pressed her closer to his nakedness.

How he had come to be in her room, naked, and ready for her, she couldn't guess. Nor, at this particular moment, did she care. All that mattered was that he was in her arms, making her feel alive again, pressing his heart to her breasts and her pussy to his arousal.

He toppled them on the bed and without further ado, plunged his cock into her heat.

She sighed, opening her legs wide in welcome.

Jordan thrust deeply into her, only stopping when his balls touched her body.

"There, Charlie. That's where I'm supposed to be. *Now* I'm home."

"But…Jordan…"

The questions began flooding Charlie's mind like her honey was flooding Jordan's cock.

But then he moved and she forgot whatever it was she was thinking about.

Forcefully claiming what was his, Jordan withdrew and thrust back again, balls deep, teasing her clit with his fingers and lifting her buttocks to his groin.

She could feel him inside her, deeper than he'd ever been. Touching places that had never been touched, never been loved like this before.

He took her to the edge of madness then let her come back a little, laughing when she begged him for more.

He withdrew and flipped her, stroking, biting, nibbling and even letting a few gentle spankings fall onto her buttocks.

She was soaked with her own juices and his, and pressed her bottom up towards him, inviting, encouraging, and offering him everything she had.

She felt him slick his hands through her honey, stroking her and moistening the little rose hidden deep in her cleft. She relaxed into his caresses, liking the feeling of him touching her there.

She knew she was trembling as he pressed himself gently against her, and it was with a mixture of excitement and trepidation that she focused on her tight ring of muscles and allowed the tension in them to ease.

Slowly, almost without detection, Jordan slipped inside her, sliding between her cheeks with a groan.

He was gentle, only intruding a little way before stopping and letting her adjust to his presence.

She found it an amazing sensation. "Jordan. I've never…"

"I know, sweetheart. I won't hurt you. Trust me." His voice was rough, husky, almost savage sounding as he slipped a little more deeply into her.

He let his fingers move to her clit and began to draw it out, back into its state of excitement.

Her hips moved and she gasped at the new sensation. His cock and his fingers were now filling her and she tensed as his skilled hands began bringing her towards the top of the mountain again.

She felt him grunt as she pushed back slightly, hungry now for his possession, feeling nothing but exquisite pleasure at his presence within her.

His fingers were pulling, teasing, flicking her clit, and her muscles began to tighten unbearably.

"Jordan…" she choked, overwhelmed by her body's response to this man.

"Let it go, Charlie, let it go…"

He pressed roughly on her clit, and it was enough.

Enough to send her mind soaring, and her body into a whirling, spinning burst of fire that seemed to consume every inch of her.

She screamed.

* * * * *

They lay in a tumbled cuddle of limbs and linens and sweat. Jordan couldn't remember the last time he'd been this happy, this sated, this relaxed or this content.

He squeezed Charlie and made her yelp. "What was that for?"

"I love you. God how I love you. And you left me." He nibbled on her shoulder with gentle but firm bites, licking her skin to ease the sensation. "I just wanted to make sure this was really happening."

That delightful giggle he loved popped out. "Oh it happened. My backside will attest to that."

Jordan cupped the soft cheeks. "Sore? Did I hurt you?"

"No, not really. It's just that I've never...well, I mean you're the first to..."

"And the only one ever to." He interrupted her with his firm comment. "You're mine, Charlie. For now and forever. There will be no one else touching you, looking at your body, or pleasing you. No one. Ever."

Charlie raised her hand and stroked a lock of hair away from his eyes. "I feel the same, Jordan. I can't stand the thought of another woman...touching..." Her hand fell to his chest and brushed his nipples.

"Well, that settles it, doesn't it?" He tugged her across him and rested his chin on her head. "We're getting married."

She stiffened, but he had her tight in his arms. He wasn't about to let her go again. He waited with interest to see her reaction.

As always, she surprised him. "I don't recall accepting a proposal."

A crack of laughter erupted from his lungs. "Well, if you don't call what we just did a pretty definite statement of future intentions..."

Charlie chuckled. "You know what I mean."

He squeezed her again. "Do I need to ask Charlie? Was I wrong in thinking that you'd be interested in spending the rest of your life with me?"

"Jordan, I…" She raised herself up on one elbow, letting her hand idly trace his features. "We women love to be asked, you arrogant male." She pinched his chin gently, then dropped a kiss on it. "But you weren't wrong. I'd like nothing better than to spend my life with you. But Jordan," she stilled his words with a finger to his lips. "You know it's impossible."

Jordan allowed his lips to curl beneath the touch of her hand. It was time to play his trump card.

"Impossible? For a member of the Fighting 95th? Shame on you, Charlie. If Wellington can defeat Boney, surely Colonel Lyndhurst can solve a simple problem."

Charlie narrowed her eyes suspiciously. "You've got a plan, haven't you?"

"Yes, and if you hadn't gone running back to London full of high principles, ethics and other such noble thoughts, we might have come up with it together." He pouted and slipped his hand across her upper thighs, making her shiver.

"How, Jordan?"

He could hear the pain in her words, the wanting, the desire for him that he knew he could match, inch for inch.

"How do you feel about a long sea voyage?"

The Colonies! He was talking about going to the Colonies.

"But, dear heavens, what about the title? Calverton Chase? Jordan, what can you be thinking?"

Charlie's heart was pounding as a tiny piece of her began to accept that there was a chance for them. A small chance, but a chance nevertheless.

For the first time in days, her spirits lifted their heads and peeked out of the bleak fog that had buried them.

"I'm thinking of the Colonies, Charlie. America. There's a new land across the ocean with new opportunities, and a new way of doing things. One where titles and relationships don't matter, but hard work and intelligence does. Where gossip probably exists, but can't ruin a reputation. Where the sun doesn't rise and set on what your title is or who you know, but what you are and what you can do. What do you think, Charlie?"

She let his words wash over her, filling her empty spaces, offering her hope — offering her something she thought she'd relinquished forever. A future.

"Would you settle for being plain Mrs. Lyndhurst? Wife to Colonel Lyndhurst? Temporarily unemployed new citizen of the town of Boston?"

"You've been planning things out, haven't you?" She needed only one look at his satisfied expression to know that this particular plan would leave no stone unturned, no loose ends to be tied.

Putting her theory to the test, she asked the most obvious question. "The title, Jordan. You can't just ignore it?"

"No I can't. But next in line to inherit is my brother-in-law, since there is no other male relative. They have several children, I forget how many." Charlie couldn't resist a sharp dig at him as he revealed a cavalier attitude towards his nephews and nieces.

"Ouch. I *do* forget. They seem to be always having 'em, or just had 'em or about to have another one. They need a bigger place, and Calverton would be perfect. They're thrilled at the prospect, my brother-in-law is a wonderful manager and will take excellent care of the property. My sister will lord it over the neighborhood and become the most obnoxious 'Lady of the Manor'. The neighbors will probably never speak to her again *or* fight for invitations to her parties. I don't know which." He grinned wickedly.

"And I'm making arrangements for the title to go to their firstborn without legal contest. I do remember *his* name. It's John. He lost his breakfast on me last time I was there."

Charlie laughed, feeling another of the dark places within her unfurling to the warmth of his eyes.

"The legalities are pretty simple, and because I'm leaving the country, there'll be no argument, I believe." He leaned back and stroked her breast softly, absently, with his hand. "I'll be an Earl in name only, Charlie. Will you mind?"

Charlie gazed at him, as her eyes filled with tears. This time around they were tears of joy. "The only thing I'd mind is being without you, Jordan. Earl or Colonel, aristocrat or boot boy, I don't care. It's not about your title, it's about you. Which is why I don't know if this will work…"

His eyebrows rose in a look that said, "My plan is perfect. It can't fail."

Sighing, Charlie began to point out the flaws. "Have you considered what will happen when someone finds out about me?"

"They'll think you're an incredibly beautiful woman, and I'm an incredibly lucky man."

"That's not what I meant, and you know it."

Jordan reached to the side table and grabbed a soft towel. He moistened it with water from the pitcher standing next to the bed, and began to cleanse her soft body. She jumped a little as the cool cloth touched her hot flesh.

"I know what you meant. And I hate to break this to you, Charlie, but Madam Charlie of the Crescent will have to disappear. For good."

Charlie frowned, even while squirming delightedly under his gentle caresses. "How? I don't see…"

"Hush. Just listen." He rinsed the cloth and cleansed himself absently as he talked.

"Charlie is going to sell, transfer ownership, otherwise dispose of, the Crescent."

"She is?"

"Yes. Be quiet." He dried their bodies, rubbing briskly.

"Sorry."

He tugged the blankets up over both of them, making sure Charlie was comfortable before he continued.

"She will then retire to parts unknown. In the meantime, Colonel Lyndhurst is going to quietly announce his wedding to Miss Charlotte Avonleigh."

Charlie gasped. "You found out," she sputtered.

"Well of course. It was only a matter of time. I told you that you were a puzzle I would solve, Charlie. I just didn't know how deeply I'd fall in love with you while I was doing it," he grinned.

Charlie shook her head, amazed once again at this man she held so tightly against her.

"So, where was I? Oh yes, we've just announced our wedding, which will, of course, have already taken place."

"Of course."

She got a squeeze for her impertinence.

"Also, we'll be announcing that the happy couple has just embarked on the Silver Dawn, bound for the New World, where they will be making their home. That Geoffrey Lyndhurst-Tremont will be assuming the rights and obligations incumbent on the Calverton Estate, etc. etc."

"Oh my. *Lyndhurst*-Tremont?"

"He had to add the Lyndhurst. Kept m'sister happy."

Her nipple was tweaked for her interruption. She liked it.

"And the Crescent?"

"Ah yes, the Crescent." Jordan slid against her, encouraging her to sprawl across him and sliding his thigh between hers, slap up against her pussy. She wiggled around, enjoying the feeling.

"Do you want to hear the rest of my incredible plan?"

"Yes, please."

"Well, stop squirming for a few minutes so I can finish it. Then we can move on to other things."

"Very well, Jordan," she said respectfully, biting her lip and pressing her mound down on his rapidly hardening erection. His gasp rewarded her and she grinned. "Just hurry up, will you?"

Jordan cleared his throat. "The Crescent," he croaked. He cleared his throat again. "Matty has said she would be very happy to take over the Crescent, subject to your approval. I should also add that, to my surprise, she's accepted Arthur's offer of marriage."

Charlie stilled in surprise. "You're joking."

"Certainly not. One doesn't joke about something as serious as marriage. Apparently while you were *not* paying attention to me at Calver House, Matty *was* paying attention to Arthur. And vice versa."

"I *was* paying attention to you. Far too much attention, as I recall."

"Never too much, my love. Never too much," grinned Jordan slipping his hands all over her body in a sensual massage that raised goosepimples on her skin.

"So you've taken care of almost everything, haven't you?" Charlie tried to absorb the enormous implications of this simple, but basically sound, plan. "You and I are pretty much going to cease to be who we are today, and become a simple married couple in the Colonies."

"Well, yes and no. We're going to leave behind two rather annoyingly burdensome identities. We're going to travel to a new life where we can be who we are not who we are titled. What will *not* change is you and me. This. What is between us. It's forever, Charlie."

She sighed with pleasure as his hands continued to stroke her. "I know, Jordan. I think I knew the minute I saw you. I certainly knew that I wanted my hands on you, not Jane's, that first night. I didn't know why, and it scared me. But I knew."

"And I knew too, in all honesty. I told myself I wanted to fuck you because you were beautiful and desirable and I wanted you. But within moments I knew there was something else going on. Something that made me want to hold you as well, wake up with you, touch you, love you…it shook my world, Charlie, this feeling I had for you."

Charlie's heart swelled and the last little piece of pain splintered into nothingness. She nuzzled against Jordan, smelling his scent, inhaling him, taking him deep into her heart and her soul.

His hands moved with more certainty, sweeping up from her thighs to her breasts and back.

She rolled under him with a sigh of contentment. "And I can continue to walk up and down your back if you need treatment. Just think, Jordan, you'll be getting a massage expert as well as a wife."

Jordan's grin was a study of sensual delight.

"Funny how I haven't had a problem with my back since I met you. And did this to you…"

And he slipped his hardened cock back into her wet heat, back into the place that seemed made just for his length. Charlie moved to give him greater access and pulled his body down to hers with a fierce surge of emotion.

"I love you, Jordan Lyndhurst. Today, tomorrow, for all the tomorrows we'll share. You are my life."

At that moment, Madam Charlie ceased to exist.

Epilogue

The Evening Gazette, Fleet Street, October 1815:

"We note an Interesting Announcement made recently from Calver House. The Marriage between Jordan Lyndhurst, Seventh Earl of Calverton, and Miss Charlotte Avonleigh of the Hampshire Avonleigh-Huntsfords, took place quietly at the end of this Past Summer. It is said that an Unfortunate Loss in the Bride's Family made a Large Wedding inappropriate. The former Miss Avonleigh is somewhat of a Mysterious Figure, for no one can claim Acquaintance with her, although her Permanent Residence in Hampshire does preclude the Possibility of her being known to the Ton. We at the Gazette certainly wish them well.

The Earl's Decision to leave for the Colonies and Relinquish all Rights and Claims to the Calverton Estate came as a Surprise on the heels of his Wedding Announcement.

We wonder what can be happening to our Nobility? Are they tiring of the onerous task of managing the Grand Estates of this Country? Of dining from Gold Plate and drinking the finest wines and brandies?

Should we prepare ourselves for Princess Esterhazy to purchase a Hotel and retire from her Public Life? Perhaps Lady Jersey might Prevail upon our Beloved Prince to forgo his Royal Duties and become a Simple Farmer. Although what Crops he might elect to raise fill the Mind of the Observer with Dubious Questions.

And speaking of the Demi-monde, Patrons of 14 Beaulieu Crescent have noticed yet another Change in Management recently. Departed forever from the Elegant Salons is its equally Elegant Owner, Madam Charlie, who has apparently retired from her Position as Hostess at the Crescent. Her Presence will be missed, although not by Sir J____ W____, who, we are reliably informed, has spent the last Seven Nights at the Crescent, enjoying the Charms of no less than four of its Residents.

We wonder upon what he fuels his Inexhaustible Stamina.

In other news about Town, the Return of one of the Season's most Incomparable Beauties was greeted with Pleasure. Lady Elizabeth Wentworth is back amongst us, after a Summer spent, in her words, "traveling different paths". Wherever these "paths" took her, they failed to quench her ever-present Desire for Pleasure, as she was seen at no less than three Balls in one night, and squired at each by a Different Gentleman.

Is it possible that This will be the Year Lady Elizabeth Surrenders her Single State? Is there a Husband in the Offing for this Vivacious Darling of Society?

That Other 'Darling', our own vaunted Byron, was discovered...."

A pair of slim hands folded the paper and set it aside on the table. The soft clatter and rumble of carriages and sleighs making their careful way over the snow-covered Boston streets echoed outside the window of the snug room.

A large mirror over the fireplace reflected the image of an elegant woman, golden of hair and large of stomach.

The door opened and a gust of wind blew in a very handsome man, who was smiling from ear to ear.

The handsome man bent and placed a cold and wet kiss on his wife's warm neck.

"Aaaargh! Jordan...you...you terror. Your nose is cold..."

Charlie giggled as she shivered, and pulled his coat away from her husband's shouders.

"I can think of at least a dozen places I could warm it," he answered, waggling his eyebrows at her. "And not one of them would bother the babe," he gave her swollen belly a gentle stroke.

"Later, you reprobate. Molly is preparing something nice and warm for you. How was the meeting?"

"Long, boring...meetings never change no matter what side of the Atlantic we're on." He nodded to the paper on the table as he pulled Charlie on to his knees and cuddled her and her precious cargo close to him. "Any news from London? "

Charlie grinned. "Well, the paper is over three months old, but you'll be pleased to know that we were married quietly because of a death in my family."

"Yes, poor Boots. I still miss him. Best barn cat we ever had, wasn't he?"

Charlie giggled. "And Sir J W somebody was known to be spending large amounts of time at the Crescent with..." she leaned forward to whisper in Jordan's ear, "...*four* women at once."

"I'll bet Arthur showed him how."

Charlie gasped, and looked daggers at Jordan. "I *don't* want to know, thank you."

Jordan held her tight. "I love you, Mrs. Lyndhurst. Little Lyndhurst been kicking around again?" He let Charlie pull his hand over her belly and place it slightly off to one side. A grin spread over his face as he felt the flutterings of their child within her.

"Anyway," continued Charlie, unperturbed at this parental bonding over her navel, "Elizabeth was mentioned. She appeared back in town last October, according to that..." She nodded at the paper. "I wonder if Spencer Marchwood was there too. I had thought that perhaps they might..."

She blushed a little, remembering a night of pleasure and exotic joys she'd shared with the other couple.

"If it's meant, they'll find a way. One thing I can assure you," Jordan leaned down and rested his head against her stomach. "Spencer Marchwood is a determined man. He'll brook no interference between him and his objective, once he sets his mind to it."

"Yes, but Elizabeth is so...so...strong, so assured. She's got a very well developed mind of her own, you know, Jordan."

"I know," grinned Jordan. "But as I said, if it's meant to be..."

"Like we were?"

"Just like we were."

And Jordan Lyndhurst cuddled his wife and their soon-to-be-born babe before his very comfortable fire in the New World, and let their warmth flood through his body and his heart.

Life was very good indeed.

THE END

About the author:

Sahara Kelly was transplanted from old England to New England where she now lives with her husband and teenage son. Making the transition from her historical regency novels to romanticas has been surprisingly easy, and now Sahara can't imagine writing anything else. She loves letting her imagination roam through wild and unpredictable times and places, creating warm and loving characters, and sharing their adventures with her readers. She is dedicated to the premise that everybody should have fantasies.

Sahara Kelly welcomes mail from readers. You can write to her c/o Ellora's Cave Publishing at P.O. Box 787, Hudson, Ohio 44236-0787.

Also by SAHARA KELLY:

- A Kink In Her Tails
- Alana's Magic Lamp
- Finding the Zero-G Spot
- Hansell and Gretty
- Mystic Visions anthology with Myra Nour and Ann Jacobs
- Persephone's Wings
- Sizzle
- Tales of the Beau Monde 1: Inside Lady Miranda
- Tales of the Beau Monde 2: Miss Beatrice's Bottom
- Tales of the Beau Monde 3: Lying With Louisa
- The Sun God's Woman

Why an electronic book?

We live in the Information Age—an exciting time in the history of human civilization in which technology rules supreme and continues to progress in leaps and bounds every minute of every hour of every day. For a multitude of reasons, more and more avid literary fans are opting to purchase e-books instead of paperbacks. The question to those not yet initiated to the world of electronic reading is simply: *why?*

1. *Price.* An electronic title at Ellora's Cave Publishing runs anywhere from 40-75% less than the cover price of the <u>exact same title</u> in paperback format. Why? Cold mathematics. It is less expensive to publish an e-book than it is to publish a paperback, so the savings are passed along to the consumer.

2. *Space.* Running out of room to house your paperback books? That is one worry you will never have with electronic novels. For a low one-time cost, you can purchase a handheld computer designed specifically for e-reading purposes. Many e-readers are larger than the average handheld, giving you plenty of screen room. Better yet, hundreds of titles can be stored within your new library—a single microchip. (Please note that Ellora's Cave does not endorse any specific brands. You can check our website at www.ellorascave.com for customer recommendations we make available to new consumers.)

3. *Mobility*. Because your new library now consists of only a microchip, your entire cache of books can be taken with you wherever you go.

4. *Personal preferences are accounted for*. Are the words you are currently reading too small? Too large? Too...**ANNOYING**? Paperback books cannot be modified according to personal preferences, but e-books can.

5. *Innovation*. The way you read a book is not the only advancement the Information Age has gifted the literary community with. There is also the factor of what you can read. Ellora's Cave Publishing will be introducing a new line of interactive titles that are available in e-book format only.

6. *Instant gratification*. Is it the middle of the night and all the bookstores are closed? Are you tired of waiting days — sometimes weeks — for online and offline bookstores to ship the novels you bought? Ellora's Cave Publishing sells instantaneous downloads 24 hours a day, 7 days a week, 365 days a year. Our e-book delivery system is 100% automated, meaning your order is filled as soon as you pay for it.

Those are a few of the top reasons why electronic novels are displacing paperbacks for many an avid reader. As always, Ellora's Cave Publishing welcomes your questions and comments. We invite you to email us at service@ellorascave.com or write to us directly at: P.O. Box 787, Hudson, Ohio 44236-0787.

Printed in the United States
24636LVS00003BA/64-348